In His Sights

A Sugarland Blue Novel

JO DAVIS

A SIGNET ECLIPSE BOOK

SIGNET ECLIPSE
Published by the Penguin Group
Penguin Group (USA) LLC, 375 Hudson Street,
New York, New York 10014

USA | Canada | UK | Ireland | Australia | New Zealand | India | South Africa | China
penguin.com
A Penguin Random House Company

First published by Signet Eclipse, an imprint of New American Library,
a division of Penguin Group (USA) LLC

First Printing, September 2014

ISBN 978-0-451-46792-8

Printed in the United States of America
10 9 8 7 6 5 4 3 2 1

PRA[redacted]
THE SUGARLA[redacted]

Hot Pursuit

"With her descriptive storytelling and sharp banter, Davis's way with words will keep the reader hooked. The passion between Taylor and Cara is hot, and their romance is sweet and sexy. Once again, Davis hits it out of the park."
—*Romantic Times*

"Scorching hot." —*Publishers Weekly*

"Romance suspense at its best . . . a wonderful series that has it all: exciting stories, superhot couple, romance, danger, suspense, friendship from a great group of secondary characters, and hot hot hot sex." —The Reading Cafe

"This exciting contemporary romantic suspense story continues the saga of the delicious detectives in the Sugarland Police Department. . . . This book can stand alone and provides a thrilling story with poignant interludes and will undoubtedly garner new fans to the series."
—The Reading Addict

"An adult romance tale which piles on the tension from the start and doesn't let up." —Fresh Fiction

"A roller coaster of emotion and action that will keep you gripped until the last page . . . with just the right combination of both romance and suspense." —Cocktails and Books

Sworn to Protect

"[A] strong series launch . . . a satisfying, fast-paced read."
—*Publishers Weekly*

"What's not to love about sexy men in blue with fast hands, true hearts, and the courage of their convictions? Davis certainly knows how to draw the perfect balance of vulnerability and strength. . . . She wraps it all up in an action novel that falls just shy of a police procedural, but with plenty of pure steamy romance and family drama. A great start to the Sugarland Blue series!" —*RT Book Reviews*

continued . . .

"Ms. Davis did a fabulous job. . . . *Sworn to Protect* is a wonderful start to the Sugarland Blue series." —Under the Covers

"If you like romance, action, and mysteries, then you will love this book." —Once Upon a Twilight

"Jo writes stories that keep you hooked until the very last page and clamoring for the next book to release."
—Book Monster Reviews

"A smart, sexy, and fast-paced read." —Fresh Fiction

PRAISE FOR THE FIREFIGHTERS OF STATION FIVE NOVELS

Ride the Fire

"The perfect blend of romance and suspense. Neither element overshadows the other. Jo Davis creates a great combination of romance, steamy love scenes with mystery and suspense mixed in. I was pulled right into the book, and before I knew it, the last page was turned. I wasn't ready to let go." —Fiction Vixen

"Once again, Jo Davis has rocked it in this series!"
—Night Owl Reviews

"Jo Davis continues her steamy, heat-packed romantic suspense stories with *Ride the Fire*. This book is a great blend of hot romance with suspenseful, well-plotted action."
—Fresh Fiction

Line of Fire

"Grab a fan and settle in for one heck of a smoking-hot read. . . . Fiery-hot love scenes and a look inside the twisted mind of a killer make *Line of Fire* stand out. Add in the behind-the-scenes look at the other characters and I could read this book over and over!" —Joyfully Reviewed

"Full of romance and steamy love scenes with a splash of mystery and suspense. This combination had me eager to turn the page and left me wanting more. The love scenes were scorching hot!" —Fiction Vixen

Hidden Fire

"Surprisingly sweet and superhot. . . . One of the best heroes I've read in a long time. If you want a hot firefighter in your room for the night, grab a copy and tuck right in with no regrets. Four hearts." —The Romance Reader

"A fast-paced romantic suspense thriller."—The Best Reviews

Under Fire

"Four stars! A totally entertaining experience."
—*Romantic Times*

"Scorching-hot kisses, smoldering sex, and explosive passion make *Under Fire* a must read! Experience the flames of *Under Fire*!" —Joyfully Reviewed

"Exhilarating [with] a two-hundred-proof heat duet . . . a strong entry [and] a terrific, action-packed thriller."
—*Midwest Book Review*

Trial by Fire

"A five-alarm read . . . riveting, sensual." —Beyond Her Book

"Jo Davis turns up the heat full-blast. Romantic suspense that has it all: a sizzling firefighter hero, a heroine you'll love, and a story that crackles and pops with sensuality and action. Keep the fire extinguisher handy or risk spontaneous combustion!"
—Linda Castillo, national bestselling author of *Gone Missing*

"Jo Davis . . . completely reeled me in. . . . Heady sexual tension, heartwarming romance, and combustible love scenes."
—Joyfully Reviewed

"One of the most exciting 'band of brothers' series since J. R. Ward's Black Dagger Brotherhood. It's sweet and sexy, tense and suspenseful." —myLifetime.com

"For a poignant and steamy romance with a great dose of suspense, be sure to pick up a copy of *Trial by Fire* as soon as it hits the bookstores! Five bookmarks!" —Wild on Books

"Hot, sizzling sex and edge-of-your-seat terror will have you glued to this fantastic romantic suspense story from the first page to the final word. Do not miss the heart-stopping, breath-stealing, incredibly well-written *Trial by Fire*."
—Romance Novel TV

ALSO BY JO DAVIS

Sugarland Blue Novels
Hot Pursuit
Sworn to Protect
Armed and Dangerous (novella)

Firefighters of Station Five Novels
Ride the Fire
Line of Fire
Hidden Fire
Under Fire
Trial by Fire

To my beautiful daughter, Kayla. You're everything a mother could wish for in a daughter, and so much more. You're a strong, smart, loving, and kind young woman. Completely individual. Trust in yourself and your gifts, and those strengths will carry you wherever you need to go for the rest of your life. You are my light and my joy.

Chris's story is for you. I love you so very much.

Love, Mom

Acknowledgments

Special thanks to:

My wonderful daughter and son for being my strength and my purpose. For always supporting and encouraging me every step of the way in whatever I do. I love you both.

My dear friend Melody Walker for coming back into my life and bringing me such happiness just when I needed it most. Because of you, I'm finding my smile again.

My agent, Roberta Brown, for always being my cheerleader and my guide.

My editor, Tracy Bernstein, for endless support, patience, and words of wisdom.

All of the crew at NAL, including the art department, marketing team, and publicists. You guys are awesome!

And the readers. Your support for our boys in blue means the world to me. You rock!

In His Sights

1

"Doctor Lassiter!"

The urgent yell from the front of the emergency room near the foyer jerked Robyn Lassiter from her exhausted stupor and got her moving.

Jogging toward the front, she met the three nurses who'd rushed through the double doors pushing a gurney. The patient was an older woman, perhaps in her seventies; her eyes were closed, her pallor gray, her lined face covered with a sheen of sweat.

"Take her to ER Two," the doctor said briskly. As they hurried down the hall, she asked, "Where are the paramedics?"

"Husband brought her in." Shea Skyler, one of the nurses, gestured behind Robyn.

Whirling, Robyn found herself with an armful of distraught husband. Catching him by the shoulders, she looked into his panicked face. "I'm sorry, but you'll have to remain outside."

"But my wife! Please, Peggy needs me!"

Robyn kept her tone firm but kind. "What Peggy

needs is for me to be in there helping her. I can't do that until you let me. Please, go to the waiting area and I'll get you as soon as possible."

Another nurse appeared, gently taking his arm. "She's in good hands. Come with me, Mr. Fields."

After a moment's hesitation, the man swallowed hard and said reluctantly, "All right. Take care of Peggy." His eyes were watery, face etched with the miserable helplessness he surely felt.

"I'll do my best, Mr. Fields." She never made promises. That was one of the first unwritten rules she'd learned as a doctor.

As soon as he turned to leave with the nurse, Robyn joined her team, taking in the unconscious woman on the table. *Peggy Fields.*

"Do we have her age? Medical history?" she asked, grabbing the ophthalmoscope and shining a beam of light into each of the woman's eyes. *Shit.* "Nonreactive."

Shea spoke up as she attached the monitors. "Seventy-one. Diabetes controlled by diet. No heart problems, no other significant health issues, according to her husband. Though he did say she'd been feeling poorly the last few weeks."

Robyn frowned, then set about taking her pulse even as she noted her blood pressure. "Vitals are unstable. Pulse is thready, BP falling rapidly. Ready the crash cart."

The woman was about to train wreck; they'd all seen the signs before. So it was no surprise when, despite their attempts to prevent disaster, the heart monitor flatlined. With fast, efficient movements, her team prepped the patient, injected the necessary meds into her IV. Robyn attached the pads on the woman's chest and waited for the all clear.

The first jolt did nothing to restart Peggy's heart. Nor did the second, or the third. Numerous tries and almost half an hour later, Shea met her eyes and shook her head, expression sad.

"Call it?"

She had no choice. Without a heartbeat, even life support wasn't a viable option. Robyn blew out a breath and stepped back, dejectedly checking the clock on the wall. "Time of death, seven twenty-three p.m. Shea, would you take her husband to the private family room to wait for me?"

"You bet," the other woman said quietly.

A nurse named Barb spoke up, glancing at the woman's body. "Must be something in the water. That's the fourth one in the last couple of months, at least that I know of."

Robyn gave the nurse her full attention. "What do you mean?"

"I've seen two other cases come in like this over the past few weeks," Barb said. "Gray pallor, sweats, nausea. Both of those died, as well as two others I heard about from some other nurses."

"Most likely heart attacks." She paused, frowning. "Though so many that close together is pretty unusual."

"The thing is, a couple of those were young. One of my patients was a man who was only twenty-two."

Staring at Peggy Fields, Robyn felt something unpleasant coil in her stomach. "That *is* unusual. I may take a look into our records of those patients and then give the medical examiner a call, see what she has to say."

"Wouldn't be a bad idea. I've just got this feeling . . ." Barb shrugged. "But it's probably nothing."

"Yeah. Probably."

But even so, it wouldn't hurt to poke around a bit.

Heart heavy, Robyn walked from the room. Detouring, she took a moment in the restroom to wash her hands and to pull herself together in order to face the worst part of her job. Then she made her way to the private family room and, taking a deep breath, pushed inside.

The elderly man's expression as he stood, so hopeful and yet afraid, tore at her soul.

"Mr. Fields, I'm so sorry," she said gently. "We did everything we could, but your wife has died."

That night, after she'd let the sitter go and tucked Maddy into bed, the memory of the man's sobs invaded her dreams, refusing to allow her to rest. Why? Why did bad things happen to good people?

Uneasy, she replayed the conversation with Barb in her head. *Must be something in the water. That's the fourth one in the last couple of months . . .*

It was likely just a terrible coincidence, but now that the question had been raised, she couldn't let the matter go without an answer. It wouldn't help the dead, but if there was something else going on, maybe more grief could be spared.

Maybe.

Try as she might, she couldn't always save them. Not even the ones she loved most.

Rolling over, she hugged Greg's pillow and pretended she could still catch the beloved scent that was no longer there.

* * *

Christian Ford burrowed into the covers, savoring the warmth. He wasn't wild about leaving his comfortable nest at oh-dark-thirty to head to the gym and then on to the station.

But that was only because of the pert, naked bottom his groin was currently nestled against. There was nothing in the world like a woman's smooth body spooned with his, and his cock took a decided interest in gearing up for round three. Or was it four?

Cracking one eye open, he raised his head and peered over the sleeping blonde at the digital clock on the nightstand. "Ugh."

Just enough time, if he hurried. With regret, he slid from the bed and padded quietly to the bathroom. He took a quick shower to wash off the pungent aroma of their sex-a-thon, even though he'd have to take another after his workout. He didn't need more ribbing from his cousin Shane, or any of the other cops, about his carousing.

Yeah, like the shower would stop them when they already knew he'd taken this one home last night. But at least he wouldn't stink.

After drying off, he dressed in warm-up pants, a T-shirt, and tennis shoes, and gathered a nice pair of dark pants, shoes, and a button-up shirt to wear to work. He folded the pants and shirt carefully, then placed them in his gym bag along with his shoes. Then he threw in his wallet and the badge he always clipped onto his belt, and headed for the safe in his closet.

Another peek showed that his one-night stand was still passed out. Satisfied, he spun the combination and opened the heavy door, removing his holster and pistol. Normally, he'd just toss the holster and ammo onto his dresser and keep the gun close to his reach—but never with a stranger in the house. He'd stashed them as soon as he'd brought her home.

Shutting the safe, he walked to the bed. Reached down and touched the woman's arm. "Hey, time to get up." She stretched, then stilled again. What was her name? Damned if he could remember. "Wake up, gorgeous."

Better to stick with something general, anyway.

This time, her eyes opened and she blinked. Looked around, and then scowled at him as she sat up. "What the hell? The sun's not even up!"

"Yeah, sorry about that. I *did* tell you I had to leave early." She was clearly unhappy, a frown marring the expression on her narrow face. He realized that she wasn't nearly as attractive as she'd been last night after a few rounds of Cuervo. Now that common sense had returned, he wasn't *that* sorry about the hour or shoving her out the door. He guessed it showed.

With a huff, she rose and began to gather her clothes. She took her sweet time pulling on her panties and donning her bra, a smirk forming on her lips as she did.

"You sure you want me dressed?" Her attitude had gone from sulky to playful, as she obviously decided to try to persuade him to be late.

"Yep. Gotta go," he said cheerfully, shoring up his willpower. Morning-after sex with this woman would definitely give her the wrong impression.

He *was* looking for forever—but not with the young

lady who'd fucked him only *after* propositioning his cousin and getting turned down flat. Even the fact that Shane was married hadn't been a deterrent to her. God, what had he been thinking? Chris forced back a shudder at the thought of how he'd allowed tequila shots and loneliness to cloud his judgment.

"Come on," she purred, stepping up to trail a nail down his chest. "Fuck me against the wall again. Please?"

Any lingering trace of lust withered and died. Now he just wanted her gone.

He stepped back, still smiling, but letting his tone cool a bit. "Look, I'm running late, which means you have to leave. It's been fun, but the real world is calling."

Snorting, she grabbed her jeans and yanked them on. "Whatever. Call me if you want another round tonight, or drinks—"

"I won't, but thanks for a great time." He cringed at the seemingly heartless, but necessary, brush-off.

Finally getting the message, she finished dressing, pulled on her spiky heels, grabbed her purse, and stormed out. Following, he winced as the front door slammed with no little force. He took a moment to be grateful she'd driven her own car, preventing the awkwardness from being any worse.

Shit, he hated hurting people's feelings. Even so, it never ceased to amaze him what some women expected from a man versus reality. Under the circumstances, was hooking up with her supposed to mean more to him than a great roll in bed? Especially when he'd been her second choice to begin with? Jesus.

With a sigh, he let himself out through the garage, where his Camaro waited. Climbing in, he stowed his bag next to him, hit the door opener, and then fired up the engine. Once he was on the road, he breathed a sigh of relief.

"Christ, that sucked. No more one-night stands."

Until the next time he got so lonely his control vanished.

At the gym, he walked inside and immediately spied his new partner, Tonio Salvatore, jogging on one of the treadmills. Tonio had moved from Texas to Sugarland, Tennessee, the year before to be closer to his brother, Julian, a firefighter and medic at Station Five. Tonio was a good guy, if a little serious—unlike his brother, who was a former womanizer of the first order.

Tonio avoided women like the plague. Badge bunnies in particular drove the guy nuts, and not in a good way. He was totally devoted to his siblings, his mother, and his job. And as far as Chris knew, he never took part in the off-color jokes other officers bandied about to blow off steam, didn't drink much, and rarely smiled. The man was an enigma, and Chris wished he'd open up some. The guy definitely had a story to tell.

But Tonio pulled his weight as a cop and had your back. That was what counted.

Leaving his partner to the treadmill, Chris did some stretches to warm up. Then he started with some easy curls, and worked up to crunches. Next came some weights to work his thighs. Last, he headed over to do some bench presses for his arms and chest. He never did too many reps, not wanting to bulk up, just enough to keep fit and toned.

"Spot you?" Tonio asked, walking over as he wiped his face with a hand towel.

"Sure, thanks."

As Chris began, falling into a comfortable rhythm of lifting the heavy bar from his chest, he could feel Tonio's penetrating gaze. He figured the third degree wasn't far behind.

"You feeling okay today?"

"Come on, man." He huffed, pushing the bar upward again. "You've asked me that every day since I came back to work."

"It's only been three days, amigo. Just answer the question."

"I'm fine." Another rep.

"Your color still isn't good. You're too pale."

"Everybody's pale next to you," he joked. Tonio was half Hispanic and half Italian.

"Smart-ass. You know what I mean. First you've been sick, and then you got into a wreck during that stupid fucking chase, got yourself banged up." Annoyance had crept into his tone, which Chris knew actually masked his worry. He'd heard his partner talk the same way to Julian. "You haven't even been out of the hospital a week, and—"

"Tonio? Give it a rest, man. Seriously."

"Fine. But if you so much as break a sweat, I'm going straight to Rainey."

Austin Rainey was their captain, and he wouldn't hesitate to put Chris back on leave if he suspected he wasn't up to par. The idea of being cooped up again, out of the loop at work, wasn't a fun one.

"Don't worry. I'm not going to fuck up and do anything to ruin your rep as the department superhero." Heaving the bar back into the holder, he sat up and caught Tonio's fierce scowl. "What?"

"What the hell is that supposed to mean?"

Reaching for his own towel, Chris rolled his eyes, then wiped his face and neck. "Come on, everybody knows about the busload of kids in San Antonio. How you jumped onto a speeding bus and saved them all, like a regular Keanu Reeves or something."

Crossing his arms over his chest, Tonio narrowed his dark eyes and ignored the repeat of the story. "I'd never put my reputation above my partner. And don't try to change the subject. I'm concerned about you."

"I wasn't trying to change the subject. Just letting you know I'm fine, but thanks." Wow, two lies in one shot.

He'd definitely been trying to steer the conversation away from himself, and the nausea he'd been striving to ignore since he'd started his workout was becoming worse. The headache was starting as well, building as an awful pressure in his skull that promised to be a screamer before long.

Not again, goddammit! I had this beat! What the fuck is wrong with me?

"Chris?"

Squinting up at Tonio, he realized the man had uncrossed his arms and was starting toward him in alarm. Pushing up from the bench, Chris stood, ignoring the sudden weakness in his legs and pasting on a cocky grin.

"Aww, you care. That's so sweet."

"God, you're such a moron. I don't know why I bother."

With that, Tonio gave up and strode for the door at the back leading to the showers. Stung, Chris watched him disappear into the other room and wondered why he and Tonio couldn't have the same relationship as Shane and his partner, Taylor Kayne. Shane and Taylor constantly traded barbs, gave each other no end of shit, but were as close as brothers.

Every time Chris tried to joke with Tonio, his attempt fell flatter than a pancake. The guy was strung tighter than a fucking banjo.

Yeah, and it didn't help that you mocked his concern. He knows something is wrong, and now he likely thinks his partner doesn't trust him.

With a sigh, Chris followed and headed to the showers. Tonio was standing in one of the stalls, only his bronzed upper body showing as he turned this way and that, rinsing off the soap. Chris took a stall next to him and made short work of cleaning up. By the time he was done, his partner was dried off and getting dressed by the lockers. Grabbing his towel, Chris dried off as well and then joined him, opening his own locker to retrieve his work clothes.

"I'm sorry," he began. "I was an asshole."

Tonio eyed him, and nodded. "Yeah, you were. But I get it."

"Do you?"

The man's expression softened in understanding. "You're still not well, and you don't want anybody to guess. Am I right?"

"How do you *know* that?" he asked in exasperation, pulling on his boxer briefs. "It's not like I've broadcast it."

"You don't have to. You're my partner, Chris," Tonio said earnestly. "I see more of you than even Shane does. He doesn't work by your side all day, so he doesn't see that you have little appetite and your energy is past gone by the end of shift. He's not always here at the gym to notice your workout gets slower every day. That yesterday you did twenty-five reps and today you only did fifteen."

Chris blinked at him, heart sinking. "Damn. You're an observant son of a bitch."

"Occupational hazard." A hint of a smile was there and gone in a flash. "I get that you want to keep this quiet, but I'm your partner and the last person who should be in the dark when it comes to your health. The same applies to me keeping you in the loop, too."

He looked away, guilt spearing his gut. "I *am* sorry. The last thing I want to do is put you or anyone else at risk on the job."

"You won't, because I'm not going to let that happen. You're going to be honest with me and let me know before it gets that far."

Blowing out a breath, he stared at the floor. What choice did he have? He'd just have to power through as long as possible. "All right. I will. But please don't say anything to anyone, including Shane."

"I'm not going to lie to your cousin if he asks me point-blank."

He knew Tonio wouldn't budge on this, so there was no point in arguing. "Fair enough."

"Are you feeling well enough to work today?"

"Yes." *But just barely.*

"Good. Now let's get to the trenches, slacker."

"Was that you *almost* making a joke?"

"In your dreams."

From the man's tone, his mood was much improved by Chris's promise. As far as his stubborn partner was concerned, he'd spoken on the matter and that was it.

If only it was that simple.

They drove to the station separately, Chris arriving right after Tonio. They walked into the crowded briefing room and took seats next to each other, waiting for Rainey to get things rolling. All around them, their friends and colleagues on the day shift, including the two female officers, were laughing and joking, sipping coffee. Spirits were high today.

Shane and Taylor strolled in, the latter in the middle of telling Shane a story, apparently about Cara, his girlfriend.

". . . and she says to me, 'Do these jeans make my butt look fat?' "

"Uh-oh," one of the guys interjected. "The loaded gun of all questions."

Taylor nodded and gestured with one arm, almost sloshing his coffee. "Right? So I say, 'They make your ass look like a ripe, juicy peach,' and she gets all pissed off and tells me peaches are fat! I said peaches are plump and sweet, but—"

"Plump?" Shane repeated, laughing. "Oh, man. Hope your couch is comfy."

"I meant it in a *good* way! Who wants a skinny, shriveled-up peach?"

Chris laughed along with the guys, and even Tonio cracked a smile. The upbeat mood was almost enough to make him forget how awful he felt, and by the time the captain walked into the room, he figured he could make it.

"All right, people," Rainey yelled over the noise. "Quiet down so we can get going."

The first part was so boring Chris almost fell asleep listening to the captain drone on and on about quotas on traffic tickets and the city being up the chief's ass like a bad enema because the number of citations was down.

Blah, blah, blah. Same shit, different day.

At the mention of the drug dog doing a sweep through a middle school and the high school, he perked up a bit. But while interesting, handling the K-9 unit wasn't his assignment and there were no plans as of yet to put someone undercover in the high school. Then the talk turned to something about the yearly presentation on Stranger Danger to the local first graders, so he drifted again and concentrated on deep breaths. Calming thoughts of the nearby Cumberland River, lazing around on the bank, anything to ease this damned headache—

"You good with that, Detective Ford?"

Blinking, he looked around and realized Rainey was speaking to him, not to Shane. He scrambled to save face. "You bet, Cap."

"Great. Thanks for volunteering," his superior said with a smirk. "You and Salvatore can pick up the suit from storage anytime."

"Suit?" Crap, what the heck had he gotten himself into now?

Beside him, Tonio groaned. "I'm not wearing that smelly fucking thing—*you* are."

Snickers sounded around the room, and Shane elbowed Taylor in the ribs, the two of them turning red from stifling their laughter. *Jerks*.

Austin strode forward with a folder in his hands and tossed it onto the table in front of Chris. "I don't care who wears it. Just follow the program and be at each school on time."

With dread, he looked down at the folder and his worst suspicion was confirmed—smiling up at him was a cartoon rendering of Valor the Crime Dog wearing a police hat.

He and Tonio had just been stuck giving the one-hour Stranger Danger program for all of Sugarland's elementary schools.

"Fuck." The others lost it, not even bothering to hide their laughter any longer, and their relief that they hadn't gotten the assignment this year. "You guys suck."

Fantastic. Other than the fact that they got squirmy if they had to sit too long and had the attention span of mayflies, what he knew about little kids could fit onto the head of a pin. Oh, he loved kids; he just didn't know what to do with so many at one time.

Tonio grabbed the folder and opened it, peering at a typed sheet of paper inside. "We start next week, one school per week."

"Like we don't have real jobs to do or anything," he grumped.

"Come on, it won't be so bad. Besides, teaching people about crime and safety is part of our job—even if they're *small* people."

"Thanks, Pollyanna. I'm sure it'll be a blast."

"If you're done bitching, we'll continue." The captain shuffled some papers on his podium. "Burglaries have risen dramatically in the last three months, most of them homes. I'm assigning Ford and Salvatore to look into these since they'll be out of the building a lot anyway."

Beside him, Tonio spoke up. "Cap, why us? I mean, the responding officers usually follow up on those."

"Good question, and you're right. Actually, they *have* followed up, and found these aren't typical burglaries. For one, there's been an entire string of them, not just one or two. Second, in the majority of these cases, little if anything was taken."

Chris frowned. "Well, that's weird."

"Yes, it is, and it raises a red flag. If the perps aren't breaking in to steal, then they're doing it for another reason. What that reason might be is what we need to find out."

"We're on it," Tonio said earnestly. "If there's a connection, we'll find it."

"Good. Next, I want to point out . . ."

Chris resisted the urge to roll his eyes at his partner as Rainey droned on. Nobody was that much of a goody two-shoes. Except Tonio, apparently. He was about as much fun as a box of rocks. Jesus, what was this guy's damage?

Finally, the briefing was over and Chris went to see Rainey for a moment, taking the report from him that contained the names and addresses of the victims of the break-ins. Bracing himself for boring grunt work, he also had to admit it was better than wearing a dog costume.

"May as well get started talking to some of these folks," Chris said to his partner as they left the room. "I'll drive."

He didn't argue. It didn't much matter to him who drove, and Tonio liked to be behind the wheel. He grimaced inwardly, though, at the sight of his partner's serviceable 2010 Taurus sitting like a dark blob in the parking lot. Not everybody was into American muscle like Shane, Taylor, and himself, but damn. Even though nobody was getting rich on a cop's salary, surely the man could afford something less grandfatherly.

In a rare moment of common sense, Chris kept the thought to himself.

Sliding into the passenger's seat, he laid the crime dog folder and burglary list on the seat between them and buckled his seat belt.

"What's the first address?" Tonio asked.

He picked up the sheet and read it off. "Home belongs to George Fell. His was one of the earliest break-ins, almost three months ago. Honestly, I don't know what we're supposed to get out of investigating these."

"That's why we're called *detectives*, Sherlock." Tonio tossed him a rare grin. "We'll figure it out."

"Ha-ha, smart-ass."

"Better than being a dumb-ass."

Chris was quiet for a minute, watching the town roll past his window. As was typical, he couldn't keep his mouth shut for long. "How's your mom and sister?"

Chris knew Tonio and Julian's family still lived in San Antonio and that their mother hadn't been happy that both of her sons had moved so far away.

"They're fine. Mamacita may come for a visit soon, but I don't know if Sis will come with her or not."

"That's good. At least you can see your mom."

"I suppose. I miss my mother, but she's a bit overwhelming."

"I miss mine, too," he replied before he thought the better of it.

"Why don't you invite her here?"

"She's dead. Cancer, when I was twelve."

"Shit, I'm sorry." His partner glanced over, his expression contrite.

"No, it's fine. I don't talk about it much. My dad's still alive, but we don't keep in touch." He could feel his partner's unspoken question, so he decided to keep it simple. "He's an asshole. I don't know how Mom stood him as long as she did."

"Ah."

The rest of the ride was quiet, Tonio forgoing any more questions. Chris honestly wouldn't have minded answering, because that meant he could ask a few more of his own. It occurred to him that was probably why the man didn't probe further.

Ten minutes later, Tonio parked in front of a modest frame house and killed the engine. They got out and walked up to the front porch, and Chris knocked. After a few moments of silence, footsteps creaked on the other side of the door, then paused as though the person on the other side was peering out of the peephole.

The door opened slowly, and an older man's face appeared in the crack. "Can I help you?"

"Mr. Fell?" Chris inquired.

"That's me." The man eyed them suspiciously.

Chris gestured to the shield clipped to his belt, and nodded. "I'm Detective Chris Ford, and this is my partner, Tonio Salvatore. May we come in for a few minutes?"

"Sure, I suppose," the man said warily, then stepped back to allow them inside.

Once they were in, he tried to give the man a reassuring smile. "We're just here to follow up on the break-in you had a few months ago. There's been a rash of them since then, and we'd like to speak with you about what happened here, see if we can find any similarities."

"Oh." Fell scratched his balding head. "I haven't thought much about that in a while. My wife passed away about a month after the bastards broke in, and it just didn't seem that important anymore."

"I'm very sorry for your loss," he said sincerely. "If you prefer, we can come back some other time."

"No, no. Might as well stay. There's not that much to tell anyhow."

"All right, if you're sure."

Tonio took a small notepad and pen from his pocket and got ready to write while Chris questioned the man.

"Mr. Fell, when did you first notice your home had been burglarized?"

"Oh, one morning after I'd been out running errands with my wife, I guess it was. No, it was afternoon, because we stopped and ate lunch before we came home."

"Do you believe the break-in took place during that morning, or could it have been the previous night while you were both sleeping?"

"It was that morning while we were out—I'm positive.

The house was fine when we left, and when we came back there was glass all over the front porch. Son of a bitch had broken out the side glass and reached in to unlock the door."

"Broad daylight, entering from the front? Pretty bold." Chris exchanged a look with his partner before returning his attention to the other man. "Okay. And when you looked around, was anything missing?"

"If he did take anything, it wasn't valuable. All of our electronics, our stash of cash in the bedroom—everything was still there. But there was something weird." He paused, as though remembering.

"What was that?"

"Stuff was moved, just slightly. We could tell because of the dust on the furniture. The lamp, some pictures, things like that. Like whoever broke in picked up certain items, examined them, and then put them back. But he didn't care if we noticed, because he didn't put them back exactly the same way."

"That's really odd," Tonio put in with a frown.

"Tell me about it." Mr. Fell sighed. "It really upset us, especially Sarah, God rest her."

There really wasn't much else George Fell could relate to them, so they politely took their leave a couple of minutes later.

"That was strange," Chris said as they climbed back into the Taurus. "Not Mr. Fell, but the burglary."

"Yeah. That's a pretty ballsy way to commit a break-in, during the day when he couldn't be sure how long they'd be gone, right on the front porch. And then to not take anything? It doesn't make sense."

"And if it's the same guy, there's a whole list of them just like that one." Chris lifted the sheet of addresses. "What the hell is he after?"

"Got no clue. Maybe he's a voyeur? Like, one of those underwear sniffers."

Chris barked a laugh. "God, I need bleach for my brain."

Tonio smiled, shook his head. "Next address?"

"Pauline Nicholson, one block over."

"Hmm. Pretty close to Mr. Fell's address. Maybe we should take a city map and place pins on the location of each home. See if there's a pattern."

"Now that's good thinkin', *Sherlock*," he drawled, throwing the term back at his partner.

The visit with Mrs. Nicholson and the next two victims as well turned out pretty much the same—not much info, and what there was didn't compute. Like items in the house being moved and the lack of theft . . .

All in all, it made for a long, tedious day. At the end of their shift, Chris was tired, but at least his headache had subsided.

By the time he fell into bed that night, he'd managed to convince himself that today had simply been a slight relapse.

Nothing more.

2

Dragging himself out of bed the next morning before sunrise, Chris ignored the aches and pains he shouldn't have been feeling and slipped on his warm-up pants and a T-shirt.

Today he decided to forgo working out at the gym in favor of going for a walk through his neighborhood. He felt fine, he told himself. He could do something more strenuous if he wanted to, but walking was just as good. And he liked his peaceful neighborhood of modest homes with their trim lawns. Taylor lived a few streets over, so maybe he'd even walk that far and bum a cup of coffee.

As he went along, he let the peace and quiet seep into his bones. He'd like to get a dog to walk with him. But while he loved animals and a dog would make a great companion, he worked too much and his hours sometimes ran long. It wasn't fair to a pup to leave it alone so often. The knowledge made him a little sad.

The sun began to peek over the horizon, and the streetlamps shut off. He hadn't been out all that long, but his limbs were starting to feel heavy and sweat trickled down his back. The headache returned as a low, ominous throb and his stomach lurched.

"Shit." Disappointed, he cut his walk short and turned down the next street he came to so he could head back home.

But with every step, the symptoms got worse. This didn't bode well for the rest of his day. Damn, he couldn't afford to miss any more work. His body didn't get the message, however, and halfway down the street he was forced to stop. Thrusting out a hand, he braced himself against a light pole and stood with his head down, panting, desperately trying to stave off being sick. Or passing out.

"Hey, mister! You okay?"

Straightening, he looked for the owner of that sweet little voice and turned. His gaze drifted downward to the cutest kid, a girl who appeared to be about seven or so. She had her brunette hair in a ponytail held on top of her head with a pink scrunchie thing, and wore a matching pink top, a backpack that was way too big, and jeans. Her small face was frowning at him, her concern clear.

"I'm all right, sweetheart," he said, mustering a smile. "Just got a bit winded."

"Oh." She seemed to consider this very seriously. "You want my mommy to take your temp-ra-ture? She's a doctor!"

What an angel. "Oh, no, that won't be necessary—"

"Madeline Jane, wait for me! And you forgot your lunch box again!" a woman's voice called. "I swear— Oh. Who are you talking to, honey?"

Chris raised his eyes to peer over the child—and forgot to breathe.

Staring back at him, holding a pink lunch box, was the most beautiful woman he'd ever seen. She was about five foot seven and had straight, silky auburn hair that fell to her shoulders. A fitted black shirt hugged her curves, emphasizing a mouthwatering busty figure that tapered to a small waist. Gray dress pants showed off long legs with just a hint of the strong thighs underneath.

As she approached, locking gazes with him, he took in the wariness in her vivid blue eyes. "Maddy, who's this?" she asked mildly, but with an unmistakable hint of warning directed at him.

"I don't know, Mommy. But he doesn't feel good," Maddy informed her mom. "You should take his temp-ra-ture."

"Maybe so." The woman stopped, handed over the lunch box, and wrapped her arms around her child, pulling Maddy's back against her front. A clearly protective stance. "But what have I told you about talking to strangers?"

Maddy dipped her head. "Sorry."

"We'll talk about it more later." She hugged her daughter in reassurance, then addressed Chris, holding out a hand. "Hello, I'm Robyn."

He shook it, a bit disappointed that she didn't share her last name. He decided to share more in his introduction. As he let go of her hand, he reached into the pocket of his warm-ups, removed his badge, and held it up. "Chris Ford. I'm a detective with the Sugarland PD." He smiled. "You and Maddy are both perfectly safe in my presence. Honest."

With that, the steel in her expression softened some. "Nice to meet you, Detective."

"Chris, please."

She nodded, but made no commitment either way. "So, you're not feeling well? Would you like to sit down on my steps? I can take a look at you or call someone to come get you."

He shook his head. "No, thanks. I just needed to catch my breath. I've been out of commission and this is only my fourth day back at work. Guess I've got to build up my strength again."

Her eyes narrowed, and she seemed to see right through him. "You don't look well. You're pale, and you're holding on to that light pole as though it's the only thing keeping you upright."

Abruptly, he pushed away from it as though it had burned him. "No, really I'm fine. But I'd better be on my way if I don't want to be late."

"Well, if you're sure . . ." She wasn't convinced. "I was just about to take Maddy to school. Would you like a ride home?"

He opened his mouth to refuse—and then thought better of it. One, he wasn't sure he'd make it. And two, he really wanted more time in Robyn's presence. "Sure, that would be great. Thanks."

"No problem." To Maddy, she said, "Would you run in and get my purse and keys? They're on the table."

"Sure!"

The girl ran inside, and Chris took the opportunity to speak privately. "I'm sorry if I scared you when you saw her talking to me. I was just resting for a minute and she surprised me."

"It's all right. No matter how I caution her, Maddy is a social butterfly." The woman gave him a real smile, and almost blinded him. "I'm Dr. Robyn Lassiter, by the way."

By God, she was gorgeous.

His mouth stretched into a wide, answering smile. "Nice to meet you, Dr. Lassiter."

"Just Robyn."

He was getting the feeling there was no Mr. Lassiter in the picture, but he couldn't be sure. How could he subtly find out?

All too fast, the little girl returned, swinging the purse and keys, and handed them to her mother.

"Ready, sweet pea?"

"Yep!" To Chris, she proudly said, "I'm in first grade!"

"Is that so?" He widened his eyes, looking impressed. "You're a big girl, then."

"Yep."

"Yes, sir," Robyn corrected the little girl.

Maddy sighed. "Yes, sir."

Something about these two made him feel warm inside. Better than he had in a long time. Maddy scrambled into the back of the car as though she was used to riding there, which was safer given her size and the air bags in the front. Chris climbed into the passenger's seat and buckled up. Once they were on their way, he gave directions to his house.

"You live pretty close by," Robyn commented.

"Yeah. I feel stupid catching a ride when I live five streets away."

"That's not what I meant. I don't mind at all."

When she pulled up in front of his house a few moments later, he turned. "Speaking of strangers, my partner and I are giving the Stranger Danger program to each of the first-grade classes starting next week. Maybe I'll see you and Maddy there." To Maddy, he turned and said in a conspiratorial voice, "I'm bringing Valor the Crime Dog."

"Yay! Can you come, Mommy?"

Put on the spot, Robyn bit her lip. "I can't promise, but I'll try."

Thank Jesus for this shitty assignment and even the smelly suit.

That was the best he was going to get, so it was time to bow out gracefully. "Thank you for the ride. Hopefully I'll see you two soon."

She smiled, but the shadows were back. "We'll see. Good to meet you, Chris."

"You, too." Winking, he got out and headed inside, glancing back once as she drove away. He wanted to know more about this gorgeous lady, and he didn't want her to go. Too bad they hadn't had time for coffee.

On the bright side, she'd called him by his first name. They lived nearby, so he could just *happen* to walk her direction again. And he'd be at her daughter's school soon.

It would do for a start.

Robyn's cell phone buzzed in her coat pocket and she pulled it out, leaning back in the chair in her office. Every second of the day had been packed, so it figured she'd get a call the one time she sat down.

On the other hand, looking at the display, she saw this was one call she had been waiting for. She answered quickly. "This is Dr. Robyn Lassiter."

"Dr. Lassiter, this is Dr. Laura Eden, Medical Examiner. I'm calling back about the message you left for me earlier."

"Yes, thank you for getting back to me so quickly."

"To be honest, your call underscored what's been nagging me for a while now. My team and I have seen reports of a higher than normal number of fatal heart attacks over the past few months. I haven't mentioned them to the police, however, because there was no indication of crime."

"Meaning the deaths appeared to be natural."

"Correct." Eden paused. "But now I'm beginning to wonder."

"So am I. At first, it was easy to overlook them, because there are various ER doctors here and we had no reason to compare notes about heart attack victims. Even if we had, we might have dismissed them as a coincidence. But now? My most recent patient died with no history of heart trouble, and one of the nurses brought the subject to my attention. That's when I started investigating, and the recent numbers are alarming."

"I crunched some numbers on my end as well. My office saw twenty-three deaths classified as heart attacks by this time last year, compared to forty-seven this year. That's a one hundred four percent increase."

Robyn sat back in her chair, shocked. "So what do we do?"

"I'll look up the recent victims' addresses and places of death, and make a call to the police departments involved. I can make them aware of our concern, but unless they can gather enough evidence to open an investigation and give me cause to exhume the remains and perform further tests, it's out of my hands."

"That's not right."

"I know." The medical examiner's voice was harried. "But for now it's the best we can do."

"All right. Thank you for taking this on."

"Not a problem. If there's something sinister going on, the victims' families deserve to know."

"Yes, they do. Call me if you need anything at all."

"Will do."

They hung up, and Robyn sat at her desk contemplating the conversation. What the hell could be causing that many deaths? Mass contamination of some kind? Something in the city's water? That didn't seem likely, considering that the water system was highly monitored, with a number of safeguards to assure quality. Contrary to what conspiracy theorists would have people believe, it would be virtually impossible to directly corrupt a city's water supply.

Then what could it be?

A knock at the door broke into her musings, and she looked up to see Shea Skyler standing just inside her office.

"Hey, come in." She smiled at the nurse who had also become a good friend since she and Maddy had moved to Sugarland two years earlier. "What's up?"

The curly-headed brunette moved into the room and sat in a chair on the other side of Robyn's desk. "Just dropping by to be sure you're still coming to the party tonight."

"Oh, I don't know," she hedged. "It's been a long week, and the sitter has plans."

"Why on earth would you need a sitter when it's just a backyard cookout? Bring Maddy along!"

"I just don't want to impose."

"Are you hearing yourself? There will be plenty of people there to spoil her. She'll have fun, so why would you want to deny her *or* yourself a good time?"

One corner of her mouth hitched up. "You really know how to hit where I live." Maddy was her weakness. Her joy. How could she keep her baby from having fun?

"You bet I do. So bring her." Shea paused, her expression softening. "You've got to stop hiding from the world eventually. Don't say no this time. Please?"

Letting out a sigh, she nodded. "Okay, I'll be there."

"Great!" The happiness on her friend's face made her smile.

"Seven?"

"Or before. Come as soon as you can, and don't worry about bringing anything. Shane and Tommy have all the food and drinks covered."

Shea's husband, Tommy, was a former firefighter/paramedic who worked for the fire marshal's office. Shane, she recalled, was Shea's twin brother who'd recently married and had a seventeen-year-old godson he was raising. Shane was a detective at the Sugarland PD.

Shane *Ford*. A click suddenly sounded in her head, a puzzle piece falling into place.

"Say, do you or Shane know a guy named *Chris* Ford?"

Shea blinked at her. "Um, yeah. Chris is our cousin, and he and Shane work together. How do you know Chris?"

Her mind whirled. Shane and the hottie from yesterday morning were related. "I don't, really. He was out walking yesterday morning and apparently wasn't feeling well, so he stopped in front of my house to rest. I was getting ready to drive Maddy to school and I looked out, saw her talking to a stranger, and I freaked for a minute. He turned out to be a nice guy, and we introduced ourselves."

"Really? Oh my God—Chris is such a sweetheart!" Shea enthused. "He's funny, smart, handsome, and better yet, *single*. I can't believe I never thought to fix you guys up!"

Robyn laughed, her interest spiking. "Do tell!"

"And he's kind of had it rough lately— Wait. You said he was sick yesterday?" Her expression morphed to worry. "He was just released from the hospital a few days ago. We thought he was on the mend."

"I don't know if he was actually sick, but he was pale and definitely had run out of steam during his walk. I drove him home."

Shea frowned. "He probably just overdid it."

"Why was Chris in the hospital? If you don't mind my asking."

"He was hurt on the job when he wrecked a surveillance van during a chase a couple of weeks ago. But that was just the icing on the cake—there were already some underlying health issues going on with him, and he won't talk much about it."

A chill traveled down her spine. "What sort of health issues?"

"I don't know much, but I'm really not at liberty to discuss what I *do* know. You'd have to ask Chris." She gave Robyn an apologetic look.

"I'm sorry. It's none of my business." She hesitated. "I guess I'm on edge, what with all the strange deaths we've had. Then you mention a man who by all appearances should be perfectly healthy yet is having problems, and the doctor in me goes on alert."

"You don't think his symptoms are related to those other cases, do you?" her friend asked in alarm.

She hurried to reassure the other woman. "I don't think anything at this point. It was something that struck me, is all."

"I'll mention it to Shane and have him keep an eye on Chris." The other woman smiled again. "Who, by the way, you'll probably see tonight."

"God," Robyn groaned. "You're incorrigible."

"I try."

"Mommy?"

"Yes, sweetie?"

Robyn hustled her daughter into the car. It was fifteen minutes until seven, and she hated being late, even to a casual party.

"When can we have a puppy?"

Oh Lord, not this again. Give me strength.

"We've talked about this," she said, sliding behind the wheel. "You know it will probably be this summer before we can get one."

"But that's too long!" Maddy wailed. "I want one now!"

Keeping her cool after the week she'd endured, and dealing with this issue yet again, took every ounce of effort she had. "Madeline, we don't have time to care for a puppy just yet. Not with my hours and you being in school."

Her daughter turned on the sniffles. "It's not fair. Amy got a puppy *and* her mommy and daddy work."

"Well, I'm sure their situation is different."

"It's not." The scowling little face assumed a stubborn pout.

I will not yell. Cleansing breath—in and out.

"I'm not discussing this anymore at the moment," she said firmly. "We're going to a party and we're going to have a good time."

Maddy didn't answer, but instead turned her head and stared out the window. In fact, she didn't speak at all, despite Robyn's attempts to draw her into conversation. Suddenly Robyn wanted to turn the car around and go home, but she'd promised to be at the party. Once she made a commitment, she hated going back on it. But days like this made it hard to remember that.

Damn you, Greg. Why did you leave me to raise our daughter alone? Why did you give up on all three of us?

Knowing the answer didn't make the loneliness any easier to bear.

Quite a few cars were parked at Shea and Tommy's

when she arrived. It was a good thing they had a sizable piece of property on the river that was perfect for having friends over. Deciding that she and Maddy wouldn't stay long, she parked in a spot that seemed easy to get out of and she shut off the ignition.

She got out and met Maddy on the other side, but her daughter didn't reach for her hand as she usually did. Letting go of a quiet sigh, Robyn walked to the front porch, climbed the steps, and knocked. Happy sounds of talking and laughter drifted from inside, and for a moment it made her a bit sad, because at one time Robyn's house had sounded much the same.

Snap out of it!

The door opened to reveal Tommy standing there with a wide smile on his adorable face. He was so darned cute with his dancing crystal blue eyes and blond hair poking in every direction, Robyn wondered if Shea had to beat the women off him.

"Hey, stranger!" he called, pulling her inside. "Glad you could make it. You, too, Miss Maddy."

Predictably, her daughter gave Tommy a smile, but withdrew a bit from the noisy scene. Edging close to Robyn, eyes wide, her upset about the puppy was clearly forgotten, for now.

"It's great to see you again," she said, letting herself be enveloped in a strong hug.

"You, too." He let her go and stood back, grinning. "Shea was so happy when you said you'd come. She tells me you work much too hard."

"Well, I'm working on that."

"Come on back to the deck—we have tons of food and whatever you want to drink."

"Thanks."

As she followed Tommy, a small hand slipped into hers and she smiled. No matter how pissed Maddy might be about something, when she wasn't sure about something, she wanted to stick close to her mom.

On the way, Tommy introduced her to several firefighters and a few police officers, plus various other people, all of them jovial and friendly. There was no way she'd remember all their names, though, so she just rolled with it and proudly thanked them when they complimented her on her pretty angel.

As they stepped onto the deck, Tommy called, "Hey, baby! Look who's here!"

Shea turned and then rushed forward to hug her and Maddy as Tommy disappeared to visit with some of his friends. "You made it!"

"Told you I would." She smiled at her friend.

"So you did." Shea turned her attention to Maddy. "Hi there, honey. I'm so glad you could come."

"Me, too." The little girl ducked her head shyly.

"Come on, fix a couple of plates. There's plenty of burgers and hot dogs, juice and soda. And some stronger stuff for the grown-ups."

"Just one beer for me," Robyn said. "I'm not on call tonight, but I've got no designated driver."

"No problem."

Robyn headed for the long folding tables filled with food, fixing a burger for herself and a plain hot dog for

Maddy. Then she allowed her daughter one root beer, her favorite soda, and chose a light beer for herself. She found a table with a couple of empty seats and led Maddy over, checking to make sure she was handling her plate and drink okay.

Then she seated herself across from one of the biggest men she'd ever seen, a bear of a man with short, spiky brown hair bleached blond at the tips. Next to him was a pretty woman with long blond hair holding a squirming baby on her lap. They were wearing matching wedding bands.

"Sweetheart," he said in a low, baritone voice, "why don't you let me hold him so you can eat?"

"No, I've got him. We're fine." Her eyes softened as she gazed back at her husband, and he kissed her gently.

There was such love between them, Robyn's throat threatened to close. She had loved Greg, and he had felt the same way, too. They had been close. But had he ever looked at *her* like that? As though she was his entire world, the moon and stars?

"Oh, hello," the woman greeted her, expression friendly. "I'm Kat Paxton, and this is my husband, Howard."

Howard? That big, sexy hunk of man didn't look like any Howard *she'd* ever seen. But hey, who cared?

"Nice to meet you both. And who's this?" She nodded to the baby.

"This is Ben," Howard said, the pride in his voice evident. "He's named after my dad."

"He's so cute. I think he looks like you," she told Howard, who immediately puffed out his chest and smirked at his wife.

"See? Told you." He grinned at Robyn. "Thank you."

"I'll never hear the end of it." Kat rolled her eyes, then smiled at Robyn. "I don't think we've met before, have we?"

"Oh! Sorry. I'm Robyn Lassiter, and this is my daughter, Maddy."

"It's great to meet you. And hello, Maddy."

"Hi." A pause. Then, in a small voice, she said, "I know you."

Kat eyed the little girl and seemed to come to a sudden realization. "Hey, I know you, too. You're in Mrs. Manning's room."

"Uh-huh."

Noting the confusion that was no doubt showing on Robyn's face, Kat explained. "I'm one of the first-grade teachers at Mendenhall Elementary. Maddy's not in my class, so I didn't recognize her at first."

Relief immediately deflated the tension that had started to knot her shoulders. "That's great! Come to think of it, I may have seen you at Back to School night and just forgot."

Kat nodded. "It's possible. So, how do you know Tommy and Shea?"

"I'm a doctor at Sterling, and I've known Shea for a couple of years, since Maddy and I moved to town. She's one of the first people I met, and she made me feel welcome right away."

"That's our Shea. She's a sweetheart."

"What do you do?" Robyn asked Howard politely.

"I'm the captain at Fire Station Five. Most of my team is wandering around here somewhere."

"I admire what you do. You guys have a dangerous job."

He shrugged. "It can be, but it's also rewarding when we're able to help people. I'm sure you feel the same way at the hospital."

"All the time. I live for the moments when I have good news to share with anxious families."

She made small talk with the Paxtons for a while, and eventually caught herself scanning the deck and backyard. She wasn't consciously aware of what, or who, she was searching for. Not until she caught sight of a familiar figure sauntering out of the house onto the deck.

Her breath hitched and her heart beat a little faster at the sight of the tall, lean figure standing a few feet away. This time, she really took the opportunity to study Chris Ford as she hadn't the other day. At a bit over six feet, brown hair streaked with blond falling into big, warm brown eyes, and a face that reminded her of Henry Cavill, the man was stunning.

He had on a pair of snug jeans that cupped his ass like a glove, and as he turned more fully in her direction she noted they did the same to his package in the front. He also wore a fitted black T-shirt that showed off a deliciously muscled chest and arms, not to mention the flat stomach.

When his gaze landed on her and Maddy sitting at the table, his eyes widened a fraction. Then his mouth curved into a broad smile that lit his face, and he started toward them.

"Well, if it isn't my beautiful neighbors," he said. Stopping next to them, he held out a hand. "Robyn, it's good to see you again."

"It's good to see you, too." She was surprised the

statement came out so calmly when inside she was quivering like a sixteen-year-old. If she'd been expecting him to simply flirt with her and ignore Maddy, as a lot of guys would have, she was surprised and pleased. He crouched next to Maddy's chair and spoke to the little girl at eye level.

"Hey, Maddy. Remember me?"

Setting down her hot dog, she studied him for a few seconds. Recognition dawned and she practically squealed. "Chris! Are you better now? Mommy never took your temp-ra-ture and I was worried that you were still sick."

Tentatively, he reached out and stroked a hand over her hair. A shadow crossed his face, there and gone. "I'm feeling okay, sweetheart. Say, I'll be at your school on Tuesday for the crime program with Valor. Isn't that great?"

Interesting, how he'd avoided getting into his health. He wasn't telling the whole truth; she was sure of it.

"Yeah! Mrs. Paxton will be there, too. She's one of the teachers," Maddy informed him, pointing to Kat.

"That's good." He nodded to the Paxtons. "Kat, Howard. How's it going?"

"Going good," Howard said. "Can't complain."

"Beautiful wife and baby, what's to complain about?" He smiled, but Robyn caught the wistful look on his face as he studied Ben.

Her heart warmed a fraction.

Chris gestured to the table. "Mind if I pull up a seat?"

Howard stood and stretched. "Actually, take one of our chairs. We're going to make the rounds inside before we have to go home and put Ben to bed."

"Oh, all right. It was good to see you guys again."

"You too, man. Take care."

Chris and Howard shook hands, and then Chris hugged Kat and kissed the baby on the cheek.

After they were gone, Chris took a vacant chair and rested his arms on the table, clasping his hands as he studied her. "I was surprised to see you here. But glad," he hurried to add.

"I have a confession to make—I wasn't surprised to see *you* at all."

He looked confused. "Really? How did you know I'd be here?"

"I work with Shea at the hospital. She's a friend of mine, and when she mentioned the party I remembered her twin brother is Shane Ford, a detective like you, with the same last name. I put the pieces together and she confirmed you're their cousin."

He smiled. "Sounds like you could be a detective yourself. Small world, huh?"

"Isn't it?"

"I'm guessing you're single?" he asked, glancing at her empty ring finger.

"For a while now." She didn't offer more and he didn't push. "You?"

"Never been married." Appearing pleased with the direction things were moving, he leaned toward her a bit. "So, what do you like to do when you're not saving lives and being a mom?"

"You mean, just for myself, for *fun*?" she said, teasing. "I'm not sure I remember what free time *is*."

"Well, according to your vague recollections, give it

your best shot." His brown eyes were dancing with humor.

"Let's see . . . I love to go boating, fishing. I prefer a quiet lake cabin over the beach. I love steaks, seafood, Italian food. I enjoy reading. Dancing."

"Wouldn't you know? I love those things, too."

"Oh, really?"

"I never lie about having fun."

As she stared into his sexy face, the intensity in his eyes, it hit her like a bolt of lightning.

Good God, he's interested in me! How did I not realize that the moment he walked over? Has it been that damned long?

Yes, it had.

And as the spit in her mouth dried up, Robyn knew she didn't have a single clue what to do about it.

3

"Robyn?"

Startled, she looked at Chris and realized he had asked her a question. "I'm sorry, what?"

"I said, speaking of fun, is it okay if I take Maddy to toss the football?"

The curve of his lips and sparkle in his eyes communicated he knew that wasn't what she'd expected him to say. Most men who were interested in Robyn tended to treat Maddy like a third wheel, or ignored her altogether. But Chris seemed sincere.

"Sure." She shrugged.

Maddy bounded from her chair, half-eaten hot dog forgotten, and raced for the grass. Giving Robyn a smile that made her heart pound again, he tagged along after his pint-sized companion. She watched as he picked up the ball and motioned for the little girl to move back a little.

Gently, he executed an underhand toss. Maddy dropped the ball, but was grinning as she picked it up and threw it back. He easily caught it and tossed it back again, and

Maddy whooped when she caught it successfully that time. His words of encouragement and praise drifted to where Robyn sat, and she couldn't help but wonder if this was for her benefit, not Maddy's.

But she just didn't believe so. One thing that was hard to fake was liking kids, and Chris appeared to be having too good a time for that to be the case. Her opinion of him thus far rose several notches.

Someone took the chair across from her, and she looked over to see Shea sitting there, gazing at her thoughtfully. "Is he always like that?" Robyn waved a hand in Chris's direction.

Her friend didn't need to ask what she meant. "Always. He's like this brilliant light who warms people wherever he goes. He's such a good man."

"He seems too good to be true."

"Chris has had his issues, but hey, don't we all?" Shea rested her arms on the table and considered her friend. "He's interested in you."

"Has he said anything?" She couldn't keep her tone casual if she tried.

"Not in so many words. But I saw the way he looked at you when he first saw you sitting there. It's the same way Tommy still looks at me."

Robyn returned her attention to Chris, who caught the ball and fell, sprawling on the grass as Maddy giggled. "That scares me a little," she admitted softly.

"I know it does, hon. Just give things a chance, maybe?"

"Maybe."

Shea knew Robyn's sad story. And she didn't push further.

The sight of Maddy crouching next to Chris, shaking his shoulder and demanding that he get up, brought Robyn to her feet. Anxiety shot through her and she started across the deck, but Shane sprinted past her and was already halfway across the yard yelling his cousin's name.

And then Chris sat upright and yelled, "Gotcha!" He made a monster face at Maddy, who squealed in delight and launched herself at him as the two of them wrestled on the ground.

Shane stopped a few feet from Chris and bent over, hands on his knees. He straightened, obviously upset and trying hard not to show it in front of the little girl. Robyn wasn't any happier, and returned to her chair on shaking legs, desperately squashing her doctor's urge to rush over and check him from head to toe. And also to keep herself from smacking him for that stunt.

Chris and her daughter stood, laughing together, and he brushed the grass off her first, then himself. Belatedly, he realized Shane was close by and seething. Bending, he said something to Maddy and pointed toward Robyn. Probably to keep her from overhearing when Shane chewed out his ass.

Indeed, Shane leaned in, and though Robyn couldn't hear what was said, it was apparent from his gestures and the tension in his body that he was making his feelings known. The smile slid off Chris's face, and immediately something strange happened in Robyn's chest. He looked sad and contrite now, and she found she didn't like that at all. Even though he'd scared her, he hadn't meant to. He had only been playing with Maddy.

After Shane stalked off, Chris hung his head for a moment. Then he heaved a sigh and headed in her direction.

Reaching her mom, Maddy was bouncing. "Did you see me throw the football? Chris showed me how!"

"I saw, sweetie! You did great." She got an exuberant hug and a smack on the cheek.

"Thanks, Mommy!"

Chris approached and gave her a sheepish smile. "I'm sorry about that. Didn't mean to scare anybody."

"That's okay—I know you were just having fun with Maddy and I appreciate it. But don't do it again or I'll be forced to whip out my stethoscope."

His eyes lit at her teasing. "Doesn't sound like much of a threat."

"More like a promise."

Maddy tugged at her sleeve, interrupting. "Can I have some cookies?"

Robyn glanced toward the dessert table. "Start with two."

"Why don't I go with her?" Shea offered, giving Robyn a knowing look.

"Okay!" The little girl took Shea's hand and went along willingly.

"She's a great kid," Chris said sincerely.

"Thank you. I think so, too."

"I really *am* sorry."

"I know. You startled several people, I think, but I'm sure they've already forgotten."

He grimaced. "I'm not so sure about Shane. I've got to see him every day at work, so I'm sure I'll hear about my stupidity again."

"Don't be too hard on yourself," she insisted. "It was a joke."

"A bad one. I wasn't thinking, and considering how worried he's been . . ." Suddenly he smiled brightly. "You're right. It made Maddy laugh, and that's all that counts."

Oh my God. Is this guy for real? Nobody is this sweet.

"So, your list of things you like to do for fun," he began, gaze intense once again. "Would that happen to include having dinner at a nice restaurant with me?"

She'd been half expecting him to ask, had been anticipating it. She liked this man, and she wanted to go. But the last time she'd been vulnerable . . . Her heart froze in her chest and she couldn't get the acceptance out if she tried.

The problem was fear, plain and simple. She'd already had her heart broken cleanly in two, and she wasn't sure she was ready to face that again.

"Surprised you, huh?" He smiled, but it didn't reach his eyes. "Tell you what. Think about it, and if you want to accept, Shea has my number. Call me anytime, okay?"

"I—I'm sorry, Chris."

"Don't be." He stood. "Guess I'd better go. I'm not really off tomorrow and I've got some leads to chase. It was great seeing you again."

"You, too," she managed. "Thanks for entertaining Maddy."

"No problem. She's an awesome little girl." He waved as he headed for the patio door. "Bye."

"Bye," she said. But he'd already disappeared inside. As soon as he was gone, it was as though a cloud had eclipsed the sunshine.

And she didn't like the sense of loss that sort of stole her breath. Not one bit.

On the Tuesday after the party, Chris was still cursing himself for being an idiot. He couldn't help but feel he'd given up too soon when Robyn had hesitated.

But he'd gotten nervous, and when she'd seemed far from thrilled at his invite, his confidence had suffered a serious blow. All he'd been able to think of was getting away as fast as possible.

Maybe it was for the best. There was no doubt that his illness, whatever it was, had him in its grip again. The downward slide was moving faster than it had last time. Steadily, it was stealing his strength, his appetite. How long before he crashed and didn't come out of it?

Helpless anger coursed through his body. Why was this happening? What was wrong with him?

He went for his walk before work, because he was a stubborn bastard; the gym was out for now, but he could do this much. Then go to work and pretend nothing was wrong. *Fake it till you make it.*

On his new route, which involved cutting down Robyn's street, he wondered where she'd been. He'd been by each morning, but hadn't seen her or Maddy out front again. Knocking on her door entered his mind, but he wasn't sure his presence would be welcome. The last thing he needed was to come across like a stalker.

So he was excited to see that this morning she was out front watering the flowers in the beds around her trees. A pair of old jeans hugged her curvy figure, and a pastel purple T-shirt emphasized her breasts. Her hair was loose around her shoulders, the strands catching fire in the sunlight. Exhaustion forgotten, he hurried his steps and called a greeting as he got closer.

"Hello."

Turning, she saw him and smiled. That she wasn't running in the opposite direction was something, at least.

"Chris! How are you?"

"Doing okay. Just been busy. You?"

"Same." She squinted at him in the sunlight. "You're late this morning. I already took Maddy to school."

"Yeah, well, I've got the crime presentation over there in a couple of hours, so I decided to fudge going in to work." He made a face. "I got stuck wearing the dog suit, so I figured they owe me."

She laughed, the musical sound going straight to his groin. "Can't say I blame you. That'll be a sight to see."

"What?"

"I'll be there." Her expression was mischievous. "I took a later shift at work so I could volunteer at school today. Can't wait to see you in action."

A groan escaped his lips. "You're not serious. I'm not going to do anything but stand around looking stupid. My partner is doing all the talking."

"So? I'm sure the kids will love it."

Fantastic. My humiliation will be complete. Valor—1; Chris—0.

"Maybe I'll call in sick."

"Oh, you won't do that."

"You sound pretty confident."

She nodded. "The guy who enjoyed playing with my

daughter the other day doesn't have it in him to disappoint a bunch of kids."

"Ugh. You're right. I *could* get hit by a bus, though. It happens."

Shaking her head, she walked over to the side of the house and turned off the water, then tossed down the hose. "You're something else—you know that?"

"Um, is that a compliment?"

Instead of answering, she walked back to him and asked, "How are you feeling?"

"Well enough to humble myself in front of ninety first graders, the staff of the school, and a few more besides. Does that satisfy you, Doc?" He hoped his grin fooled her, and it seemed to work.

"I suppose."

He checked his watch and felt a surge of disappointment. "Better go. I have to get home, change, and go pick up the stuff for the presentation before Tonio and I head to the school."

"Tonio?"

"Tonio Salvatore. He's my partner. He wasn't at the party, so you probably haven't met him."

"No, I don't know him. Well, I guess I'll see you later."

"All right. See you."

This time, she didn't offer him a ride home, and he fought a sense of discouragement. On one hand, she seemed reluctant to spend more time with him. On the other, it almost seemed that she had wanted to make a point to let him know she'd be at the school today. Perhaps she'd been burned before, but it could be that she just wasn't into him. After all, she hadn't mentioned his dinner invite.

Maybe she'd accept if he asked again? Should he? He wanted to spend time with her so badly. He'd never felt like this before.

He made it home with barely enough time to shower and get dressed. Then he drove to the station and picked up the awful brown suit, dragging the thing through the hallways taking *endless* amounts of shit from the guys.

There were times in a man's career when he was way underpaid for what he did. This was one of those times. The only thing keeping him from going right back home was what Robyn had said about the kids enjoying the presentation. He knew she was right.

Damn him and his soft spot for the little ankle-biters.

"Pop the trunk," he said shortly, waving a hand at Tonio, who was climbing into the driver's side of the Taurus. The trunk opened, and he stowed the suit in the back before assuming his spot in the front. "Don't say a word."

"I wasn't going to." But the asshole was smirking.

"Yes, you were."

"But if you're good, I'll toss you a bone when we're done."

He snorted in spite of himself. "Fuck you, man."

"Not even on your best hair day."

When they arrived at the school, his partner found a visitor's parking spot in front and pulled in. Tonio grabbed the handouts and some age-appropriate swag, including Valor the Crime Dog bookmarks, pencils, and coloring books, while Chris retrieved the suit.

In the office, they signed in and the principal, a

friendly older woman, welcomed them. After they'd been fussed over and flirted with by several of the office ladies, which the normally reserved Tonio completely lapped up like a cat with a bowl of cream, the secretary directed Chris to the staff restroom to put on the suit.

In the small room, he struggled to get the thing on over his clothes and pulled up. Finally, he secured the bottom half with the suspenders and stared at himself in the mirror. Without the head, he looked more like a sasquatch than a dog. Picking up the head, he left the bathroom and found Tonio waiting in the office.

"Ready?" his partner asked.

"As I'll ever be."

"They said the kids are assembled in the cafeteria."

"Lead the way."

As they exited the office, Chris finally bit the bullet and stuck on the head of the costume—and almost gagged. "Jesus, it smells like a gym locker in here."

"I can imagine. I doubt they sanitize it when they put it away each time."

"Oh, gross."

Their entrance at the front of the cafeteria caused an excited buzz. As the teachers quieted the students and made the introductions, Chris scanned the edge of the sea of small bodies for Robyn. He found her toward the back, smiling and chatting with a man Chris assumed was another parent. She and the good-looking guy seemed pretty chummy and something unpleasant unfurled in his gut—jealousy. He didn't like the feeling.

Belatedly he realized that Tonio had introduced him, and everyone was waiting for him to wave or something.

He did, and was gratified at the kids' happy faces. Somehow that made wearing the stinky costume, not to mention feeling like a giant ass, worthwhile.

The presentation wore on, and Chris did his job, walking around some but mostly standing off to the side while Tonio outlined crime prevention and how to get help in case of emergency.

And as the hour wore on, Chris began to get hot. Dizzy.

The familiar nausea began to build in his stomach, the feeling of lead weighing his limbs. It was getting harder to breathe. Casually, he made his way to the side, where he leaned against the wall, but that didn't help much.

If he didn't get some air and sit down, he was going to pass out.

Pushing off the wall, he waited until Tonio paused to have the teachers pass out the bookmarks before approaching and tapping him on the shoulder. Tonio turned, a question in his eyes.

"Tell them Valor has to leave," he whispered.

"What? Why?"

"Just tell them . . ." Spots encroached on his vision. "I'm about to hit the floor, man."

Tonio's expression mirrored alarm, which he quickly masked. "Go, I'll take care of the rest."

"Thanks."

"Kids, Valor has to go fight crime now," his partner said loudly. "But why don't we all wave good-bye to him and show him how much we appreciate him being here today?"

The man was good, he'd give him that much.

The students waved, calling out their good-byes with enthusiasm, and he waved back until he'd exited the cafeteria. Then he staggered down the hallway, rounded a corner, and ripped off the costume's head, letting it hit the tiled floor. Leaning against the wall, he wiped the sweat from his face and struggled to pull the cool, fresh air into his lungs.

"Chris?"

Struggling to appear normal, he straightened and faced Robyn, who was bearing down on him with rapid steps and worry etched on her pretty face. His dignity was officially shredded. Stopping in front of him, she pushed a lock of sweaty hair off his forehead and then felt the skin there with the back of her hand.

"I saw you leaning against the wall, and then you left so suddenly. I was worried," she said, voice soft.

"Oh, it's just this damned suit. This thing is way too hot and I had to get some air. No worries."

Not swayed, she took his wrist and held it between her fingers for a few seconds. "Your pulse is racing."

He mustered a grin. "That's because of you, gorgeous."

Letting go of him, she huffed a laugh. "Right. You never quit, do you?"

"I don't know the meaning of that word." He took a deep breath. "In fact, I was wondering if you'd thought about—"

Just then, Tonio rounded the corner carrying the leftovers of their materials. "Hey, are you—? Oh. Didn't mean to interrupt."

Damn his timing!

Robyn eyed Tonio, offering him her hand. "Hello, I'm an acquaintance of Chris's. We're neighbors."

"Oh?" He shook her hand, glancing between them.

"I'm also a doctor, actually. I know he hasn't been well, and I was just checking on him."

"Not feeling well? Is that so?" His partner shot him a pointed look.

"Isn't there something called a HIPAA law?" he muttered.

"You're not my patient," she shot back. "That makes me simply a concerned friend."

"Friend?" That perked him up. Now they were getting somewhere.

Whatever she might have said was cut off as the phone in his jeans buzzed. Stifling a curse, he slipped off the suspenders and dug around in his suit until he snagged the device.

He glanced at the display and then to Tonio. "It's Rainey." Punching the button, he answered. "Hey, Cap."

"You two done playing Wonder Dog? I've got a homicide with your names on it."

His adrenaline kicked into overdrive as he fumbled in his pocket for his notepad. "Address?" He scribbled as the captain rattled it off.

"I know you two are backed up, but from all appearances this one started as a burglary. Seems the victim may have surprised the intruder."

"You think it's related to the other break-ins?"

"That's what we pay you the big bucks for. Go find out."

"Yes, sir." Ending the call, he jumped around, kicking off the suit before gathering it. He looked at Robyn with real regret. "I'm sorry, that was our captain. We have to go."

"Oh." She seemed to deflate a little. "No problem. I'll talk to you soon?"

His heart lightened. "I'll look forward to it."

He and Tonio hurried from the building, not bothering to sign out. Once they were in the car and on their way, Chris told him what little he knew.

"We caught a homicide. It appears the victim surprised an intruder."

"That's why you asked Rainey if it could be related to our burglaries."

"Yeah. It might be a stretch."

"Or not. Guess we'll have to wait and see."

Tonio followed the directions to the address Chris loaded into the GPS, and soon they were parking in front of a nice home in a newer neighborhood. A couple of uniformed officers were waiting, and had stretched yellow crime scene tape around the perimeter of the yard and driveway.

One of them was young Officer Jenkins, or "Jenk" around the station, who had had his homicide cherry popped a few weeks earlier when he'd responded to a call at a motel and ended up with a murder victim. That had turned out to be Shane and Taylor's case, the one that had caused Chris to crash the surveillance van and almost get himself killed.

Jenk didn't seem any happier now than he had back

then. "Hey, guys. Brace yourselves, it's a real fucking mess in there."

"Never saw a pretty murder," Tonio said shortly.

Jenk flushed. "Just sayin'. Anyway, we're still waiting on the ME."

Chris nodded. "All right, we'll be careful."

He and Tonio donned latex gloves and pulled covers over their shoes. Then they made their way inside, where Chris saw that Jenk was right—the house was a disaster. At least the living room was. Lamps were on the floor, smashed, as were picture frames, books, magazines, and various knickknacks. A fight had taken place, and every item in the battle zone had fallen victim.

The *real* victim was sprawled in the middle of the mess on the living room floor, next to the mangled coffee table. The man appeared to be about seventy years old and was wearing jeans and a polo shirt. He was lying in a huge pool of blood that spread from his abdomen, head turned to the side, eyes wide and sightless.

Chris looked around. "I don't see a murder weapon yet."

"Me, neither. Could be underneath his body. We'll have to wait for Eden."

Walking into the kitchen, Chris examined a stack of mail, all addressed to the same man. "Edward Burke. He's got junk, bills, and a social security check. His wallet is on the table." Picking it up, he examined the contents carefully. "It has more than a hundred dollars cash inside."

"So, assuming nothing else is missing, it would appear that robbery is not the motive."

"Seems so, which is weird."

"Right? Why break in if not to steal something?" Tonio frowned as he took in the scene.

"Reminds me of what Mr. Fell told us about the burglary at his home. Front entry in broad daylight, items moved slightly but nothing taken." Retracing his steps to the open front door, Chris examined the doorframe and was gratified to see deep gouges in the wood.

"Bingo. Our perp jimmied the door."

Tonio pointed to a couple of items on a side table that had survived the scuffle. "This picture and the figurine beside it were moved. See the dust?"

He walked over to examine them. "Yep. What the hell is he getting out of this? And why commit murder over a simple break and enter? Why not just run away when he heard the owner come home?"

"Beats me. But we're gonna find out when we bust his ass and toss him in prison."

A search of the rest of the house turned up zilch. As they exited to stand on the front porch, Jenk hurried, waving an arm.

"We found something back here you'll want to see."

Curious, Chris followed. The other officer, Troy Hillman, was already there, standing next to a grassy patch beyond the borders of the yard. When Chris drew closer, Hillman pointed to a slender object on the ground.

It was a small glass vial with a rubber top and a tiny hole for a needle to be pushed into, the kind one might find in a doctor's office. Crouching, he saw it was almost full of clear liquid. Rolling it gently with a latex-covered finger, he saw there was no label.

"Over here, too," Jenk said, hitching a thumb.

A few feet away from the vial was a syringe. The cap was still on, and unlike the vial, there was nothing in the reservoir. Chris speculated out loud. "Doesn't look like it's been used. Wonder if our suspect dropped these. Could be he broke in the front, crept around doing whatever he does, was surprised by the home owner, and they fought. He killed the victim and fled around the back, dropping these."

"It's as good a theory as any," Tonio said. "The vial and syringe might shed some light on what his game is."

"Or they could add more questions." Chris sighed. "Let's bag 'em."

Tonio pulled a couple of baggies from his pants pocket and sealed them separately. By the time they'd walked back to the front, Medical Examiner Laura Eden and the department's forensics unit were on-site doing their thing. Chris and Tonio went inside the house again to watch Eden work, asking her questions now and then but staying out of her way.

After she'd cataloged all of the evidence she could get from the body—at least until she did the autopsy and further tests—she gestured for them.

"Help me roll the body, and we'll take a look at the wound." She waited until Chris and Tonio were positioned on opposite sides of the dead man before nodding. "Now."

They rolled him over carefully, and then stood back to let Eden work. The woman was a machine, a brilliant scientist who missed nothing, and most everyone Chris knew admired her. She was real easy on the eyes, too, though Chris had never been interested her in *that* way.

She cut the polo shirt away and hummed, peering at the wound. "Knife wound, large blade, very sharp. See the edges here?"

Chris's stomach got a bit queasy, and he marveled at how she could remain so clinical. Some guys joked about her icy calm, but Chris believed she really could eat a sandwich while performing an autopsy, if she were ever inclined to be that unprofessional.

Tonio spoke up. "So, our vic wasn't shot."

"Nope."

"And he fought like Mike Tyson," she observed, picking up one hand to study it. "He did some damage to these knuckles, and to whoever was on the receiving end of them. Tough old guy, and in pretty good shape for a man his age. Too bad the killer fought dirty."

"Yeah." Poor bastard.

"Wonder if he's former military, or law enforcement?" Tonio speculated aloud.

Chris gestured toward the kitchen. "I saw an envelope from the American Bar Association on the table, addressed to him. Could be a lawyer, if our victim is Edward Burke, that is."

There wasn't much more to do except get the victim loaded and let the crime scene techs do their thing. After Eden had taken the body and gone, he and Tonio watched the techs work for a while, then made their exit.

"Something doesn't sit right about this whole thing," Chris told his partner. "The burglaries, and now a dead guy. We have a few giant pieces of the puzzle missing, and this feels more disjointed than usual."

"And when we put them together, the solution will be so obvious, we'll be kicking ourselves."

"Maybe so." He eyed the other man. "Sounds like you have some experience in that area."

"More than I'd like."

Chris waited for him to elaborate on that cryptic statement, but let it alone when he didn't. As much as he wanted to know more about his partner, he'd respect the man's privacy.

His thoughts drifted back to Robyn and he wondered whether he'd ever hear from her again. And whether he should stop walking by her house.

No. If she wanted him to back off, she'd have to tell him to his face.

Satisfied with that plan, he focused on feeling better. One hour at a time.

It had to get better. *Worse* was a scenario he didn't want to think about.

The young man huddled in the corner of his room, terrified.

Dried blood coated his hands, and was starting to itch. But he wrapped his arms around his knees and made himself small. Maybe small enough to disappear?

But no. They'd find him. They always did, and there was hell to pay then. Always.

They'd make him cry and there was nobody who cared. He wanted to be held, to be safe, but he was ignored. Left to suffer alone and bear the brunt of their wrath. To scream while the blows rained down and the demon took off his belt. Made him beg and scream more.

"No!"

The sharp sound of his own voice had him looking around, frantically searching for *him.* But *he* was long gone and the boy was left in the here and now, with nothing but his broken mind for company. The fear and the anger. The knowledge that he hadn't deserved this, and they all needed to pay.

Nobody had helped him. Not a single one of the *caring professionals* who were supposed to save kids from monsters. Not the principal, the teachers, the counselor, the lawyer. Not the doctor, next-door neighbor, or countless others who should've stepped in. Not even the cop.

Especially not him.

Dad cracked open the door and talked in soft, persuasive tones to the cop as he crept closer, heart pounding in his thin chest. This was it, the moment he'd been praying for. After the latest beating, he'd finally summoned the courage to call 9-1-1.

He peered around the corner—and fear seized his lungs.

The cop's eyes met his, over his dad's shoulder. A slight smirk tilted the corner of the man's mouth, and then he returned his attention to the other man. What was that about? Couldn't he see the busted lip, the torn clothes, the bruises? Just to be sure, the little boy stepped into full view of the officer.

But the cop never looked his way again. Instead, he closed his hand around a wad of bills pressed into his palm. And then he turned and walked away without a backward glance.

Dad had nearly killed him afterward.

That had been the day he'd truly lost hope. When the son of a bitch had walked away, that had been the end. The last slam of the cell door. The moment he knew: *You're in hell and never getting out. Nobody cares.*

Unfortunately, that cop was gone from the earth long before his plans for revenge had taken flight. But then he'd spotted Detective Ford. The man looked so much like that other cop he'd known it was meant to be.

Ford was the perfect substitute. If the original sinner had already escaped him through death, a stand-in would do. They were all alike anyway.

Pushing himself to his feet, he walked on trembling legs to the bathroom. There, he scrubbed his hands, watching blood and soap suds swirl down the drain. He'd made a bad mistake. It wasn't supposed to be like that, quick and easy. Yes, it was messy, but the bastard didn't *suffer*! Well, only for a minute. But not nearly enough.

"Not like I've suffered my whole life!"

He shouldn't have risked another so soon; he shouldn't have gotten impatient with the slow as shit pace his plans were progressing. He'd already taken measures to gain the attention of the authorities, and that should have been enough for now. He knew that. But the temptation had been too much to resist. All their pretty things! He loved looking at the riches he never had. Gazing upon the treasured mementos knowing he was going to crush the happiness they represented, just as his had been crushed.

He'd almost been caught today. It would have been over much too soon.

It had to end; he was cool with that. But he wasn't ready. There was still so much more left to do.

When he'd shown them all the error of their ways, he'd go gladly.

And not one second before.

4

"Okay, are you going to tell me what has you in such a funk?" Shea asked.

Sitting at the break room table, Robyn looked up from her unappetizing turkey sandwich and pretended not to have a clue what her friend was talking about. "The cafeteria food," she quipped, poking at the hoagie roll. "I think I saw it move a second ago."

Pulling up a chair, Shea shot her friend a droll look. "Really? That's the story you're going with?"

"Have you taken a look at the meat? It's as gray as one of the cadavers we worked on in medical school."

"I don't think your problem involves bad turkey. In fact, I happen to know someone who's walking around lately with a very similar expression to yours." Leaning back, Shea crossed her arms over her chest.

Robyn's heart did a funny little dance. "Who?"

"Oh, come on," her friend said with a snort. "Chris is moping around like he lost his best friend, which is very unlike him."

"That doesn't mean it has anything to do with *me*." Though she sort of hoped it did.

"It's you, trust me. I don't think he's ever heard the word *no* before. Women are usually throwing themselves at him."

That was an annoying thought. "First time for everything," she muttered.

Shea laughed. "You've got it so bad. You two are going to be a perfect match. I just know it."

"Um, we've only met a couple of times and I haven't even agreed to go out with him."

"But you will!" She leaned forward. "You like him and he likes you, so let me ask—what the hell are you waiting for?"

Some of the old hurt rose and she tamped it down with an effort. "You know why I don't date, Shea. It's been tough to let myself get too close to a man. Or anyone new at all, for that matter."

"I get that. But, honey, it's not like he's proposing marriage. What's it going to hurt to have a meal with the man?"

"I don't know if—"

"Look, at worst, you'll hate each other, which I don't think is going to happen. At best, you get closer to someone who could become a good friend and companion, maybe more. What do you have to lose?"

"My peace of mind?"

"Do you really have much of that?" Shea questioned gently. "You stand to gain so much more than you'd lose at this point. And you know, if we were talking about anyone but Chris, I wouldn't be pushing. I know my cousin, and he's solid gold."

Robyn bit her lip, thinking about everything her friend had said. "It's not just me. I have to think about Maddy, too."

"Yes, and that's understandable after what both of you have been through. But you can't cushion her with bubble wrap. Didn't she have a great time at the party the other day?"

"She did."

"And didn't she hit it off with Chris right away?"

"Yes, and he was wonderful with her," Robyn admitted. "She hasn't stopped talking about him since."

"Well, there you go."

Doesn't Maddy deserve an awesome man like that in her life? Don't I?

"Listen, I'll think about it. That's all I can promise right now."

Shea beamed at her, probably sensing Robyn was ready to cave. "That'll do."

"So glad you approve."

Ignoring Robyn's sarcasm, her friend pulled out her cell phone and sent a quick text. Immediately, Robyn's phone vibrated and she saw that Shea had texted her Chris's number.

"That's his cell," Shea told her.

"Okay. Thanks."

Then Shea launched into the most recent hospital gossip. Robyn, however, was listening with only half an ear while the other woman chattered about who was dating whom, hospital politics, and whether any money would be spent to improve the staff lounge. There wasn't a ton of hope among the staff for the last item.

By the time she and Shea departed and Robyn had thrown away her unfinished lunch, she'd come to a decision. One that involved making a phone call to a man she hoped hadn't yet written her off.

Checking her watch, she decided she had just enough time to find out if Chris was still interested. Excited, she hurried outside, pushing through a side door into a peaceful area sculpted to look like a garden. Visitors and staff alike were welcome to use it to take a break, gather their thoughts, or whatever they needed. It was currently unoccupied, and the perfect place for a private call.

Quickly, she checked the text again and repeated the number to herself. Then she placed the call, waiting on pins and needles as it rang. A familiar voice answered on the third ring.

"Detective Ford."

She tried to sound confident, not nervous, and wasn't quite sure she succeeded. "Chris? This is Robyn. I hope it's okay that Shea gave me your number."

"Oh, hey, Robyn! Of course, that's more than okay." He sounded really happy to hear from her, and that made her insides quiver. "So, does this mean you've done some thinking about having dinner with me?"

"Yes, and I'd love to. If you're still interested, that is." There were those nerves, making an appearance and doing their best to rattle her composure.

"You're kidding, right?" He laughed. "I feel like I've just won the lottery."

Her face stretched into a broad smile. "I wouldn't go that far."

"Believe me, I *would*. So, when are you free?"

"I'm off tomorrow night, if that works."

"Perfect. What's your favorite kind of food?"

"I'm not picky," she said honestly. "I can eat almost any kind of food except Indian. I can't stand curry."

He chuckled. "I'm with you there. How about I give it some thought and surprise you?"

"Sounds fine." Inside, she felt giddy. When was the last time she'd been surprised?

"What about Maddy?" She tensed, but before she could say anything, he rushed to reassure her. "Don't get me wrong, she's more than welcome on our first date. I just need to know so I can choose accordingly."

He was officially too good to be true.

"I'll get a sitter," she told him. "I'd like to get to know you before I bring her along."

"That's more than fine. Pick you up at seven thirty?"

"That will be great."

"All right, see you then, gorgeous."

"I'm looking forward to it."

"Me, too."

She hung up, almost drunk on the rush. The pure joy. *I did it. I'm going on a date with a handsome, charming man for the first time in two years.*

Well, longer than that if she was counting. Because it had been much longer than two years since Greg had been any kind of companion. She wasn't going to think about that, though. Not when she finally had a nice evening to look forward to.

Sticking her phone in her coat pocket, she walked back inside to see Shea and Lee, a male nurse, standing at the nurses' station. They were talking, looking over a chart, Shea no doubt having to take the man in hand again for screwing something up. Honestly, Robyn didn't know how much longer the director could put up with him. Shea spotted Robyn and then waved as she approached, giving her a tentative smile.

"Well?"

"Date, tomorrow night!"

"That's great." Her friend gave her a brisk hug.

"A date?" Lee studied the two women with a curious expression on his face.

Shea let go of Robyn and made a face at him. "Yes, you know—two people go out and have dinner, maybe get some nooky for dessert?"

"Shea!" Robyn's face flamed. "Okay, this is where I get back to work. See you later."

"Don't do anything I wouldn't do," Shea called out, looking downright smug.

Shaking her head at their antics, Robyn hurried back into the building. But she was lighter in spirit than she had been in a very long time.

Tomorrow night. She couldn't wait.

Chris was flying high as he pulled onto his street. So much so that at first his brain didn't register the water flowing like a mini river down his driveway.

Water line break.

"Shit!"

Throwing the Camaro into park, he shut off the ignition and ran into the house, searching everywhere for running water and damage as he went. He was relieved to find that the break wasn't inside the house—that would've been a major disaster, considering the new carpet, furnishings, and God knows what else.

Continuing his search, he found a soggy patch of grass in the backyard, water gurgling and spewing at a rate that made him cringe to think of his next water bill—especially if this had been gushing all day. Why the hell hadn't one of the neighbors called him? The people on each side of him had his cell phone number, but they must not have been home.

First, he found the meter and shut off the water. Once inside again, he phoned the utility company and was informed that the earliest they could send someone out to look at the pipe was tomorrow. But in all reality, it would be several days before the actual repair could be made. It seemed their schedule was very backed up.

That meant he couldn't stay here. No running water for dishes, the toilet, or the shower made that impossible. He considered his options. A hotel would be easy, but over several days could get expensive. He could stay with Shea and Tommy, but the thought of cohabitating with his nosy cousin and having her grill him about Robyn didn't appeal at all.

Staying with Shane and Daisy made the most sense. Their house was a bit more crowded now that they had Drew with them, and the teen was always having friends over, but he could deal if they could. With a sigh, he pulled out his phone and went back into the house. It rang a couple of times before Shane answered.

"Hey, cuz. What's up?"

"Not my impressive ten inches, that's for sure."

Shane laughed. "Ten? Who's delusional?"

"Not me. But I didn't call to make you feel inadequate," he joked. "Especially when I need a favor."

"Anything, you know that. As long as it's legal, that is."

"Good, because I need a place to crash, maybe for a few days. I have a water line break here at the house."

"Ouch." His cousin's voice was sympathetic.

"Yeah. I'm not going to have any water until they can get it fixed, so I'm kind of in a spot. I know you've got more people in the house these days, though, so if it's a problem I can go somewhere else."

"Say no more, and bring your ass over before I kick it. We've got four bedrooms, and the spare two are rarely used unless Blake stays over in one of them."

Blake was a young man of about nineteen that Taylor and his girlfriend Cara had recently helped to get his life together. Everyone really liked him, including Chris. He was a good kid who'd once had it pretty rough, and he had become Drew's best friend.

"Thanks, man. I'll be over after I scrounge up some dinner."

"Nah, fuck that. Daisy's making fried chicken and mashed potatoes. Pack, then get over here and come help us eat it all."

His mouth watered. "Well, twist my arm . . ."

"Ha! No force involved, I'm thinking."

"You're right. See you soon."

Moving quickly, he pulled a duffel bag from the closet and threw in enough clothes for two days, both work and casual. A pair of lightweight shorts for jogging followed, tennis shoes, plus socks and underwear, his toothbrush and his deodorant. After a brief inspection, he was satisfied. Shane and Daisy would have anything else he needed.

He locked up, then made his way back to the car, tossed in his bag, and left. Briefly, he worried that the utility people coming to look at the pipe might interfere with his date, but then he cast that fear aside. Nothing was getting in the way of his evening with Robyn. Not going to happen.

Twenty minutes later he was turning down Shane's driveway. Well, the place was Daisy's now also, but this property and the one next door, beautiful tracts of land located right on the Cumberland River, had been left to Shane and his sister, respectively, by their parents. Shane had built his house here a few years earlier, and then Shea and Tommy had built on her portion after they'd gotten married. The siblings and their families lived barely a few hundred yards away from each other.

Chris couldn't help but feel a bit jealous. And a little left out sometimes.

But that feeling was false, and totally on Chris. Shane and Shea were more like siblings to him than cousins, which was the main reason he'd moved to Sugarland a few months back. He had badly needed family, people who cared for him, and he'd been welcomed with open arms. Why would he ever feel left out?

Because they have families that take up their time and attention now, and you don't.

Shutting out that destructive voice, he grabbed his

bag and headed for the porch. There he rang the doorbell and was greeted by an enthusiastic Daisy. She flung her arms around him, giving him a big hug as the aroma of fried chicken drifted out to assault his nose.

"Hey, stranger!" The tall blond juvenile officer gave his cheek a kiss and pulled back to smile at him. "Get in here. Where the hell have you been lately?"

"What do you mean? I just saw you at work three days ago." He stepped inside to see Shane rise from his recliner and stretch, then start toward him and Daisy.

"Work doesn't count! I've been inviting you over to dinner for weeks, and it takes a busted water pipe to get you here? I don't know whether to be happy or insulted." The quirk of her mouth and humor in her blue eyes told him which it was.

"Can we settle for happy?" He sniffed appreciatively at the air.

Laughing, she draped an arm over his shoulders and guided him into the living room. Shane met them halfway and thumped his cousin on the back.

"That didn't take long."

"Food was mentioned," he said. "I have my priorities in order."

Daisy gestured toward a hallway that Chris knew led to the guest rooms. The master bedroom and Drew's room were on the other side of the house. "Why don't you go put your bag in the second guest room and wash up. We're about ready to eat."

"Yes, ma'am."

She took a swat at him and muttered something about not calling her *ma'am* as he sauntered off. Doing as she said, he put his bag on the bed in the second room and then washed his hands. As he did, he took a few moments to study himself in the mirror.

There were still faint circles under his eyes, but he felt a little better than he had that morning. For some reason, his illness seemed to hit the worst after he'd gotten ready for work, and so the sickness and fatigue dragged at him throughout the day. He'd lost a little weight, but not too much. Having a healthy appetite wasn't the problem—the nausea was, and it didn't seem to be related to eating, which was strange. He was *always* hungry.

And terribly thirsty. That was an odd realization that hadn't occurred to him as possibly being related before: that he couldn't drink enough water. That, along with his other particular symptoms, would've had him convinced he was diabetic if the doctors hadn't already ruled it out.

Cataloging how he felt now, he leaned on the sink. He was tired. A little shaky. But the feverish sickness, the racing pulse, was absent for the time being. Thank God.

He didn't want to wonder how short the respite might be.

Pushing that to the back of his mind, he made his way to the kitchen. There he found Daisy using a pair of tongs trying to place the pieces of chicken on a platter. *Trying* being the operative word, as Shane was wrapped around her like a burrito, kissing her neck and making her giggle. She almost dropped one of the legs.

"All right, you two," he drawled, pulling up a chair beside Drew. "No fair taunting those of us who don't have a significant other to nibble as an appetizer."

"And they're at it *all* the time." Drew rolled his eyes

and snagged a roll from a bowl on the table. "I *so* don't want to watch old people get their groove on."

"Old!" Daisy's mouth dropped open.

"You're just jealous," Shane said with a wink. "You'll change your tune fast enough when you have someone special of your own."

"Who says I don't?" the teen shot back.

Chris watched the verbal sparring match between Drew and his guardians in amusement. Over the summer, the seventeen-year-old had shot up to nearly six feet and had filled out. Tanned and developing muscle from regular workouts, he was a good-looking guy, with a strong resemblance to his late father. Drew was coming into his own, the man peeking out now and then from behind the kid, and it was cool to see.

Not that Shane always agreed. He was staring at his godson, the tables suddenly turned. "Is there something I should know?"

The teen smirked, lips quirking up. "Nope. Unlike you, I don't flaunt my biz to the world."

Shane narrowed his eyes. Letting go of Daisy, he moved to the table and took a seat across from the young man. "It's not *flaunting my biz*, as you put it, to kiss my wife in the privacy of my own home. So no deflecting. Is there someone special?"

"Wouldn't you like to know?"

"Actually, I would."

Drew glanced at Chris, then back to Shane, and some of the cockiness drained from his demeanor. "Nah, I'm just givin' ya a hard time. There's not really anybody."

Shane opened his mouth to say something else, but

Daisy appeared and caught her husband's attention as she set the platter of chicken on the table. An imperceptible shake of her head and Shane dropped the subject, though it was clear he wanted to push harder.

His cousin didn't believe Drew, and neither did Chris. Especially when Drew didn't join in the small talk for the rest of the meal, instead checking his text messages under the table with almost religious fervor. Chris knew the couple preferred that Drew not have his cell phone at the table, but that was a tough rule to enforce, the two of them being cops and needing their own phones to be handy at all times in case of emergency.

Shane gave his boy the stink eye, but let it go. In turn, he was roundly ignored.

Eventually, the conversation turned to work, as it tended to do with a room full of cops. "So, what's going on with the body you and Tonio caught the other day?" Daisy asked.

"Not much. We think it's one of the rash of burglaries we've had lately, but this one went south when he surprised the intruder." Chris shook his head. "We've got a burglar who doesn't take anything of value, whose point seems to be creeping through people's things. Weird, but not violent. Then he kills the first person who catches him in the act. We just can't seem to grasp the thread we're missing."

Daisy made a face. "That's damned strange."

"What about the vial and the syringe that was found out back of the victim's place?" Shane asked. "Got the test results on those yet?"

"Not yet. The lab is *really backed up*," he emphasized with air quotes.

Shane snorted. "There's a news flash."

"Yeah. It's a miracle crimes ever get solved, as slow as things move."

Drew looked up from his texting. "So, does anybody have any *good* news?"

Chris shrugged, but was unable to contain the bubble of happiness that welled inside him. "I've got a date tomorrow night."

"Awesome," the boy said with a grin. "Is it the hot chick who was at the party the other day?"

"Her name is Robyn, and she's a doctor. She's smart *and* hot."

"Dude, that rocks. What else do you know about her?"

He thought about that. "Not as much as I'd like, but I hope to change that. I know there's no husband in the picture, but not why. She's warm and kind, if a bit reserved, like she's been burned before. And she's got a little girl who's in first grade."

Drew made a face. "A kid? Wow, what a buzzkill."

"That's rude," Shane began.

Chris waved off his cousin with a laugh. "It wasn't too many years ago that I would've agreed with you. But attitudes change as you get older and spend more time alone. Trust me."

"I can't imagine being saddled with a kid, much less somebody else's, but I'll take your word for it," Drew said.

Shane's tone cooled. "Excuse me? Want to run that by me again?"

The teen looked to Shane and his eyes widened as he

realized what he'd said. "I was thinking of a *little* kid, not . . . Anyway, may I be excused?"

"Sure." Shane frowned after the young man as he put his plate in the sink and left the room. "I worry about him."

"He's a normal teenager," Chris said. "He's fine."

"I guess." Shane looked at Chris thoughtfully. "But he's right about one thing—be sure you know what you're getting into. Getting involved with a woman who has a small child is no light responsibility."

He struggled to keep the annoyance from his tone. "I'm quite aware that's a huge game changer, okay? I'm looking to settle down with someone special, not tap a piece of pretty ass and run. Plus, I like kids and I want some of my own."

Shane held up a hand. "All right, sorry. I care about you and I want you to be happy, no matter what. You know that."

"Yeah, I do. Sorry for getting defensive." He blew out a breath.

"Not a problem."

Shane and Daisy rose and started clearing the table. Chris tried to help, but Daisy shooed him away. With nothing else to do, he wandered into the living room and turned on the television, killing time until they joined him.

The three of them shot the breeze until Chris yawned, realizing that the week had caught up with him. Excusing himself, he retired to the guest room, closed the door, and undressed. Then he slid naked between the sheets, enjoying the sensation of them on his skin.

Rolling to his back, he closed his eyes and pictured Robyn. Her auburn hair and big blue eyes. He couldn't help but imagine her lush figure bared to his gaze, his palms tracing her curves. Was her ass the nice handful it appeared to be? How would it feel to squeeze the mounds in his hands as he drove between those long thighs?

Arousal woke his cock, and he groaned as it thickened, the length brushing against the cool sheets. God, he wanted her. His fantasy fueled his desire, and needed an outlet. Reaching down, he palmed the hardening flesh. Stroked the warm skin, bringing his rod to full attention. Delicious tingles skittered from the weeping tip to his balls, and he spread the pearl around the head. Then gave himself a few strokes, worked down to his sac to cup and massage it.

So good. Gripping his cock again, he made a snug fist and began a slow rhythm, pushing the turgid length through the warm tunnel. Nerve endings began to fire, licking at his shaft like a thousand tongues. Driving him crazy, spiraling his need higher.

All too soon, his balls drew up tight, signaling the impending orgasm. With a few last pulls, he sent himself over the edge with a hoarse cry. Spurts of hot cum bathed his abdomen and chest, painting him with creamy stripes. As he came down from the high and reality set in, he stared at the ceiling and let himself hope.

He hoped like hell that, very soon, making love was just that—and not an empty, lonely fantasy.

5

"Mommy, what's wrong?"

Robyn paused in the act of wearing a hole in the living room carpet and looked down into Maddy's face, realizing her anxiety wasn't lost on her daughter. She hadn't kept her date with Chris from Maddy. Her little girl liked the man, and besides, the idea of keeping something as important as a potential new person in their lives from Maddy didn't sit well. Smiling, she bent down and gave her a quick hug.

"Can you keep a secret?" she asked in a stage whisper.

"Uh-huh!"

"I'm a little nervous about having dinner with Chris," she admitted.

"Why? You like Chris and he's nice." Her cute face scrunched as she pondered this.

Kids, God love them. She hardly recalled a time when life was that simple, and you either liked someone or you didn't. "Yes, I do like him, very much. But what if he doesn't like me as much as I like him?"

Maddy nodded. "Like when Tara invited Danny to

her birthday party but he said no 'cause he didn't want to go to no stinky girl's party. Tara cried."

"Well, that was very rude of Danny to hurt Tara's feelings. And yes, it's sort of like that."

"But Chris invited *you*, so why would he be mean?"

Laughing, she threw her arms around her baby, squeezed her tight, and gave her a big kiss. "Why, indeed? How come you're so smart?"

"Because!" Giggling, Maddy tried to squirm away. Robyn held fast and tickled her ribs.

"Because *why*?"

"I don't know!"

The doorbell interrupted their silly fun, and for a second her heart lurched. Then she saw the form standing on the other side of the frosted glass and knew it had to be Rachel. She walked over and let her in.

"Hi, hon," she said to the girl. "Thanks for sitting tonight."

"Hey, no problem. It's not every day you have a hot date."

"I'm pretty sure we had a different president the last time it occurred."

Rachel laughed and Robyn set about giving the sitter instructions.

"No soda with Maddy's dinner tonight. She chose to have hers with her after-school snack."

"Mooommy!" her daughter whined.

Robyn ignored her, refusing to engage in a battle of wills. "Bedtime at eight thirty if she's been a good girl. That's thirty minutes longer than usual," she told Maddy, cutting off her protest. "Take it or leave it."

"O-*kay*." Crossing her arms over her thin chest, she pouted for about five seconds. Then the doorbell rang again and she forgot all about being annoyed with her mom. "He's here!"

A tall form stood on the other side of the glass, shifting slightly from side to side. Maddy bolted before Robyn could stop her, and threw open the door to reveal Sugarland's sexiest detective standing on the threshold.

"Chris, hi!" Maddy was practically bouncing.

"Hey, munchkin," he said warmly. "I have something for you, if you want it. Sort of a thank-you for letting me take your mom to dinner."

His arms were full of flowers and some sort of stuffed animal, and as Maddy reached for it, Robyn saw it was a purple teddy bear. There wasn't anything more disarming than seeing the pleasure on Chris's face at making her daughter so happy. Having seen him interact with her before, Robyn knew it was genuine.

She looked over at Rachel to see the twenty-year-old staring at Chris like he was a steak on a dinner plate. A tiny surge of possessiveness rose in her, though she couldn't blame the girl. Just then Rachel glanced at Robyn and mouthed, *Wow!*

Robyn smiled. That was an understatement. The man looked heart-stoppingly gorgeous in black jeans and a silky-looking gray-and-black fitted shirt. His brown-gold hair was artfully mussed with a bit of product, much more so than the previous times she'd met him. He'd gone to some trouble with his appearance, and she liked that.

Not that the man had needed any improvement. He was already hot enough to melt her panties.

Maddy was suddenly shy, burying her face in the bear's soft fur. "I love him. Thank you."

"I'm glad, sweetheart, and you're welcome." He turned to face Robyn and handed her a vase of mixed flowers. "These are for you, pretty lady."

She took them, thrilled to her toes. "Thank you, they're beautiful. I don't remember the last time anyone gave me flowers."

"Well, that's not right. I'm a firm believer that a woman should get flowers all the time, especially for no reason other than she's perfect." His smile was breath-taking.

"I think that's an opinion I could get behind. Thank you again." Impulsively, she gave him a hug and inhaled his spicy scent. He smelled damned good, and that brief moment of contact with his hard, muscled body had her yearning for more.

With regret, she let him go. Carrying the flowers to the sofa table, she moved a couple of framed pictures and placed the vase in the middle. Then she waved a hand at the sitter. "Oh, this is Rachel, Maddy's sitter. Rachel, Chris."

"Nice to meet you," he said politely. Robyn was gratified to note he barely spared a glance for the pretty young woman before returning his focus to her. "Are you ready to go?"

"If you are."

"I am." Turning to Maddy, he said, "I promise not to keep your mom out too late, okay?"

"You'll keep her safe 'cause you're a policeman, right?" She was as serious as could be.

His mouth quirked, but his tone was equally solemn. "That's right. She's in good hands."

"Okay." And that was that.

Robyn hugged her daughter good-bye, and then waved to Rachel, who assured her that Maddy would be in bed by eight thirty. Then she let Chris guide her down the sidewalk, loving the feeling of his hand on her lower back.

When they approached his car, she ogled the shiny black Camaro with the dark tinted windows. "Damn, sweet ride."

"Glad you approve," he said, opening the door for her. "I saved for ages to afford the down payment. Worth every penny."

Shutting her door, he hurried around to the driver's side and slid behind the wheel. "Are you into cars?"

"I am," she admitted. "I love good old American muscle. If I was rich, I'd have an entire temperature-controlled warehouse full of classic cars just like Jay Leno does."

"Me, too. That's something else we have in common."

"So, where are we going?"

"I was thinking Italian food, if that's okay with you? There's a new restaurant that opened on the river and I've been meaning to try it."

"Sounds fabulous. I could eat Italian every other day."

"Great." He glanced at her. "You look beautiful, by the way."

"Thanks. You look very handsome yourself."

He smiled, shaking his head as if he didn't really believe her.

She admired his profile as he drove. Again, she was

struck by how the gorgeous outside of him, so far, seemed to match the inside. How many men brought a gift to their date's child?

"You've lived in Sugarland for two years, right?" he asked, breaking into her thoughts.

"Yes. We moved here from Phoenix, Arizona, after my husband, Greg . . . passed away." That term was so innocuous. So far removed from the real tragedy.

"I'm so sorry," he said sincerely. "He was Maddy's father?"

Not so much—at least not at the end. But she wasn't ready to go there just yet. Too many horrible memories, and too much sadness for a first date.

"He was. Her memories of him are pretty dim, though." Seeking to change the subject, she asked, "What about you? Have you always lived here?"

"No, I moved here from the Dallas area a few months ago. I wanted to be close to my cousins, and I'm glad I made the move. I love the people and the scenery."

"That's good. What about your folks? Do they live in Dallas?"

His jaw clenched and he hesitated. She realized too late she'd probably hit a nerve, but he gave no further indication as he answered. "Cancer took my mom when I was twelve. My dad lives north of Dallas, but we don't stay in touch. He's a drunk who used my mom as a verbal punching bag for as long as I can remember, and then shifted his focus to me when he didn't have her to demean anymore."

"I'm so sorry," she said gently. "That must have been rough growing up."

"Could've been worse, I guess. I've *seen* worse, like

women and children being physically abused. My father never hit us, but he made our lives miserable just the same. I have no respect for him."

"Is that part of the reason you have a soft spot for kids?"

"I suppose," he mused. "Someday I'd like to give my kid the happy childhood I didn't have. Disney World, late-night movies with pizza and popcorn, picnics in the park, a dog, the whole works."

An emotional lump formed in her throat. "I have no doubt you'll make some boy or girl very lucky one day by being their dad."

"I sure hope so." He grinned. "I want a houseful."

She laughed, imagining him with children hanging off him, climbing him like a jungle gym. She'd like to do the same thing, for entirely different reasons.

"What about you?" He slid a glance at her. "Would you like more kids someday?"

She thought about that. "Yes, eventually. I think Maddy would love a little brother or sister. If that ever happens, though, I'll need to be in the position to take a long hiatus from work. My hours aren't very conducive to taking care of a new baby."

"Do you ever wish you were a stay-at-home mom?"

"It's the American dream, isn't it?"

"Not for everyone."

"I was teasing. Honestly, I'm not sure if I'd want to go back after having more children. I feel bad missing out on so much time with Maddy, what with the long hours and late nights. Sometimes I feel like the sitter spends more time with her than I do," she said quietly.

Reaching over, he put his hand on top of hers. "I'm

sure that's not true. It just feels that way when your heart is at home."

"I know. I love my job, but it's hard sometimes, feeling like I'm taking care of everyone except my own family."

"I get that."

Chris turned onto the road leading down the hill to the restaurant and found a parking place. As they walked toward the entrance, he took her hand in his larger, rougher one. The simple contact was nice and she relished it until they got inside, and he asked for a table for two.

The hostess took them to a table next to a window with a nice view of the river. Darkness had fallen, and the water reflected the twinkling of lights from piers and other businesses across the way.

"This is a great view," she said, admiring it.

"It's spectacular," he answered softly. And he wasn't looking at the river.

Their eyes met and held. Robyn had heard mutual attraction described in all sorts of ways. That moment when two people recognize the spark between them without a word being spoken—from angels singing to fireworks to electricity, and everything in between.

But for her, that recognition was gentle and quiet. It was a shift in her soul as she stared deep into his kind brown eyes and saw all that he was reflected there—sweet, honorable, intelligent, a good cop, a great friend, a man of hidden passion. All the qualities she'd ever wanted in one complete package, one incredible man who she sensed could be hers for the taking.

And it scared her in a way nothing had in a very long time.

"Can I start you with something to drink? Wine, iced tea, soda?" A handsome, dark-haired waiter smiled down at them.

"A beer for me, draft." The waiter made a suggestion, and Chris said that sounded fine.

"A glass of Chardonnay for me," she said.

The young man made a quick bow and left.

"I'd heard this place was family owned," Chris said.

"That would explain the sexy Italian accent."

"Uh-oh. I can't compete with the Latin-lover appeal." The humor on his face said he wasn't too worried.

"I don't think it'll be an issue."

"Like your men a little more . . . homegrown, do you?" he teased.

"Something like that." It felt good to flirt. "I'm a sucker for a Southern accent, brown-gold hair, and big brown eyes."

"And big *weapons*?" His grin was boyish, mischievous.

"Especially the weapons. As long as they don't discharge prematurely."

He laughed out loud, and she liked the sound and sight of him with his inhibitions stripped. The man was simply stunning.

"Sweetheart, not a chance of that. I take weapon maintenance very seriously."

"Good to know."

The waiter brought their drinks and gave them time to look at the menu. Robyn scanned the selections, then took advantage of studying Chris while he made up his mind. What Shea had told her in private the other day, about him battling some sort of health problem, weighed on her mind. Chris seemed to be the real deal, but she didn't want to come to care for another man only to have him leave her and Maddy. She couldn't go through that horrible pain again.

No, she was borrowing trouble and needed to stop. He looked good tonight, the shadows under his eyes faded. Perhaps whatever had afflicted him was becoming a thing of the past. She hoped that was so.

"The menu looks awesome," he said, setting it down. "Between eating out and Daisy's cooking, I'm going to get as big as a barn."

"Do you eat at your cousin's house quite often?"

"Sometimes, but not as much as I am right now. I'm staying with them for the time being because I had a water line break at my house yesterday."

She grimaced. "Oh, what a pain. No major damage, I hope."

"No, the break was outside, thank God. But I've got no running water and won't for several days, until it's fixed. The utility company said they went by my house while I was at work today and took a look, but who knows."

"So you have to put up with home-cooked meals for a bit. Bummer."

"Yeah, poor me."

An idea formed, but she decided to hold off mentioning anything. Best to see how their date went first. The waiter came back and took their order. Robyn decided on shrimp and linguine in a white wine cream sauce, and Chris went for the lasagna. Then the waiter disappeared briefly, came back to drop off some garlic rolls, plates, and butter, and left again. They both plucked rolls from the basket.

"You look like you're feeling better," Robyn said.

He took a bite of his roll and nodded. "I am. Thanks. It's weird how I feel better when I'm not home. Maybe I'm allergic to my own house," he joked.

She chuckled, but quickly reverted to doctor mode as his words sank in. "You could be closer to the truth than you think. Have you considered an environmental cause for your ailments, like black mold or clogged air filters?"

He blinked at her. "Not really. But that's an excellent point. We live in an older neighborhood, so those aren't out of the realm of possibility. I'll do an inspection once my water line is fixed."

"It's worth a look." She paused, uncertain. "This may sound like a strange question, but . . . Do you think it's possible we have some sort of mass contamination going on in the city that's affecting people's health?"

"I don't know," he said slowly. "What makes you ask?"

"It's just that something's been bugging me about the symptoms you've been battling. They're very similar to a few other patients we've seen at the hospital in the last couple of months. Actually, many of those people have died." He was staring at her, all ears, but at least he wasn't looking at her like she was crazy. Fortifying herself, she continued. "The deaths were brought to my attention by one of the nurses. I started looking into it and got concerned, so I called the medical examiner. She's notified the authorities, but I don't think she's gotten anywhere."

Chris nodded. "We'd need solid evidence, or probable cause at the very least, to open an investigation into the deaths. Something more than coincidence."

"That's the frustrating part. I think there really is something going on and so does Eden. But there's nothing she can do now that the bodies in question have been released, and it's a tricky proposition to ask those families to consent to more in-depth toxicology testing."

"If anyone can convince the survivors to consent, it's Eden," he said. "She's like a dog with a bone when she's onto something."

"Yeah."

"But I don't see what those deaths could possibly have to do with me. Besides, I'm sure whatever has been kicking my butt is finally working itself out of my system."

"I hope you're right." She put a lid on her worry in front of him, though, and shot him a bright smile. "Gosh, what morbid dinner conversation. My apologies."

His eyes danced with humor. "None necessary. We're a doctor and a cop, so that sort of makes it an occupational hazard with us. What're you gonna do?"

Their food arrived and they dug in, moaning over the delicious, rich flavors.

"That's some of the best Italian I've ever had," she said, rolling her eyes in pleasure.

"Wasn't it? I'm so glad you like this place."

They made small talk for a while, and inevitably the

conversation turned back to their work—but this time they kept it to the lighter side. Chris entertained her with funny stories of calls they'd answered and some of the witnesses they'd talked to, making her laugh.

She shook her head. "I'd say I'm shocked at the number of calls the police get about naked people running around, but many of them wind up in our emergency room being treated or held for psychiatric observation."

"I'll bet! What is it with the drunk and disorderly wanting to shuck their clothes and take off down the street?"

All too soon the meal was over, and they were regretfully too full for dessert. Chris paid the bill, flatly refusing to let her even pay half, and as they took their leave she felt a pang of regret that their evening was drawing to a close. However, when they stepped outside, he took her hand and paused instead of leading them to the car.

"Someone—I'm guessing the city—has built scenic walkways down by the river. Would you like to take a stroll with me?"

"I'd love that."

He took her hand and together they walked around the side of the restaurant, where the concrete walk continued for a short ways. Soon there was a sign pointing them toward a set of steps descending to the scenic boardwalk. The path was illuminated by attractive lighting, which lent a certain romance to the setting by the water.

Romance. She'd experienced so little of that in the past few years and suddenly she wanted that for herself with a fierce yearning that stole her breath. Was it so wrong to want happiness for herself? To be more than a doctor and Maddy's mother?

"What are you thinking?" he asked as they started down the steps.

"That it's been too long since I was in the company of someone I like, doing something for *me*." That was close enough to the truth.

"I know what you mean. It seems like I'm either involved with work or I'm the sidekick at someone else's party, if that makes sense. I watch all my friends pair off and I wonder when it's my turn. Does that sound selfish?"

"Not at all."

At the bottom, they walked to the wooden railing and stood in silence for a few moments, taking in the lapping of the water, the blanket of stars that lit the inky sky. Somewhere downriver a motor hummed, perhaps someone getting in a little night fishing.

Robyn was increasingly aware of the vital man at her side. How he moved in close, slowly wrapping an arm about her waist as though giving her time to move away or protest. She did neither, instead leaning into him more, letting him know without words that this closeness was more than okay.

Eventually he turned to face her and pulled her closer, tucking her head under his chin. With a content sigh she locked her arms around his waist and let herself be held, curling into his warm body and breathing his male scent. She could hear his heartbeat, steady and strong, part of the solidness of him that made her feel safe and protected.

"Robyn," he breathed into her hair.

"Mmm?"

"This feels so good, holding you. I've wanted to do this since we met."

"God, me too," she admitted. "Please, kiss me."

He sucked in a breath, his expression showing surprise. But he recovered quickly. "My pleasure."

His mouth covered hers, his lips full and firm. Warm. She melted against him and buried her fingers in his soft hair, tangling her tongue with his.

The first stirrings of arousal were a welcome surprise. She wasn't surprised that she was aroused by him, but it had simply been so long she'd forgotten this feeling. The wonder of having a man pressed against her, his hard length trapped in his jeans between them, evidence that he felt the same. It was so normal. And yet such a revelation.

His hands slid under the hem of her blouse, palms skimming her abdomen. Her skin tingled where he touched and she shivered. Desire flared, tightening her nipples. The place between her thighs heated and she wanted more. To get closer.

Breaking the kiss, he framed her face with his hands. "I don't want to push too hard."

"You're not pushing. If you do, I'll let you know."

"All right." He gave her a rueful smile. "I want you so bad it hurts, just so you know."

Her pulse leapt and she laid a hand on the front of his shirt, reveling in the muscles of his chest underneath her fingertips. "I want you, too. You have no idea how much. Come back to my place for a nightcap?"

"What about Maddy? Will it freak her out if I'm there?" His concern was sweet.

"She'll be in bed by now," she reminded him. "And besides, even if she wasn't, she thinks you're awesome."

"We'll see if that lasts when she spies me kissing the crap out of her mom."

When, not if. She liked that. "My daughter is made of strong stuff."

"If you're sure . . ."

"Positive."

"To your place, then."

The trip back to the car wasn't rushed, but neither did they linger. He opened the door to the vehicle and helped her in, then jogged to his side and soon they were on their way. The ride to her house was charged with desire. Robyn couldn't speak for Chris, but finding him had been like stumbling from the desert into an oasis.

She wanted to drink until she was sated.

When they arrived, she used her key to let them in. Quietly, they made their way to the living room, where Rachel was curled up on the sofa watching TV in the darkness. On seeing them, the sitter stretched and yawned.

"Did you guys have a good time?"

"We sure did," Robyn told her with a grin. "How were things here?"

"The usual. Maddy colored for a while, then we played a couple of games, and she had her bath. She went to bed at eight twenty, after her snack, and she was out like a light by eight forty. She squirmed around some before she fell asleep, but I think that was because you were out on your date."

"So she was no trouble?"

"Are you kidding?" Rachel snorted. "She's the best kid ever."

"Well, I happen to agree, but then I'm biased." Slipping off her purse, Robyn dug for her wallet and extracted the money she owed Rachel. After counting it out, she handed over the bills. "There you go."

"Thanks, Dr. Lassiter."

"Thank you. I appreciate you watching Maddy."

"No problem."

Robyn saw her to the door, and then locked up behind her. When she returned to the living room, Chris was sitting on the sofa watching her with pure male interest. The heat was unmistakable.

"That was hot."

"What?" Puzzled, she took a seat next to him.

"*Dr.* Lassiter," he emphasized. "I like that. Who would believe I snagged a smart, beautiful doc of my very own?"

"Oh, I don't know if you've *snagged* me just yet," she began. But she found herself wrapped in his arms as he growled playfully.

"Oh, you don't, huh?"

"Nope."

Turning, he leaned over her and cupped her face, planting another skillful kiss on her lips. His mouth devoured hers and she went with it. Let need take over and fuel the fire, licking at her body higher and higher with each passing second. His hands roamed, caressed her thighs. Stroked.

They explored each other's mouth, touched as much

as they could there on the sofa, where they could be discovered any second. Finally she could take no more.

"Do you have protection?"

"Never leave home without it."

A small laugh escaped her. "I'm not sure whether that's a comfort."

"Can we go with yes?"

"We'd better, or I'm going to combust," she told him. "Come on."

Taking his hand, she led him down the hallway, tiptoeing past Maddy's room. The door was open and she glimpsed her little girl's sleeping face in the glow of the night-light before moving on. She felt a bit guilty, but why she wasn't sure. She was a grown woman with all the desires that came with it. And hers had been sorely neglected for years.

Once they were in her room, she closed and locked the door. "If she gets up and needs me, she'll knock."

"You sure this is all right?" he asked softly.

She tugged on his shirt. "Never more so than I am right now. And you're way overdressed, my sexy detective."

He helped her off with his shirt. "Have a fetish for a man in uniform, by any chance?"

"Nah, it's not the uniform that does it for me," she said breathlessly, working on the button on his jeans. "More like the total package. The smokin' body, the weapon—both kinds—and the whole authority figure thing. Turns me on."

"Lucky me."

There wasn't a lot of talking after that, which was fine by Robyn.

With his shirt discarded, she got his jeans undone and pushed them down his thighs to reveal strong, sculpted legs. From head to toe, he looked like he could've played football at one time, though he was built more like a quarterback than a linebacker—lean, toned muscle. He had a light dusting of dark hair on his chest that matched the neatly trimmed bush surrounding his cock.

And what a cock. Mother nature had blessed Chris with what she guessed was a good nine inches, thicker at the base and tapering to a flared mushroom head that was weeping little pearls at the slit. She needed a tiny taste, had to have him.

Kneeling, she grasped the base of him and guided the tip to her mouth. He groaned, hips pitching forward some as she swirled it with her tongue. Lapped and enjoyed the salty-sweet essence. Wrapping her fingers around his girth, she began to pump. As she inched him farther into her mouth and sucked, she used her hand to work the rest that wouldn't fit. She enjoyed sucking but wasn't good at deep-throating.

He didn't seem to mind. A moan rumbled in his chest as he found a rhythm, fucking into her mouth at a pace that wouldn't hurt her. She was working on making him come when he suddenly, but carefully, pulled back.

"I'm going to come if we keep that up, honey. Your turn."

Taking her hand, he helped her up and then got busy removing her clothes. He unbuttoned her blouse first, parted the material, and pushed off her shoulders, letting it slide to the floor. Then he reached around her and unclasped her bra, eased off the straps. The bra joined her blouse and he sucked in a breath, cupping her breasts reverently.

"You're beautiful."

She wanted to duck her head and avoid his gaze, but she didn't. Even though it seemed like a lifetime since a man had seen her body, she wouldn't shy away. "Thank you."

His thumbs brushed her nipples, hardening the already pert peaks to bullet points. Bending, he flicked one of the little points with his tongue, sending small tremors of delight through her nerve endings. He laved first that nipple, then the other, before working to unfasten her pants.

He pushed them down, along with her lacy panties, and she stepped out of them. Bared to his hungry gaze, her desire mounted. "I need you. Now."

His lazy grin was disarming. "You've got me."

Crowding close, she walked him backward until the backs of his legs touched the mattress. Then she gave him a playful shove, enjoying a sense of satisfaction to see the hotter-than-hell detective sprawled on her bed. Pouncing, she quickly crawled over him to straddle his waist and bent to spread kisses on his yummy chest.

"Damn, that feels good," he whispered. "You have magic lips."

"Mmm, but *you* have the magic wand." Scooting down some, she reached for him and began to stroke the rigid length.

Chuckling, he raised his hips, making it clear how much he loved the attention. She gave him a few more strokes and then reached for the square packet on the nightstand. Quickly she tore it open and sheathed his cock. She held him while she got into position, then slowly lowered herself, working him inside.

"It's been so long . . ." she breathed. He was a tight fit. So snug the stretch almost burned.

"Don't hurt yourself, honey."

"I won't. Just need to adjust."

Gradually, her channel relaxed to accommodate him and the burn began to ease. As she moved up and down, riding him, the discomfort gave way to heat that started in her sex and spread to her limbs. She wanted to get under his skin, merge, become a part of him.

As she rode him, the way he gazed up at her, as though she was the most beautiful thing he'd ever seen, spiraled her desire out of control. His big hands spanned her waist and held on as she increased the tempo, bouncing on his lap. Breathy moans filled the air. Hers and his mingled, along with the musky scent of sex.

All too soon, her passion was driven over the edge. "Oh! I'm gonna—"

"Do it," he urged, fucking her hard. "Come all over my cock, baby."

Unable to hold back, she shattered. The orgasm rolled over her in a tidal wave of ecstasy, shaking her to the foundations. Her lover quickly followed, burying himself deep and grinding his hips, head thrown back as he spasmed on and on, filling her with heat.

Spent, she draped herself across his chest and kissed his lips. He responded with enthusiasm, returning the kiss for a long moment. Pulling back, she smiled down at him.

"Stay for a while?"

"I'd love to. I'll be up early, though, before Maddy stirs. I've got some witnesses to see in the morning, anyway."

She didn't want him to go, but knew that was for the best. "Okay. But you're all mine for now."

"And you're mine."

She snuggled into his side and drifted. As she did, it occurred to her that she hadn't thought of Greg at all, except for when Chris had asked about him at dinner. *Am I really ready to move on? Can I open myself up to more pain?*

She didn't know about the future.

But the here and now felt pretty damned good.

He waited for hours.

Seething, he watched the darkened house, positive his special chosen one would come home. The others were vital, but this one . . . he was the culmination of all the careful plans. He was the one who must suffer the most, which was why he was still breathing. The others were dying swiftly, as planned.

But not him. The bastard must suffer the most horrendous death possible.

But why isn't he home? What if he suspects? Could he have figured out why he's in such agony? Does he know why he's dying, and how?

Shifting from foot to foot, he began to sweat. *No. If the cop knew, I'd be in handcuffs already. There's still time to make sure everything happens as it should.*

So the cop probably didn't know. But there was one way to find out.

Making his way to the back of the house, he kept to the shadows. Using the trees and bushes as cover, he trod as silently as possible, careful not to alert the neighbor's yappy dog. Pets were always a problem and sometimes he had to shut them up. Not that he liked hurting animals. They were mostly nice, but he had to do what was necessary.

Moving slowly, he skirted the backyard and was halfway to the back patio door when he saw something interesting. In the light coming from the back porch bulb, he saw there was a hole in the grass, obviously dug on purpose. Dirt was piled to one side of the hole, and there was a wire with a small red flag to mark the spot. As if the big pile of fucking dirt wasn't a clue about the hole.

Briefly, he wondered what sort of work was being done, then shrugged. Who the hell cared? Hurrying, he made his way to the back door. This was the tricky part—he was exposed, unscrewing the hot bulb with a cloth from his pocket. If anyone saw him, the chase was on.

But nobody did. In seconds, he had his special tools out and had jimmied the door open, and was stepping inside.

It had been a calculated risk, targeting the cop. But this was meant to be. The bastard had to pay. Justice would be done for the wrongs he'd suffered.

Inside, he shook himself from his musings and took a look around. He didn't dare turn on a light, so he fished the small penlight from his jeans and used it instead. The house was tidy, not much out of place. The kitchen had a couple of dishes in the sink, two bills tossed onto the counter. Also on the counter was a scrap of paper with a number scrawled on it, and above that the words *City of Sugarland Utilities*.

Could that be the reason for the small mess in the backyard? Going on a hunch, he walked over to the sink and turned on the water. Bingo! Nothing came out. The water had been turned off, which meant his target was likely staying somewhere else until it was fixed.

Dammit—now his plans had been put on hold.

He took a calming breath. The important thing was that they were merely on hold, not destroyed.

Just to be sure, he went to check on the items most crucial to his revenge. Heart pounding, he searched, fearful that the ace up his sleeve had been discovered too soon. But no!

The items were still there. Relief made his limbs grow weak. Now he needed to get out of here before he was found. Quickly, he retraced his steps and let himself out, then, after some debate, screwed the bulb back in over the porch. He could've left it, but if the cop got curious, he might snoop around. And if he did that, he might find the very faint scratches around the lock on his door.

One thing could lead to another. So the bulb was put back to rights.

He'd gotten away clean and congratulated himself for a covert operation well done.

One more step toward his goal.

6

"Do I need to ask what—or who—is responsible for putting that stupid grin on your face?"

Chris looked up from the file he was holding and saw Taylor Kayne standing just inside Chris's office, his expression open and betraying his good humor. "I guess the rumors are flying, huh?"

"About you and the foxy doc? Hell yeah, what else is there to gossip about?" Taylor leaned against the wall. "When are you going to introduce me? I somehow missed the pleasure at the party."

"You have your own pretty lady," he said, sharper than he'd intended.

The detective laughed. "Relax. I'm quite happy with Cara. You've got it bad already, man."

"Sorry." He forced himself to relax. "I'll introduce you guys soon."

"Been going out a lot?"

"We had our first big date last Friday night," he said, warming to Taylor's interest. "I took Robyn to that new

Italian place on the river. It was great. *She's* great, and so is her little girl. We—"

"Whoa, a kid?" Taylor whistled, arching a brow. "That sounds real domestic."

"So what? Maddy's a sweet girl, and she hasn't had a father figure in her life for a while now. She and I get along really well."

"It's cool," Taylor said, nodding. "I was just wondering if you were ready for an instant family, that's all. I mean, I've watched Shane go through it with Drew, and even though the boy is older and is a good kid, that doesn't make the adjustment any easier."

"I know. Shane's my cousin and I saw all that go down, remember? Anyway, I don't want to jump the gun, but things are going well. I've taken lunch to Robyn at the hospital twice since our date, and it's been fun. We've got plans to take Maddy out together tonight when I get off."

"That's cool. I'm glad to see you so happy. For real."

"Thanks. Like I said, it's early. And there's this hesitance in Robyn that worries me." He paused, trying to find the right words. "We get along great, and the chemistry is off the charts. But when I hint at getting serious, she changes the subject or clams up."

"Ah," his friend said sagely. "A woman with baggage. Don't worry, it sounds like she's really into you."

"I think she is. I just wish she'd open up more about her past, particularly with her husband." He ran a hand through his hair in frustration. "Robyn told me that he passed away two years ago, but I get the distinct impression there's more to it than that. Whatever happened has left her scarred, and afraid."

Taylor clamped a hand on his shoulder. "Don't sweat this, and don't push too hard. She'll tell you when she's ready."

He sighed. "Yeah, you're right. It's just hard not to push when it's in my nature."

Just then, Shane stuck his head in the door, leaned in, and smacked his partner on the arm. "You gonna stand in here and shoot the shit with my cuz all day? Come on, lazy ass, we've got cases to solve."

"Yeah, yeah, suck my dick."

"Not even for a million dollars. Let's go, shithead."

With that he was gone, leaving Taylor to glare after him. "Some days I wonder how I ended up with that asshole for my partner."

Chris rolled his eyes. "Right. Says the guy who about lost his mind both times Shane was nearly killed on the job."

"Well, that was different."

"Sure." Those two were best friends, and they weren't fooling anybody.

"Gotta run. Good luck with the female thing." Taylor started out the door, then stopped and turned. "Just so you know, it never gets any easier to understand them."

"Thanks. That's uplifting advice."

"You're welcome."

Chris left his office a step behind Taylor and went in search of the captain. He found Rainey in the break room, munching on a bagel.

"Hey, you know those have been out on the table for two days," Chris told him with a smirk.

Rainey stopped chewing for a second, then shook his head. "Don't care. I'm starving." He paused, eyeing Chris. "What's up?"

"I need to ask you something. It's kind of strange and it's not even a case yet. In fact, it may be nothing at all."

Rainey frowned. "We need to go to my office?"

"No, I think this is fine. It's not top secret, that I know of." Where to start? "Have you heard anything about the medical examiner being concerned about a number of deaths in the area?"

The captain's expression cleared, and he nodded. "Yeah. She phoned the chief and he told a select few of us, mostly the captains and lieutenants. Of course, he wants it kept quiet for now, pending any evidence that she could be right, enough to start an official investigation. How'd *you* learn about it?"

"I'm seeing one of the doctors from the hospital, Robyn Lassiter. She's the one who first spoke to Eden about the suspicious rise in the number of heart attack deaths the hospital is seeing. The victims are coming in with the same symptoms, and most of them have died."

"I heard. But there's not much we can do when the autopsies haven't shown anything beyond heart failure, and nothing to pinpoint a culprit, either natural or man-made."

"Nothing to pinpoint it *yet*. The thing is . . . you know about my health issues," he said quietly, though the break room was still empty. "You're one of only a handful of people who does. What you don't know—that I didn't either until recently—is that my symptoms are the same as those people who've died."

Rainey's eyes widened. "Shit. You sure?"

Chris rested his hip on a table and stared at the floor. "Nausea, sweats, weakness in my limbs, general exhaustion, dizziness, and a racing heart. That last one is the scariest. Right now I'm fine, or at least better than I've been. This has been a good week—I'm just tired instead of all the rest."

"But they've done all sorts of tests. They haven't found anything wrong."

"You don't think that's weird in itself? These are common symptoms that overlap with any number of diseases and conditions and yet they've found *nothing*?" Chris asked, looking him in the eye. "I'm not a hypochondriac. I'm *sick*, Cap. And I'm starting to get scared. There's something going on and we need to find out what, before more people end up like the rest, including me."

"What would you have me do?" Rainey spread his hands in frustration. "There's nothing to investigate yet. Give me something to go on and I'll back you."

"Let me do some poking around," he urged. "I need a list of those victims who've died of heart failure after showing the same symptoms, not just from Sugarland, but the whole county. The ME will help me with that, I know she will."

Rainey wasn't convinced. "You're borrowing trouble. If you go stirring up folks, start a panic, and get our asses in a sling—"

"Cap, I swear there's something to this." Lowering his voice, he made a last appeal. "I'm fighting for my life here. I can *feel* it. Give me a chance to figure out what's going on."

Rainey was quiet for a long moment. At last, he gave in reluctantly. "All right. Look into it, *off* the record. Tread lightly if you question any of the survivors. I swear to you if you get us in trouble, I will fuck you over so hard you'll be calling me sweetheart."

Chris smiled. "Thanks, Cap! You won't regret this. I promise."

"That remains to be seen. One more thing—you start having those symptoms again, you let me know. Don't keep this to yourself, or you could end up on that list."

"I hear you. And thanks."

Rainey walked out, snagging another stale bagel, leaving Chris to ponder his last words. The other man had no idea how afraid Chris truly was. Nobody did.

He suspected it wouldn't be long before something came to a head. He just hoped he survived long enough to solve the case.

With that squared away, he returned to his office and placed a call to Laura Eden. The medical examiner wasn't in her office, so he left a message that didn't say too much, in case someone else heard it. But he did say it was urgent, so hopefully she'd call back soon.

In the meantime, other cases awaited. And another elementary school visit with Valor this afternoon. One more outing in the smelly suit before he could go home and get ready for his date with two special girls.

He grinned a little at that. Who'da thought?

Pushing to his feet, he started to skirt his desk when a wave of dizziness hit him hard, making his head swim. The room dipped, and for a second he thought he'd fall. Fumbling, he reached out blindly for the desktop and steadied himself. After a few seconds, the feeling passed.

But the fear remained.

He wondered how long he had before the grim reaper came to call—and he was forced to answer the door.

Chris was beyond tired as he pulled his car into Robyn's driveway.

He'd come straight from work, not even stopping at his own house first even though he needed a change of clothes for one more night at Shane and Daisy's. The water line should be fixed by tomorrow. The city had declared it wasn't their problem since it was on his property. Of course, the plumber was backed up but had sworn it would be taken care of.

He wouldn't hold his breath.

Robyn opened the door just as he stepped onto the porch. Swiftly, he moved in for a kiss and held her tight, liking how she pressed her body to his and played with his hair.

"Is the munchkin ready to go?" he asked.

She gave a laugh. "Since the crack of dawn, bugging me every five minutes before I took her to school about when you were coming, and starting right up again after we got home."

That made him feel pretty damned good. "Where is she?"

"In the kitchen, making sure we have plenty of snacks. But don't worry," she said, giving him one last squeeze and then stepping back to let him in. "I made sure you and I have stuff to nibble on besides Pop-Tarts and fruit chews."

"You are a very wise woman."

"I have my moments."

"Hey, Maddy!" he called. "You gonna come see me or what?"

"Chris!" The sound of a chair scraping across the tiled floor came from the kitchen; then the little girl bolted toward him.

Bending, he spread his arms and braced himself for impact. She launched herself into his arms and he caught her with an exaggerated huff, then swung her around as she squealed.

"Oh my gosh, you're heavy!" he teased.

"Nuh-uh!"

Setting her down, he ruffled her hair. "You ready to go?"

"Yep!"

"Yes, sir," Robyn corrected gently.

"Yes, sir." Maddy wrinkled her nose and pouted for a second, but instantly forgot about it, her attention more focused on their upcoming outing. "I wanna help carry the picnic basket!"

Robyn shook her head. "Sweet pea, it's too heavy. You can take the bag with the chips."

"Okay."

Chris watched her dash to the kitchen. "I'm not sure I ever had that much energy."

"She can be a handful. You sure you want to do this?" Her question was half teasing, but there was something else in her eyes and tone. As if she almost expected him to back out.

"Are you kidding? I've been looking forward to this all day. And I told you before, Maddy's a great kid. Gets it from her mother."

Robyn's cheeks flushed, making her look even more beautiful—if that was possible. Before she could respond, Maddy came bounding back in with a plastic grocery sack in hand.

"We got two kinds of chips," she announced. "Sour cream and onion, and cheese puffs."

"Sour cream and onion are my favorite," he told her, and was rewarded with a wide smile.

"Me, too."

He looked to Robyn. "I've got the cooler in the car with the drinks in it. If you're ready, I'll grab the picnic basket from the kitchen."

"I'm ready."

"Yay!" Maddy sprinted out the door, oblivious to Robyn calling out to wait.

"That child." She sighed, hurrying after her daughter.

Chuckling, Chris walked into the kitchen and retrieved the basket. He hauled it outside, where Robyn was waiting to lock the house, and then started down the steps. Maddy was jumping up and down beside the Camaro, singing to herself a song that sounded suspiciously like one by Katy Perry. Not that he listened to that stuff, but hell, he didn't live under a rock.

Privately, Chris thought the munchkin was way too young for that sort of music, but it wasn't his place to say.

Unlocking the car, he placed the basket in the trunk

next to the cooler. Neither one was overly large, so they fit fine. Robyn got Maddy buckled in the backseat and then climbed into the front. Chris slid behind the wheel, and then they were on their way for an afternoon of fun at Cheatham Dam Park.

The day had turned out to be gorgeous, a bit on the hot side still but not unbearable. Chris listened to Maddy chatter about school, mostly who was mean and who was nice among both students and teachers—of supreme importance to a first grader, apparently—and how she loved PE, hated math, and brought her own lunch because the cafeteria food was gross. She was inexhaustible.

And she was just about the cutest thing he'd ever seen.

A few minutes later, he turned down Cheatham Dam Road, enjoying the winding path with its hills. Soon he was pulling into the park, where the hills and trees parted, giving way to the flatter area of the park next to the Cumberland River. He found a spot near the playground that had a table where they could set up.

As soon as the car was parked, Maddy bolted for the playground. Robyn, he noted, held back from admonishing her, probably because they were so close to the area. But she scowled after her daughter, lips thinned.

Then she sighed and turned to Chris, annoyance replaced by worry. "She has a bad habit of dashing off when she's excited. I know the impulsiveness is mostly her age, but it still scares me sometimes."

"That's understandable. I'm no expert on kids, but it seems many of them go through that stage. That's why we do safety programs and such—to try to get them to stop and think before they act. We know it works because we hear from parents who've said their children remembered our lessons and saved their own lives or someone else's."

"That's so impressive. You really make a difference."

"Not in the same way you do. You're the one with all the smarts, but thanks."

"Hey, that's not true. And we both save lives, so we're the same in that regard. Come on—let's get the stuff out."

He got the heavier basket and cooler, then Robyn helped him with the tablecloth and putting out the chips and plastic cups. He also grabbed a gym bag and tossed it to the ground by the table. When everything was ready, they sat next to each other on the table's bench seat facing the playground, and Chris put his arm around her shoulders. He liked that she scooted closer, leaning into him.

"What's in the gym bag?" she asked, pointing.

"I brought some things for Maddy to play with, like a football. She and I had a lot of fun the other day with that."

Robyn smiled. "You just happened to have a football lying around?"

"No," he admitted. "I bought it a couple of days ago. But I used to have one, back when I played in high school."

"I knew it. I had you figured for a jock. Did you play in college?"

"For a while, quarterback. Had a couple of scouts from the NFL eyeing me at one point, but then I blew out my shoulder and that was the end of it. I went into law enforcement instead and I've never regretted it."

"I'm glad. If you had taken a different path, I might never have met you."

"That's the nicest thing anybody's said to me in a long time," he told her softly. Then he leaned in and stole a chaste kiss, mindful of Maddy nearby.

"It's the truth." Her eyes were warm.

"I'm glad, too."

They sat quietly for a moment, enjoying each other's company. "So, what else is in the bag?"

"A Frisbee, a set of horseshoes, and a remote-controlled helicopter."

"A what? Um, we're next to the *river*. If it goes for a swim, it's a goner."

"Yeah, maybe that one wasn't the best idea. But I think we can walk to that field over there, away from the water, and give it a try."

"I know why you get along with kids—you're a big kid yourself."

"I can't deny that."

Maddy called out for someone to push her on the swings, so Robyn did that for a while. Chris soaked up the sight of them, and the awesome day, perfectly content. By the time Maddy was tired of swinging, everyone was hungry.

Robyn opened the basket and unwrapped turkey and bacon sandwiches on ciabatta rolls, putting a plain one on a plate for Maddy. His and Robyn's had lettuce, tomato, and mayo, and he was practically salivating when they were ready to eat.

That simple meal went down on his list of all-time favorites.

Not so much for the food, but just being here with Robyn and Maddy. Feeling part of two other people in a way he never had before. *This* was how it should have been when he was a kid. He should have been like Maddy, happy and well adjusted. Loved by both of his parents. They'd never had days like this in all his life.

He stopped chewing as a realization smacked him between the eyes. He was thinking in terms of a family. With these two, who were slowly worming their way into his heart. Hadn't he known that's what was happening? Maybe, deep down. But acknowledging what he wanted—even just to himself—was sort of scary.

How could he be any kind of positive role model for Maddy when his own childhood had sucked so badly?

"Chris?"

His gaze snapped to hers to find her staring at him from across the table. "Hmm?" Quickly, he finished chewing the bite of sandwich.

"You okay?"

"Oh, sure. Just thinking about work." He wasn't sure why he lied. Except it just seemed too soon to broach the possibility of his being a part of their future. Instead, he went with something he *could* speak about. "I talked to my captain about that issue we were discussing, the one involving Eden." He was well aware of small ears, and was careful.

Glancing at Maddy, she nodded. "What did he say?"

"The chief made them aware of the concerns you and the ME have, and I've been given permission to unofficially take a look at the list of people affected."

"That's good," she said with relief. "Maybe you'll find a connection somewhere."

"I'm sure going to try."

After that, talk was kept lighthearted, and he made sure to include Maddy in the conversation. He wouldn't tolerate her feeling left out or ignored—by himself or anyone else. The protectiveness that came over him where she was concerned still amazed him. She wasn't his, and damned if that didn't sting a little.

After dinner was cleared away, it was time for football. He and Maddy even coaxed Robyn into participating, despite her protests that athletics were not her thing. They tossed the ball back and forth for a while, letting the little girl "score" now and then and spike the ball.

Horseshoes were a bit out of Maddy's skill set just yet—her arms were too short and skinny to throw the U-shaped irons with much strength, so that game quickly waned.

The remote-controlled helicopter, however, was another matter. The gadget was met with unbridled enthusiasm, and so he took her over to the field to try her hand at junior piloting. He demonstrated a couple of runs, showing her how to work the controls, and then relinquished them to her.

It soon became clear that the small copter was not going home in the same shape in which it had arrived. He didn't mind—he simply enjoyed watching her have such fun. Robyn called out encouragement and tried to give her directions, but the toy crashed again and again, spending more time on the ground than it did in the air. Maddy didn't care.

Then suddenly the thing remained aloft for an extended run, the little girl shouting in delight at her improved flying. Inevitably, however, the copter got away from her. But this time it soared away from the water and directly into a stand of trees some forty yards away. The toy was totally swallowed by the foliage.

"I'll get it!" she yelled. Then she took off after it like a bullet.

"Maddy, wait!"

The girl paid no heed, and Chris gave her mother a rueful smile. "I'll go help her look for it."

The kid was fast, disappearing into the trees before he could catch up. Stopping, he listened and could hear her crashing through the undergrowth—and suddenly the noise stopped. He waited a few heartbeats, but there was no sound at all. A chill crept down his spine.

"Maddy? Where are you?" Nothing. "Maddy!"

His feet got moving, jumping over logs and dodging branches. Getting desperate, he looked all around, calling her name with increasing worry. *Don't panic. She's fine.*

Then she was there, jogging back toward him with the toy in hand, grinning triumphantly. He blew out a breath and met her halfway, then crouched in front of her and put his hands on her slim shoulders.

"Maddy, listen to me." At his firm, serious tone, her smile slid off her face and her eyes widened. "Never go running off like that again where your mom and I can't see you. I was getting scared when I couldn't find you. Do you understand?"

"Yeah," she said in a small voice. "But I was okay. The man helped me find it."

His blood turned to ice. "What man?"

"The man in the trees." Turning, she pointed behind her in the direction from which she'd come. "Back there. I saw him and he had the helicopter. Then he gave it back to me."

Oh God. "Did he say anything to you?"

"He said I should be more careful not to lose my toys."

All right, that's not really threatening. Breathe. "Anything else?"

She shrugged. "He told me kids get hurt when they don't stay with their mommies and daddies. And even sometimes when they do."

Chris swallowed hard. "Is that all?"

"Uh-huh."

"Okay. Let's go find your mom."

Putting a hand on her shoulder, he guided her out of the trees and over to where Robyn waited. There was a smile on her face—until she noted the expression on his.

"What's wrong?"

Fishing in his pocket, he dug out his keys. "Take these and go wait in the car, please. And lock the doors."

"Why? Where are you going?"

"I'm going to see if I can find the man Maddy was talking to in the woods and thank him for being so helpful in finding her toy," he said in an even voice. But she read the truth on his face. The incident had rattled him, and he wanted to find this man, check him out.

She nodded, striving to keep her voice light. "All right. We'll be waiting."

Turning, he jogged back to the area that Maddy had come from. He searched for a good ten minutes but found no trace of the mysterious man, or anyone else. No cigarette butts, no footprints on the ground. No piece of clothing. Nothing.

Arriving back at the car, he'd almost convinced himself it really was someone trying to help. Almost. But that explanation didn't sit well with him. In that case, the man should have come to meet Chris, made sure to see Maddy was safely returned to where she belonged. He sure as hell wouldn't be hinting to her that sometimes kids weren't safe with their parents. What sort of freak said shit like that to a little kid?

Maddy had already dismissed him, but Chris couldn't.

Robyn helped him stow their picnic stuff in the back of the car once more. Their outing had been wonderful, up to the strange ending, and they were all ready to go back. Even Maddy was so tired she didn't beg for more playground time, which was fine by him. He wanted some distance between the girls and this place.

There was an itch between his shoulder blades he couldn't quite scratch.

Reaching for Robyn's hand, he was gratified when she took it and curled her fingers into his. They rode quietly as he drove them home, and he soaked up the last of the evening with his new lover. He wondered whether he should stay overnight. But who was he kidding? If she asked, he wasn't strong enough to say no.

They arrived and he carried the basket and other stuff

inside that belonged to Robyn. In the kitchen he helped throw the rest of the trash away, clean out the basket, and put away the leftover chips.

Then Robyn disappeared to make sure Maddy got started with her bath, returning a few minutes later wearing a worried frown.

"Who was this man she was talking about?"

He related the whole story to her, emphasizing that it could've been nothing. Robyn wasn't buying it.

"That's just too weird, Chris. Why was he even hanging out in the woods? There aren't any houses or trails right where we were, no reason for him to be there."

"I don't know. I took a good look around, but I didn't find anything."

"What he said . . . the last part could be construed as a threat."

"It could," he agreed. "But it's equally likely it was the ramblings of a vagrant, and that the words meant nothing to anyone but him."

"Could be." Her blue eyes hardened. "I'm going to be extra careful for a while, though. There's no telling what he was up to."

"I'm sorry," he said, dejected. "I should have caught up with her faster. I didn't— "

"No! I didn't mean you should've done anything different." Moving to him, she touched his face. "Wasn't I just telling you how she runs off when she's excited? I have to find a way to get through to her about that before she gets hurt."

"I may have overstepped." The confession was heavy on his tongue. "When I found her, I crouched down and told her rather firmly not to run off like that again. I don't know if she'll remember next time, but it scared me so bad when I couldn't find her. I had to say something, but I didn't yell at her."

"It's all right. I believe you. In fact, when you spend time with us, I want you to feel comfortable correcting her as needed—if you want us to continue to see each other, that is."

"Of course I do, gorgeous." He smiled. "You're both getting under my skin faster than you realize."

"Same here," she said softly.

He paused, let that sink in. "Well, I should go, I suppose."

"You don't say that with much conviction."

"None whatsoever," he admitted.

"Then stay. Maddy's going to be finished with her bath and asleep before we know it."

"And then?" His pulse quickened.

"And then we reward ourselves for being so good today . . . by being very bad."

He almost came in his jeans. "That's a plan I can get behind."

Worn out from their big day, the little girl finished her bath and went to bed without a fuss. While Robyn was tucking her in, Chris snuck into the kitchen and fished around in the pantry until he found the item he was looking for. With a grin, he took it to the master bedroom with him and shut the door.

Naked or dressed? Taking a chance, he set the pilfered item on the nightstand, then stripped to his skin and crawled beneath the covers. He was sprawled on his back, stroking his hardening length under the sheets, when Robyn walked in, firmly shutting and locking the door behind her.

"Well, someone's eager to get started," she commented, arching a brow.

"Is the coast clear?"

"Completely."

"In that case . . ." Flinging back the covers, he let her have an eyeful as he continued to stroke. His cock turned to steel as she licked her lips, riveted. With his other hand, he reached out and grabbed the plastic bottle on the nightstand.

She gave him a wicked smile as she moved to the bed, pulling her shirt over her head. "You're a bad boy, Detective."

"Me? I'm a good boy, really. I just like to get a little dirty sometimes." He waggled the bottle of honey in his hand. "Wanna help me?"

Giving a husky laugh, she finished undressing as she spoke. "Would I? With the proper motivation, getting sticky can be one of my favorite things."

Sweet Jesus, she was beautiful. Auburn hair fell around her shoulders, surrounding her face. Pouty lips were made for kissing and sucking. Her full breasts were begging for his hands and mouth, and those thighs went on forever.

"Why don't you show me?" he murmured. He had to let go of his erection, or risk shooting too soon.

She crawled onto the bed, stalking him like a pretty cat, and crouched over him. Bending, she braced her hands on his chest and took his mouth, tongue slipping inside to taste. He returned the kiss wholeheartedly, until she pulled back and peppered kisses on his jaw. Then down his neck, to his chest. There she nibbled on each of his nipples, making him suck in a breath as his dick twitched, aching to be buried inside her.

"Shit, that feels good," he breathed.

"That's nothing. Just wait."

Snatching the honey bottle from his hand, she flipped the cap and scooted down on the bed. Then she grasped his straining cock and drizzled the sweet liquid all over it and his balls before setting the bottle aside.

When she began to lap up the honey with slow, sensual licks, he nearly came. She laved his cock and balls, getting every drop, sending shivers of pure pleasure through his body. When she took the bottle and started to add more, he gently grabbed her wrist.

"My turn. If you do that again, I'm going to go off like a rocket."

"And that's a bad thing?"

"It is when I want to be inside you when I do." Sitting up, he gestured with the bottle. "On your back, gorgeous."

"I love it when you get all bossy in bed." She complied, spreading her legs.

He gave a playful growl and then upended the bottle, pouring a generous amount of the golden treat on each nipple. Then he sucked each one, loving the taste of the sweet honey combined with her skin. It made for a heady aphrodisiac, and he added more, cleaning off each nipple again.

When he moved on to her sex, spreading apart the delicate lips to drizzle some honey there, she began to writhe in anticipation.

"Please," she begged.

"Please, what? Say it."

"Lick me."

He couldn't refuse such a heartfelt request. Setting the bottle aside, he crouched and gave her exactly what she'd asked for. He licked and sucked the golden sweetness until she moaned his name, buried her hands in his hair and started to pull.

"Chris, fuck me."

At her plea, he retrieved a condom from his shorts pocket and covered his cock. Then he moved over her and positioned himself at her entrance. He pushed inside slow and easy, resisting the urge to come too quickly. He wasn't going to last long, though. The fire already burned too high, his balls aching for release.

He began to move inside her, loving how she clung to his back. How her long legs wrapped around his waist and held on as he made love to her. He especially loved the breathy sounds of passion coming from her throat as she surrendered. They were connected not just physically, but emotionally.

It had never been this way with anyone else.

They came together again and again, until he couldn't hold back a second longer. He stiffened and his release exploded, his cock jerking. She joined him with a cry, and they trembled in each other's arms until they were spent.

Eventually, he moved off her and pulled her into his

arms. She rested her head on his chest and they simply enjoyed the closeness for a while.

"I'm not done with you yet," he whispered, pressing a kiss into her hair. "I plan on loving you again."

And he did, twice more that night.

7

Robyn awoke to the sound of her cell phone buzzing on the nightstand. Not a welcome noise to hear when tangled with a sexy naked man in her bed.

Stifling a curse, she managed to wiggle from under Chris's supine body and reach for the phone. When she saw the hospital's number on the display, she slid from bed and padded from the bedroom, easing the door shut behind her before she answered.

"Dr. Lassiter."

"Doctor, this is Lee Miller from the hospital. I know you weren't scheduled to come in until ten and I'm so sorry to bother you, but we've got multiple victims coming in from a bad wreck on I-40."

Immediately, she turned and dashed back into the bedroom, heading for the master closet. "ETA?"

"First ones are arriving in about fifteen minutes. The paramedics advise they're almost ready to transport."

She glanced at the clock—barely six a.m. Not quite light out. "All right, getting dressed now. Hopefully I'll beat them there, but if not, I won't be far behind. Thanks for calling, Lee."

"I'll let everyone know. Thanks, Dr. Lassiter."

Swiftly, she pulled on her underwear and a bra, a pair of dark pants, and a blouse. Emergencies happened, and she was glad that she had taken the time to shower after their last lovemaking session.

"Hey," a sleepy male voice called. "What's going on?"

"I'm sorry," she said, turning toward Chris, who was blinking at her from the bed. "I got called in. We have victims from a bad wreck on the way into the ER and I have to go— Shit! Maddy. I'll have to call Rachel and see if she can come over early."

Pushing from the bed, a mouthwateringly naked Chris pulled her in for a hug. "No worries. Let Maddy and Rachel sleep. I can go in to work later. There's no rush. Plus it's Sunday and there's no school, so I'll stay until Rachel gets here at her normal time."

Robyn bit her lip. God, she had to leave, and she didn't know what to do. "I can't impose on you like that. This is so new, and *so* not what you signed up for—"

"Stop." He kissed her on the forehead. "Do you trust me here, alone with your daughter?"

Her hesitation stung him. She could see the hurt in his liquid brown gaze. But it didn't take her long to answer that question. "I *do* trust you. I know you'll watch over her and keep her safe."

"Always, whenever you need me to. So go, and focus on what you have to do. Maddy and I will be fine until Rachel shows up."

Relieved, she squeezed him tight and gave him a sound kiss. "Thank you. I'll make this up to you."

Teasing, he waggled his brows. "I'll entertain myself by thinking up all sorts of ways you can do that."

She laughed, and stepped back to slip on her shoes. "I just bet you will."

He started backing up toward the bathroom and hitched a thumb over his shoulder. "I'm going to get cleaned up and dressed so I can be ready when Maddy gets up. And if she asks, I'll tell her I came back this morning to stay with her until Rachel arrives."

"Thank you."

"No prob. Have a good day, and don't stress too much. I'll text you later."

With that, he disappeared and the water came on from inside the bathroom. Rushing out, she closed the bedroom door and hurried for the living room, where she collected her keys and purse. This was going to be a long day, starting it off with a tough call like this one.

But as she pulled out of the driveway and headed to work, a sense of calm washed over her. Whatever was developing between her and Chris felt *right*. She really did trust him, and she was comfortable leaving Maddy in his care.

He belongs already, in our home and in our lives. Is that insane?

The thought filled her with budding happiness—and more fear than before. The strengthening of his presence in her and Maddy's lives came with the brand-new problem of having to *face* the fear of letting another man into her heart, and finally overcoming it.

Once she arrived at the hospital, however, treating the victims of the wreck took her entire focus. As the first two came in, she was shocked to learn that an eighteen-wheeler had run a red light and broadsided an ambulance that had been on its way to a call. She recognized the pair of paramedics from Station Two who were rushing into the ER, pushing a gurney with a third medic lying on it. The victim, firefighter/paramedic Clay Montana from Station Five, was bleeding profusely from multiple lacerations, and had several broken bones and a traumatic head injury.

The man would be lucky to survive.

Another doctor, a couple of residents, and nurses took over with the other victims of the chain reaction wreck, none as badly injured as the paramedic. Robyn ordered him prepped for surgery, and the fight to save his life was on.

Clay made it through surgery, just barely, and nearly three excruciating hours later he was taken to the ICU, where he would remain in a coma for the next few days, or weeks. He might never wake at all, and Robyn's soul was heavy as she cleaned up and then checked on the condition of the other paramedic who'd been hit. Then she went to the waiting room in search of relatives.

She wasn't surprised to find the man's team from the station instead, some pacing and some sitting, all anxious. The group parted and she was faced with Howard Paxton—the big captain she'd met at Shea and Tommy's party.

"First of all," the captain said, "Clay's mother died

seven months ago and he has no siblings. No family. So he's got nobody but us. Lay it on me straight."

She took a deep breath. "If any of you are inclined, prayers wouldn't hurt. He has several broken bones, massive internal injuries, and a traumatic head injury. He's in a coma, and with the swelling we won't know about brain function for some time. If he survives, and that's by no means certain, he's got a long road ahead of him. I'm so sorry."

Heads hung low and a few turned away, wiping at their eyes.

Howard cleared his throat. "When can he have visitors?" he asked hoarsely.

"They'll have him settled shortly, and I'll send someone to let you know. Two visitors at a time, for no more than fifteen minutes. I know there will be a lot of friends who want to come visit him, but please urge them to keep the numbers down, at least in these first few days. He'll need to rest."

The big man nodded. "I'll see to it. How's Julian Salvatore, the other medic who was riding with him? He's family—he's married to my wife's sister. Kat and Grace are with him but I've been waiting out here for word on Clay. I had trouble reaching Julian's brother, but he'll be here soon also."

"He escaped with relatively minor injuries, including a concussion, bruised ribs, and torn ligaments in his ankle. He'll be fine after he rests for a few days."

"Thank God," Howard said, swallowing hard. He looked ready to fall down. "I can't believe this happened, especially to someone as vibrant as Clay."

Sympathy welled in her and she patted the captain on the arm. "He's getting the best care possible, and we've got a top neurologist on staff who's already with him. Plus he's young and strong, so hold on to that. I'll talk to you soon."

"Thanks, Doc. I can't tell you how much I appreciate all you've done."

She kept it together until she got to the staff lounge, and then she collapsed into a chair. The stress caught up with her and tears threatened as she rested her elbows on her knees and buried her face in her hands.

"Hey," Shea's voice said from beside her. "I heard about Clay. Are you all right?"

Sitting up, she gave her friend a slight smile. "I'm okay. I don't know him personally, but we have friends in common, and sometimes that makes it hit home a little harder, you know?"

"Yeah, I do." Her voice cracked. "Clay's an awesome guy, and this is so unfair. He's got to make it. He was Tommy's replacement on A-shift at Station Five after Tommy was injured and couldn't be a firefighter anymore. Did you know that?"

"No, I didn't." How awful.

"That could've been Tommy driving today when that truck hit them. As stupid as it sounds, that's what keeps going through my head. It could've been the man I love in there, but for a set of circumstances that put Clay in his place behind the wheel of the ambulance."

"That's not stupid at all. It's human nature to think about twists of fate, especially in our jobs."

"Yeah. I feel so bad for Clay, and his friends."

"He's strong, or he wouldn't have made it through surgery." Robyn wrapped an arm around her friend's shoulders and gave her a hug. "We have to hope that's enough."

Reluctantly, they both left the break room and got back to work. Robyn checked on Clay from time to time, and found he was holding on. His friends were keeping the ICU staff on edge with their sheer numbers, so Robyn had to impose orders restricting his visitors to the captain and a couple of others.

That afternoon another patient arrived that took her mind off the paramedic for a while. A well-dressed man in his forties was rushed in by ambulance. He was pale, sweating, nauseated, experiencing chest pain, heart racing. Classic symptoms of a heart attack.

Despite their best efforts, he didn't survive. As Lee draped the sheet over the man's body, covering up what appeared to have been a perfectly healthy businessman in good shape, a quiet anger began to take root.

I'm going to get to the bottom of this if it's the very last thing I do.

In the privacy of her office, she placed a call to Laura Eden, but was told the ME had been out sick and to leave a message. "Please tell her that I need toxicology on the deceased we're sending over, Robert Woodrow. Cause of death appears to be a heart attack, but I'm not convinced."

Hanging up, she sat for a few minutes trying to restore her equilibrium. What a fantastically hellish day. And it wasn't quite over yet.

Her only consolations were thoughts of her sweet

baby girl . . . and her sexy new lover to drive away the lonely nights.

Those were more than enough.

Chris and Tonio were in the middle of questioning another burglary victim when his partner got a call on his cell phone.

And for the first time since they'd met, he witnessed his normally serious, self-contained partner fall completely apart.

"Hey, Howard. What's up?" Tonio's expression was puzzled—but only for a few seconds. Confusion morphed to horror. "Oh my God. When? What happened?"

The witness glanced at Chris, startled. Tonio listened for a few more seconds, groaning in clear anguish before answering again.

"Sweet Christ. I'm on my way." Ending the call, he raked a hand through his hair. "I need to get to the hospital. My brother's been in an accident."

Chris immediately took control, starting with the witness. "I'm sorry, we'll have to continue this another day."

"Hey, no problem," the younger man said. "Hope your brother's okay."

"Thanks." Tonio gave the man a polite nod.

Chris steered him to the car, then held out his hand. "Give me the keys."

"But—"

"You're in no condition to drive. Keys."

Thankfully, Tonio surrendered them without further argument, which turned out to be a good thing. The man was in shock, swiping a shaking hand down his pale face as Chris navigated through town.

"What happened?" Chris asked quietly.

"Julian and Clay Montana were on their way to a call when an eighteen-wheeler ran a red light. Clay was driving and it hit on his side."

"Shit." Chris breathed. "How are they?"

"He just said to get there quick."

That wasn't good. At all. Chris wondered whether Robyn was treating either of the men, and figured she probably was. There were a limited number of doctors working at any one time, especially for traumatic injuries.

They arrived at the hospital and Chris parked the Taurus right outside the ER, making sure not to block the driveway. Then he jogged inside on Tonio's heels, hanging back a bit so he could be there for his partner and hear him talking to Howard Paxton without being in the way.

The big captain placed both meaty palms on Tonio's shoulders. "I'm so glad I finally reached you. First, Julian's going to be all right. I just spoke with Dr. Lassiter." Tonio visibly sagged with relief.

"Is he hurt?"

"He's got a concussion, some banged-up ribs, and a messed-up ankle. Some TLC from Grace and he'll be fine."

Tonio closed his eyes and pulled a silver cross from under his shirt. "Thank you, God. Thank you." Opening them again, he asked, "What about Clay?"

Howard's face became miserable as he dropped his hands. "Not as lucky. He might not make it, Tonio."

The other man stared at the captain in shock. "Clay's

so full of life, so . . . so fucking *awesome.* I can't imagine anything bad happening to him."

"Me neither, but we've got to say our prayers now. He's so busted up, there's not much holding him together, and it's not looking good. The doc said he's in a coma and they don't know when, or if, he'll come out of it."

Tonio looked positively gray under his bronzed skin, and Chris knew what he was thinking—only a toss of the coin had put Clay in the driver's seat rather than Julian. He was likely both relieved and feeling guilty about that at the same time. The man was only human.

"Where is he?" Tonio demanded. "I want to see my brother."

A nurse directed him, and he hurried together through the ER's doors to the treatment bays beyond them.

Tonio would likely be here for a while with his family. At loose ends, Chris pulled out his phone and texted Robyn.

I'm here at the hospital. Can you talk?

No answer was immediately forthcoming, so he entertained himself by taking a walk on the grounds. He ended up in the small garden area where visitors and staff sometimes took refuge, sitting on a bench for a bit. Almost half an hour had passed before his phone buzzed. He read the display.

Sorry, it's been hell. Where are you?

Still here, in the garden area.

On my way.

A few minutes later he spotted her coming through the doors, and rose to meet her. She launched herself into his arms and held on as if she'd never let go, and it made him feel good that she was using him as her life raft in the storm.

"Rough day, huh?" he commented softly. It wasn't really a question, more of a statement.

"One of the worst in quite a while, and that's saying something." As she drew back, he saw her eyes were red rimmed. Whether from exhaustion or tears, he didn't know.

"I heard about Clay. That's rough stuff."

"Just about the worst it can get, short of death," she agreed dejectedly. "If he survives, he's going to need extensive physical therapy and the support of every one of his friends to recover. But at least he's holding on, which is more than I can say for the other victim we had today."

Reaching out, he took her hand. "You lost one?"

"Another heart attack." Her expression was haunted. "This one was in his forties, a businessman named Robert Woodrow. He appeared to be in terrific shape—and I'm betting he had no blockages in his heart."

"Another of our suspicious victims?" His gut clenched.

"I'm willing to bet my license on it. I put in a call to the ME about doing more extensive testing, including toxicology, but Eden is out sick."

"That must be why she hasn't called me back yet about that list."

"Give her a few days. I'm sure she's going to be swamped."

"I will." He touched her face. "Do you have time for a quick sandwich in the cafeteria?"

She nodded eagerly. "That sounds great. I'm so hungry, but it's been too insane to stop and eat."

"Let's go."

In the cafeteria, they picked out some chicken wraps and small salads and a couple of bottles of water. Chris insisted on paying; then they found a table in a corner. They ate for a few moments before Robyn picked up the conversation.

"Where's your partner? Aren't you working?"

"I am." He swallowed a bite of his wrap. "Tonio's brother, Julian, was the other paramedic who was injured with Clay. As soon as he got the call from Howard, I drove him over. He's in with the family visiting Julian."

Her eyes widened. "That's terrible! But at least Julian is going to be okay."

"That's one miracle today, anyway."

"I'll say." She paused. "How was Maddy this morning? I've been so busy I haven't been able to call you."

"She was fine. When she got up and saw me, but not you, I think she was thrown and a little nervous. But when I explained you had to go to work and Rachel was coming over soon, she got over it. And I *may* have bribed her with Pop-Tarts, but I'll never tell."

Robyn's laugh went straight to the happy place in his groin. "Why doesn't that surprise me?"

"Hey, I'm a guy. You're lucky I didn't feed her chocolate cake and soda."

"True."

They finished eating, making small talk until Robyn looked at him with regret. "I have to get going. I need to check on Julian and Clay and make the rounds."

"Okay." Just then, his phone buzzed and he eyed the text on the screen. "That's Tonio."

I'm done. They r keeping J 2nite 4 observation.

Coming, he texted back.

"Is everything all right?" she asked.

"Yes. His brother is being kept overnight. Your doing?"

"Just as a precaution, due to the concussion. He can probably go home tomorrow."

"That's good news."

He walked her to the entrance of the ER, where Tonio caught sight of them and watched with open curiosity. Ignoring his partner, he wrapped her in his arms briefly and gave her a chaste kiss. No need to get her in trouble with the hospital brass.

As they pulled apart, she nodded toward Tonio. "I want to speak to him before you guys leave." Chris stayed at her side as she reached the other detective. She held out a hand, which the other man took. "Detective Salvatore, I'm Dr. Robyn Lassiter. One of my residents is the one who actually treated your brother, as I was busy in surgery. Did Dr. Rocha speak to you?"

Tonio nodded, his expression grateful. "He did. Thanks. I understand the decision to keep him overnight was yours?"

"It was," she confirmed. "Dr. Rocha consulted with me, and we feel that's best. If all goes well, he can go home tomorrow."

"Good. You don't know how much I appreciate you all taking good care of him." The man's eyes grew suspiciously bright. "He's my only brother."

She patted his arm, then dug in the pocket of her white coat and handed him a card. "Well, he's going to be fine. That's my number. If you have any questions or concerns, give me a call."

"Thanks." He paused, then his lips curved upward. His tone was friendly. "So, you and my partner, huh?"

"Um, I suppose you could say that." Her cheeks flushed. "Though I'm sorry we had to meet like this."

"Me, too. Maybe Chris can bring you out to the Waterin' Hole for a beer soon, so you can meet the guys from the station."

She shot a glance at Chris, who nodded. He should've thought of that first, and it annoyed him that he hadn't.

"That sounds like fun. Hopefully it'll be soon." She smiled at them both. "I have to go. See you later."

They both stared at her backside hard as she walked away. Tonio was the first to find his voice, giving a low whistle.

"Hot *damn*, my friend," he said appreciatively. "You are one lucky son of a bitch."

Chris blinked at him, torn between being irritated at the man for openly ogling his lady and astonished that the man's uptight facade had crumbled. The latter won. And he realized this was the first time he truly felt like the man was being himself in Chris's presence. That they could be friends as well as partners. A wide smile stretched his face.

"I am, aren't I?"

It seemed things were finally going his way.

"Your water line is fixed."

Five awesome words that meant Chris could leave his cousin's house and get back to his own. Finally. He loved his family, but there was definitely such a thing as too much closeness.

A little more than a week after leaving, he walked into his house and took his gym bag to the bedroom, tossing it on the bed. His body followed and he flopped onto his back, stretching like a lazy old cat and for a few minutes just savoring being on his own comfortable mattress again.

That lasted all of seven minutes or so before he got restless. Fishing out his cell phone, he checked his texts. One from Tonio saying his brother was home and resting, so Chris sent one back saying he was glad. There was nothing from Robyn, though Chris knew she had the day off. Should he send a text, or call? Was he pushing too hard?

No. He'd continue to take his cues from her. If he was moving too fast, she'd let him know. He decided on a text.

Dinner tonight? My house?

Her answer wasn't long in coming. Alone?

If that's okay? Want some serious snuggle time with you . . . But don't get me wrong, Maddy is always welcome!!

No, I need some alone time with you too. 7:00?

Great! See you then. ;)

:D

As an afterthought, he added his address since it occurred to him that she'd only been by that one time she dropped him off. Then he got up and began inspecting the house and realized it wasn't nearly clean enough to have his lady over for the first time. Wanting to make a good impression, he started throwing away trash and tidying up. Then he vacuumed, mopped the kitchen, and washed the few dirty dishes. A couple of weeks' worth of dust had accumulated on the furniture, so he took care of that, a task he typically hated.

When he was done, he was proud of his efforts. But now he was sweaty and disgusting, so a shower was in order. He took care of that, and in a half hour was ready to go to the store. The question was what to fix for dinner. Something simple, but good.

On the way to the store he mulled it over. It was hard to concentrate on food when he was suddenly so hot that a bead of sweat trickled down his face. He turned up the air in the car, and that helped. But by the time he got to the store, the nausea was making an appearance for the first time in three or four days.

If the customers coming to and from the store wouldn't have thought he was having a breakdown, he would've cried.

I can do this. I'm okay.

As he searched the aisles, he kept repeating that to himself. He managed to immerse himself in hunting for dinner ingredients, and set about purchasing chicken breasts, jerk sauce, and some fresh veggies. At the last minute he threw in a frozen chocolate ice box cream pie, because he had a sweet tooth and he was no chef.

Happy with what he'd chosen, he checked out and was soon on his way home. Once there, he brought the bags in and started dinner, putting the chicken in a dish and heating the oven. The fresh broccoli and carrots went in a pan to sauté with a liberal amount of butter, something simple he could handle with no problem.

When the doorbell rang about forty-five minutes later, he had to admit the house was smelling pretty damned good. However, it didn't smell nearly as good as Robyn when he flung open the door and pulled her into his arms. He buried his nose in her hair, inhaling the sweet scent of strawberries and some sort of light, fruity perfume that made him want to eat her like a piece of candy.

"I'm so glad you're here," he said, tilting her face up for a kiss. He took her mouth slowly, getting a good taste, a preview of what he hoped was to come.

"Me, too." She stepped back and sniffed. "Oh, something smells wonderful."

"Yeah—you." He grinned.

She gave a laugh. "Thanks. But seriously, what's cooking?"

"Jerk chicken and sautéed vegetables. Hope that's okay?" He tried to keep the sudden anxiety from his voice.

"That sounds terrific! I haven't eaten today."

"Seems like you make a habit of that," he commented with a frown.

"One of the downsides of being a doctor, I guess."

"Well, you obviously need a keeper, and I'm the perfect guy for the job."

"You think?" Her eyes were filled with warmth.

"I know." He took her hand. "Come on in, put your feet up. Can I get you a glass of wine, beer, or soda?"

"Wine sounds good, whatever's open."

She sat while he opened a bottle of Cabernet for them. After turning down the oven to warm, he slid the vegetables in and then poured them each a glass. He went into the living room and handed her one, taking a seat beside her on the sofa as he proposed a toast.

"To the future, whatever it may bring."

Her lips curved up. "I'll drink to that."

Taking a sip, he set his glass aside. He was really more of a beer guy, but he wasn't about to complain. "How did you spend your day off?"

"After I took Maddy to school, I did some shopping, then came home and went for a run. Then I did some laundry, caught up on a good thriller I've been neglecting, and took a nap. Pretty pathetic, huh?"

"Actually, that sounds really good. Next time maybe we can run together," he suggested.

She brightened. "I'd like that. I should've thought of it before."

"Then it's a date." He refused to think he couldn't handle a run.

He studied her for a moment, drinking in the sight of her. The auburn hair falling around her shoulders, those blue eyes staring back with such emotion in them. She had on a pink cotton pullover shirt and a pair of soft, faded jeans that hugged her figure without being too tight.

"You're beautiful," he said quietly. He reached out and ran a finger down her cheek.

"I haven't felt that way in a long time." She paused, leaning into his touch. "But you've changed that."

"I'm glad, because it's true. And I don't mean just on the outside. You're a gorgeous person, Robyn, inside and out. The way you love Maddy, and how you care for your patients. You're simply amazing."

A pained expression crossed her features, and he frowned. "Hey, what's that for?"

She wasn't looking at him, her voice a murmur. "*Amazing* isn't the word I'd use to describe myself. I've got a lot of sins to make up for."

Something unpleasant lodged behind his sternum. "What do you mean?"

Raising her head, she looked up at him, shadows in her stunning eyes. "Never mind. I want to forget about the past tonight. I just want to be with you."

"Will you tell me someday?"

She nodded. "One day."

"That's good enough for me."

He tried not to be stung, to think she didn't trust him with her secrets. Deep down, he knew that wasn't it. She was fighting her own demons, and it took a lot for her to let someone else in, to lance the hurt in her soul and let it out.

He would wait as long as he needed.

Robyn moved as close as she could and captured his mouth with hers. Her breasts pushed against his chest, pliant, inviting.

"Can dinner wait for a while?" she asked in a breathy voice.

"As long as we need it to, honey."

Taking her hand, he led her to his bedroom, not giving a damn about anything but making love to his lady.

8

"I love your bedroom," Robyn said, looking around as he led her inside.

"I love the sight of you in it."

His king-sized cherrywood bed dominated the room, with its four posters and dark comforter. She looked perfect in his room, and now he regretted ever bringing anyone else here. Not that he would mention that to her. Ever.

Slowly he undressed her, revealing her sun-kissed skin inch by inch. He couldn't resist spreading kisses over her, starting with her face and neck, then working his way downward until he was on his knees at her feet, where he'd stay forever if she'd let him.

He urged her thighs apart and parted her sex with his fingers, rubbing. She didn't protest—far from it. Widening her stance, she moaned when he tasted, running his tongue along her slit to the nub near the front. Back and forth, getting her nice and wet, making her boneless with want.

Gently he sucked her clit, working the magic button until she pulled at his hair.

"Chris," she breathed. "I don't want to come yet."

Chuckling, he wiped his mouth and stood, pulling her over to the bed. He flung the covers back and they crawled onto the mattress together. She pushed him onto his back and began to explore his body much the same as he had hers. Kisses were peppered over his chest and abs. Then lower as she lavished attention on his cock.

God, she could suck like nobody, ever. Her pink tongue darted around the head, lapping at the precum weeping from it. He spread his legs, giving her access to do what she wanted. She cradled his balls in one hand, manipulating them, driving him crazy. Then she took him deep in her throat, something he knew wasn't easy for her, and rendered him almost incoherent with lust.

"Baby—" He gasped. "Need to fuck you."

"Please!"

Rolling over, he grabbed a condom from the bedside drawer and ripped open the package. With swift movements he sheathed his cock. Then he pressed her onto her back and moved between her legs, bringing the head to her entrance.

Pushing inside her was simply heaven. She was tight and slick, so hot. Her sex gripped him like a vise, stroking him from base to tip. He slid in to his balls, then out again. In and out, savoring the rhythm their bodies made, how attuned to each other they were.

The delicious friction drove him higher. As he increased the tempo, she wrapped her legs around his waist and met him thrust for thrust, nails digging into his back. That was such a turn-on; knowing that she could lose herself, come unraveled in his arms, he couldn't hold back anymore.

His release exploded and he drove home with a hoarse cry, and remained there, shuddering as he emptied his balls. His heat filled her and she cried out as well, bucking against him, riding out her orgasm.

Spent, he cradled her for a few minutes, enjoying the feeling of being connected. But too soon, his erection softened and he had to pull out. So he rolled onto his back and brought her with him, settling her head on his chest.

"Hungry?"

"Famished. That was quite a workout."

He felt her smile against his chest. "Maybe we'll have time for a repeat after we eat and before you have to get home? When do you have to let Rachel go?"

"I've got a couple of hours," she said.

"All right." He kissed the top of her head. "I'll take whatever I can get."

"I know this isn't what you signed up for—"

"Stop." He rubbed her back, kept his tone soothing. "I want all of you, Robyn. Even the part of you who's a mom. Haven't I made that clear?"

"Yeah. I guess you have." She burrowed closer.

"Then don't worry about anything right now. Let's enjoy every moment and let things happen."

"You make it hard to say no."

"So don't."

"That simple." Hesitation colored her voice.

"It can be."

With that, she became quiet and relaxed in his arms.

He wasn't ready to put a name on his growing feelings, but he knew he didn't want to let her out of his home, or his bed.

Not now. Not ever.

The next few days passed by in a blur of happiness. There was only one blight on Chris's world: his illness was back with a vengeance, worse than ever before.

He started to think Robyn might have a point about black mold or some other contamination, so he placed calls to experts. Several of them. He had men trooping in and out, going over every square inch of the house and property with a fine-toothed comb. If there was anything in or around the house causing him to get sick, they assured him they'd find it.

But they found *nothing*. The problem was baffling, and disheartening.

He didn't know what to do, other than move back in with his cousin or go to a hotel room, but he was reluctant to do either. No way did he want to impose on Shane and his family more than he had, and his relationship with Robyn was too new to ask to stay there. Nor did he want to stay in a hotel. Something had to give, though. He only knew that whenever he was away from home for a couple of days or more, he started to improve.

What the hell is in my house? This is not my imagination!

A week later, he woke up barely able to get out of bed. In the bathroom, a wave of horrible sickness overwhelmed him and he fell to his knees, vomiting into the toilet.

And was shocked to see crimson. *Blood.* He blinked hazily, a tendril of fear snaking down his spine. He thought at first he must be imagining things, but no. There was no mistaking that he was in real trouble.

After his stomach was emptied and raw, he flushed and pulled himself up with difficulty. His legs were weak, shaky. In fact, his whole body was trembling like he was a geriatric Chihuahua on speed. He broke into a cold sweat, and his heart was racing.

Quickly, he brushed his teeth and considered whether to attempt a shower and get changed for work. Immediately he discarded that idea. There was just no way he was going to make it to the station. In fact, he should probably call Tonio.

Wearing only his sleep pants, he started from the bathroom and was scared to realize he had to brace a hand on the wall in order to walk. God, where was his phone? Sofa table? Kitchen counter? He had to find it. Now.

It took him at least five minutes to make it from the bedroom down the hall to the living room. Wobbling to the sofa, he held on to the back of it and scanned for his cell phone. Spotting it on the coffee table with his keys, he started around the arm of the sofa—and fell.

His legs gave way like someone had cut the muscle and tendon holding him together. His knees hit the carpet, the blow somewhat cushioned, and his vision swam. He crawled to his cell phone and fumbled to unlock the screen. Finally he made out Tonio's name on the contact list and punched the button to dial him.

"Come on," he said, anxious. "Answer."

The man picked up, thank God. "Hello?"

"Tonio? Hey, it's Chris." He stopped, panting. Why couldn't he get enough air? "I—I can't make it in today. I can't . . . I'm not . . ." The room dipped and the phone slipped from nerveless fingers, then bounced under the couch.

"Help me." Distantly, he could hear Tonio's voice raised in concern.

He got on his stomach and fished for the phone, but it was out of his reach. He'd seriously fucked up. Should've called 9-1-1 instead of using his cell to call his partner. That would've been quicker to get help on the way, more direct. Using all his strength, he pushed up and stumbled for the kitchen, the closest landline phone. The other was in his bedroom—he'd never make it back there.

God, he couldn't breathe. His heart was threatening to explode, and agony was ripping his chest in two.

Lurching for the kitchen counter, he grabbed for the phone, felt his fingers wrap around the cool metal. But he fell again, taking the base, cord, and all with him, felt the line jerk from the wall. The phone clattered across the tile a few feet away, and he stared at it.

Horror swept him in an icy embrace. His body was done. He couldn't move. Couldn't get air. The pain was so intense, spots began to swim in front of his face. Black spots growing larger and larger. Like spilled ink, obliterating everything.

He felt himself go. Knew he was falling into a black

abyss that he might never awaken from. And there wasn't a damned thing he could do about it.

Then there was nothing.

"Chris! Chris! Breathe, goddamn you!"

He wanted to obey the voice. Couldn't.

"Oh God. Hello? Somebody help me!"

Nobody could help. Too late.

The voice rattled off something. Numbers, a street. He couldn't make sense of it. Or of the pounding on his chest when more voices joined the first one. They were trying to crack his chest open, and he didn't understand why.

Hurts. So much. He tried to tell them. But they weren't listening. They kept right on trying to rip him apart, while demanding he live. He didn't know how.

When the blackness engulfed him again, he sank into the ether. He had no choice.

"Dr. Lassiter, we've got a victim coming in hot. ETA five minutes," Lee told her. "Another heart attack, according to the paramedics."

Dammit, this could not be happening again! "Okay, thank you. Let's get prepped."

"Already on it."

Nerves strung taut, she paced the floor, double-checked that everything was ready. But she couldn't have been prepared to see the paramedics rushing through the doors with a very familiar man on the gurney.

Chris's hair was plastered to his head with sweat and his face was pale, eyes closed. Her lover was in real trouble.

"In the first room," she called sharply, pointing. Then she whirled and found Shea. "I need another doctor here, now!"

Shea's eyes were wide. "There's nobody else available! You don't have a choice."

Spinning on her heel, she rushed into the room, where one medic was hanging Chris's IV on the pole and the other reported on his vitals: his blood pressure was not low and sluggish, as expected, but extremely high.

"He's also vomiting blood, and in respiratory distress," the medic said, stepping back to let the nurses take over.

Her mind went cold, clinical. "Vomiting blood?"

"Yes, Doctor."

Sure enough, she noted the traces of pink froth around his mouth.

None of the other victims had arrived with this symptom—and it made all the difference. Nausea, sweats, general fatigue, racing heart, trouble breathing—and vomiting blood. In that instant, one terrifying word jumped to the forefront of possible diagnosis: *poison*.

"Get him intubated," she snapped to Cori, one of the nurses. To Shea, she ordered, "Draw blood. We need a full tox screen from the lab, right fucking now. Include tests for the big three poisons—cyanide, arsenic, and strychnine."

"Poison?" Shea gasped.

"Just do it."

How could she have missed this before? But clever killers knew that poisons were most often completely missed by doctors and medical examiners, misdiagnosed from the start because the poisons, especially cyanide, were virtually undetectable and mimicked any number of diseases. Especially heart disease resulting in heart failure. Killers were also well aware that tests for these poisons were not standard, and the poison wouldn't simply show up in routine blood work. Doctors had to know *exactly* what they were looking for in order to find it.

And she would goddamned well find it. Chris was *not* going to die. She wouldn't allow that to happen.

Even if her team thought she was crazy, they obeyed her instructions without question. Faced with a ticking clock and little recourse, she couldn't wait on the test results. Working quickly and with the help of her nurses, she administered two common antidotes for the poisons she suspected.

She knew that, if it was going to work at all, the treatment should be effective within minutes. "Hold on, Chris, do you hear me? Hang in there."

His heart rate was so high, she was terrified the organ would give out. If it hadn't been for the breathing tube and oxygen, he would've asphyxiated already. His vitals were erratic, but gradually his pulse slowed, his pressure stabilizing. When his pulse finally fell within the normal range and stayed there, the room breathed a collective sigh of relief.

"My God," Shea said quietly. "How did you know it was poison?"

"The froth around his mouth and the vomiting blood. Combined with the other symptoms he's been complaining about, it finally clicked." She put a hand over her mouth as she stared at her unconscious lover. "With a man who seemed so perfectly healthy otherwise, it should have occurred to me sooner to look toward a more sinister cause."

"That's not true," Shea said. "Statistically, poisonings are extremely rare, especially those done with intent to harm. And the symptoms are too common to raise suspicion."

"I know. I just have to get my head wrapped around this. I need to see him settled into a room and talk to his partner. Then I've got a few phone calls to make."

Reaching down, she touched Chris's hair. His eyes were still closed, and he'd be out for a while. But she'd take it over the alternative any day. Glancing at Shea, she saw concern and understanding on the other woman's face. Shea knew without saying anything that the detective had come to mean so much more to Robyn than just a friend.

She had spent the last few years so afraid to get close to another man, to fall in love with someone who might leave her, as Greg had. Now she'd gone and done it anyway, and had almost lost Chris.

She didn't have a damned clue what to do about these rampant feelings.

With dread, she went in search of Tonio and found him practically wearing a hole in the tile, along with Shane and a tall, ruggedly handsome man she didn't recognize. This man appeared to be a few years older than the detectives, perhaps in his mid-forties. As she approached, they turned to her, naked fear etched on their faces.

"Tonio called and told me what happened," Shane rasped. "Got here as fast as I could. How is he?"

"Chris is stable now," she told them. Shane actually sagged and braced himself by holding on to the back of a plastic chair.

"What the hell happened?" Tonio asked. His raven hair was poking in every direction like he'd been running his hands through it. "I've never seen anything like that in my life. He called me and was telling me he couldn't come in, and then I heard the phone drop and he called out, 'Help me.' I got there as fast as I could, and he was lying on the kitchen floor with blood trickling from his mouth. He couldn't breathe, and I thought he was going to die."

This wasn't going to be easy. They were going to *freak* when she told them.

"Chris was the victim of poisoning." Their identical expressions of shock stared back at her. "I ordered a full tox screen on his blood, specifically for arsenic, strychnine, and cyanide. We won't know which one is the culprit until the tests come back."

The tall man regained his wits first and held out his hand. "I'm sorry—I'm Captain Austin Rainey, and Chris is one of my men, along with these guys." He nodded to the other two detectives. She shook his hand as he asked, "How the hell did this happen?"

"That's going to be a question for the police to answer," she said, indicating all of them. "All I can say is that it's highly unlikely Chris arrived at a critical state of poisoning by accident. Especially since he hasn't been well for some time and suddenly the symptoms take a dramatic turn for the worse. You could find a natural culprit in his home, a liquid or some type of chemical spill, or something slowly burning to create lethal gas, but I would be surprised if that was the case."

"Poison," Shane repeated, rubbing his eyes. "God, that's insane. Evil."

"I agree. And speaking of evil, there's more." She paused. "I'm more sure now than ever that the string of deaths we've had here at the hospital are *not* natural. Chris was waiting on Laura Eden to get back to him with a list of similar deaths, but she's been out sick and a list like that can take a while to put together."

"I'm aware of Chris's request to the ME for that list," the captain put in, eyes hard and angry. "I gave the okay for him to poke into the deaths, unofficially. I've just made it official. We're going to find out what the fuck is going on and who's behind it—that I can promise."

Shane gave a humorless laugh. "This just keeps getting better."

"I'll see where Eden is at," Tonio said grimly.

Robyn checked her watch. "That's all I can tell you for now. I have to get back to my patients, particularly Chris."

"When can I see my cousin?" Shane pressed anxiously.

"Soon," she said gently. "Let us get him settled and his visitors can take turns. Keep it brief, though, so you don't wear him out."

Shane agreed and Robyn bid them good-bye for the time being.

She had a very special patient to tend to.

Consciousness returned slowly.

The first thing Chris became aware of was the deep

ache. In his gut, his limbs. Everywhere in his muscles and bones as he tried to shift a little, feeling like he'd been beaten by a baseball bat.

The next thing that filtered through to his brain was his surroundings. He was lying on something soft. A mattress. He was covered by blankets, but was still cold. A shiver shook him and he tried to open his eyes. Too bright.

So he listened to distant sounds, beeps from equipment, voices, a squeaky cart rolling along a hallway. A hospital? He tried to remember what had happened before *here*.

His throat was raw, he discovered upon swallowing. Same with his stomach, which cramped as though the lining had been scraped with razor blades. His right hand felt heavy and, flexing his fingers, he found that the skin pulled. Cracking one eye open, he focused enough to see the IV taped to the back of his hand.

Footsteps approached, and the door opened with a quiet whoosh. Braving the light again, he blinked and found himself peering up at Robyn—who looked like she'd been crying. Her expression was also relieved.

"You're awake," she said, squeezing his shoulder. "You don't know how happy that makes me."

"Makes one of us," he croaked. "Feel like shit."

Her smile was watery. "I imagine you do, after what you've been through. Do you remember what happened?"

Frowning, he tried to recall. Bits and pieces were coming back, but the picture wasn't making sense. "I was home. I was going to shower, but I didn't."

"You were feeling sick. Do you remember?"

"Yes," he said slowly. It was becoming clearer. "I—I went for my cell phone. I was going to call someone."

"You called Tonio. He said you were telling him you couldn't come in to work, but then he heard you drop the phone and say, 'Help me.' You didn't come back on the line, so he drove right over."

"He found me?"

"Yes. He had to break down your front door, and he found you on the kitchen floor." Pausing, she smoothed back his hair. "You were in bad shape. If he hadn't found you when he did and called the paramedics, you wouldn't have made it. You'd been vomiting blood and your blood pressure was so high, you were in danger of heart failure or stroking out."

"Jesus." His eyes widened. "What's wrong with me? Do I . . . do I have a terminal illness or something? Be straight with me."

Her face grew grim. "No, nothing like that. But what I found out isn't much easier to grasp. Chris, you're being poisoned," she said quietly.

For several moments, he stared into her face, stunned. "What?"

"You're a victim of cyanide poisoning—and a very lucky one at that."

Cyanide. What. The. Fuck?

He struggled to make sense of that and couldn't. "Isn't that the stuff used in the CIA and spy movies and shit?"

"Yes, but it's a more common substance than a lot of people know. It's present in small doses in everyday items like cigarettes, fabric, and even some foods, like almonds."

"Okay. So there's some normal little thing in my house causing all this?" It would be weird, but a much better alternative to what he feared.

"I'm sorry. That's not what I meant to imply. But for the sake of ruling out causes, have you been handling any chemicals in the past few weeks?"

"No."

"You're sure?"

"Positive."

"Have you been burning anything? Cyanide can be released as a lethal gas when certain materials are burned—in which case you probably would have died on the spot, but I have to ask."

He shook his head slightly, making it swim. "No, nothing."

"Then considering the severity of your poisoning, and the symptoms that have occurred over a period of time, getting progressively worse, I have to conclude that your poisoning was intentional."

"Christ, that's insane," he whispered. "Why would anybody do that to me? How?"

"I don't know, but you've got a lot of people in your corner working to find out, including me. Tonio, a couple of other detectives, and a team of crime scene techs from the department are hauling items out of your house as we speak, taking samples for testing. We might not learn the *who* right away, but they'll have the *how* soon enough."

His brain was engaging now, and he started to recall facts he'd learned about that particular poison. "I should have died."

"Yes," she said, pretty blue eyes filling with tears. "The hallmark of this poison is that it's vicious and instantaneous. People rarely survive it. Whoever is using it knows that, and worse, knows exactly the dosage to keep you sick without killing you right away."

"Like he was getting his kicks by torturing me."

"Exactly. To me, this means he or she may be someone with a medical or scientific background. Someone with access to a very restricted dangerous substance. You don't just drive to Walmart and buy cyanide."

"So it's highly controlled and difficult to purchase."

She nodded. "And very traceable once you have a suspect. It's a fact that the perpetrator is almost always caught because of the paper trail of the purchase."

"You know more about this than me and I'm the cop." He smiled a bit, hoping to erase those sad shadows from her eyes.

"We learned about these sorts of things in medical school. Medicine and crime do overlap from time to time, unfortunately."

Another thought hit him hard. "I'm not the only one this has happened to. I bet those suspicious deaths *are* related to me, somehow. If you hadn't figured out I was poisoned, it would have looked like a heart attack."

"Yes. We'll have the first of the toxicology results back soon. We have yours because we rushed it to our own lab, and now we're waiting on results for the lawyer who died to come back from Eden. He's the most recent one before you."

"Let me know as soon as you have them."

"Of course."

"When can I go home?"

"A couple of days," she said firmly, ignoring his groan. "We're running more tests to make sure your internal organs haven't suffered permanent damage, particularly your heart, liver, and kidneys."

Fear gripped his gut. "Is that common?"

"No, surprisingly. Cyanide is metabolized quickly by the body in lower doses, and filtered from the person's system. Thus its use in common items like cigarettes. It's a very strange poison. Lethal in large doses, yet almost impotent in smaller ones, leaving little to no damage. You were straddling the line, so to speak."

He relaxed into the pillows, exhaustion taking over. "I guess I can't complain too much. Could've been worse."

"Exponentially." Leaning over, she pressed her lips to his. "Get some rest."

"Okay."

She left and he drifted off again. His dreams were troubled, frightening.

Because the immediate danger was past, but it was far from over.

The next morning, Robyn walked in to check on her sexy patient. Going home and leaving him at the hospital all night was the hardest thing she'd ever done. But her mind was eased by the cop posted outside his door.

Seemed that the higher-ups at the Sugarland PD took the attempted murder of one of their own very seriously. They weren't leaving anything to chance—even the food brought to Chris's room was closely monitored from preparation to serving.

Chris was lying on his back sleeping. She took a moment to study him, and emotion clogged her throat and made it burn. Her mind was a whirl of confusion now that the immediate danger to him was past. Their evening together at his house, his declaration of wanting all of her, even her daughter, as his own, filled her with wonder.

It also made her very afraid, because this thing between them was suddenly getting very real. She and Maddy had both heard promises before. Greg had promised to get well. Claimed he was getting better. Stronger.

He'd left them anyway, and that sort of pain and heartbreak didn't simply vanish. His death had left a ragged hole inside her that she'd believed would never be filled. In truth, she had been sure she never *wanted* it to be. Letting others in was dangerous. Too risky.

Then she'd met a handsome detective with brown-gold hair and big brown eyes, and he was trying to break down those defenses.

On the bed, Chris stirred, and her trepidation was put aside. His eyes opened slowly and his face brightened as he blinked at her sleepily. "There you are."

"Here I am," she said softly, brushing a lock of hair from his eyes. "How are you feeling?"

"Better. What's the verdict on me?"

"Your organs are clear and functional," she said. "No permanent damage."

"Thank God. Check me out, Doc, I'm ready to split." He sat up eagerly, then winced.

"Not so fast, hon. You're still recovering and you don't want to end up back in here because you were pushing too soon. Right?"

"I know," he said, pouting a little. "I won't push, I promise. I just want out of here."

"You will be. One condition, though: you're not going home. You'll stay with me and Maddy until the suspect is caught." Whether she was afraid of letting him into her life permanently or not, there was no way she was sending him back into a dangerous environment.

He frowned. "That could be indefinitely. What if he's never apprehended? Or worse, what if he comes after me at your house? No way will I put you and Maddy in danger."

She thought about that. "He could come after us anyway. I think I'd feel a lot safer with a cop in the house."

He paled. "I hadn't thought of it that way. I'm not letting him get near you or Maddy. The sooner he's caught and put in prison, the better."

"I have faith that he will be. In the meantime, you'll be away from the source of your illness, getting pampered by two doting girls. How can you top that?"

"Mmm, you're right. I can't. Will you make me chicken soup?"

"Whatever you want."

"Okay, it's a deal."

Just then Tonio walked in wearing a broad smile. He was a stunning man, though in her eyes he had nothing on Chris. He seemed like a good friend, though he attempted to hide behind a wall of stoicism. The man gave Chris a small smile as he went to his bedside.

"Hey. I came to see you yesterday and brought you some clothes, but you were zonked. Had no clue I was here."

"Sorry about that. I hear I owe you a huge thanks for saving my ass." Chris smiled. "Thanks, man."

"Don't mention it. Just don't pull that shit again. You scared the hell out of me." Tonio glanced between Chris and Robyn. "You got a place to stay when they let you go? If not, you can crash at my apartment."

"Thanks, but I just agreed to stay with Robyn until my house is cleared."

Tonio shot Robyn a speculative look. "Oh, okay. That's cool."

"How's it coming with the testing on the stuff they took from my house?"

"Slow. I'll let you know when they pinpoint the source, believe me. I want that bastard caught and punished for what he did to you."

Except for in the emergency room, this was the most emotion Robyn had seen him express in the few times they'd met.

"Me, too. It takes a pretty sick mind to do something like this. There's no telling how many people he's killed and how many are suffering."

"True. And by the way, speaking of the sicko, the clothes I brought for you are from the mall. Couldn't risk bringing your own clothes until the techs are done with them."

"Jeez, I owe you one."

"No, you don't. So forget it." Tonio clamped a hand on Chris's shoulder. "Listen, I'm going to go for now. I'll be back later, or I'll come by the doc's house if you've been discharged once I have some news."

"That works. Thanks again."

"Anytime."

After the other detective left, a surge of visitors from the station came to his room. Word was obviously out that Chris was better. Robyn had to make rounds but kept an eye on the flow of people. Finally she shooed the last of them out and ordered the nurses to make sure he rested.

The next day, the final round of Chris's tests came back clear, and she decided to discharge him with some restrictions. First and foremost, he had to rest for a few days, no argument. She had a feeling he'd agree to just about anything to be able to leave.

She managed to time his release with her getting off shift, and after he was dressed in the fresh clothes Tonio brought him, a nurse wheeled him out to her car.

Almost as soon as the car began moving, Chris leaned his head against the window and passed out. She felt so bad for him, but she'd help him all she could.

At home, she had to wake him to get him out of the car and inside. Even though Rachel rushed to help her—with Maddy fluttering around *thinking* she was helping—it was still quite a challenge to get him into the guest bedroom. Once they did, he went out like a light again, and so the three of them tiptoed out to let him sleep.

Maddy had a hundred questions about what was wrong with Chris and why he was there. She might be only seven, but she was a smart girl and knew something was wrong. Keeping it simple, Robyn told her Chris was sick and couldn't stay home alone. Truth enough. Maddy accepted that and threw herself into the role of caregiver with relish.

Robyn smiled in spite of herself, putting her feet up in her easy chair for a bit. Maddy really loved Chris. And the feeling appeared to be mutual. Throughout the evening, he woke up to ask where the little munchkin was, and she'd magically appear with tea or water to help him feel better. He declared it did, and Maddy was happy.

Only after Maddy was in bed did Robyn sneak down the hallway to the guest room. There, she closed and locked the door and slid underneath the sheets with him. As she did, something he'd said to her before he'd gotten sick came rushing back. *I want all of you, Robyn.* Even if she was afraid of saying those words back to him, she couldn't deny to herself that she felt the same way: she wanted all of Chris. She held him all night long, grateful beyond words that she still could.

They had to catch the murdering bastard soon. The connections had to be made soon.

And Robyn hoped like hell she would be the one to do it.

9

Chris awoke to an unfamiliar bedroom, and it took him a few minutes to get his bearings. Rolling over, he pressed his face into the pillow and postponed getting out of bed as long as possible.

At least until he recalled Robyn sliding in next to him last night, and that made him wonder where she'd gone. Maybe he'd slept so long, she'd taken Maddy to school and had gone to work already.

Curiosity propelled him to push himself upright. He sat for a moment, testing the waters just in case he got sick or dizzy. When neither of those things happened, he got out of bed and stood. So far, so good.

By the time he got to the en suite bathroom, he realized he was still tired and a bit weak. The cyanide had done a number on him for sure. Nothing he couldn't overcome, though, with another day of rest. Moving slowly, he showered and dressed in some jeans and a T-shirt.

Then he went in search of Robyn. And coffee. What he found was one of those fancy one-cup automatic machines and several types of brew to choose from. But no Robyn. A piece of paper on the kitchen table caught his attention, and he walked over to read it.

Took Maddy to school. Running a few errands, be home soon. Bringing pastries. ☺

His stomach growled and he went back to the coffeemaker. After investigating the choices, he settled on a French roast that he hoped was strong enough to revive his brain and get the juices flowing. Might take two cups.

After making his coffee, he took the steaming mug and tried to sit still at the kitchen table. But he got restless and decided to wander to the living room. There, he turned on the TV and watched a bit of *Good Morning America*. Soon his attention strayed and he found himself looking around the room, focusing on the photos Robyn had displayed.

The ones on the end tables were mostly of Maddy. On the wall were pictures of two different older couples, and he figured these must be Maddy's grandparents.

But it was the pictures on the mantel that drew him in like the proverbial moth to the flame. Unable to help himself, he rose from the sofa and padded to the fireplace, studying the studio photo of the man he assumed was Greg, who had once held Robyn's heart.

The man was handsome, he had to admit. He'd have to be, Chris thought, to snag a woman like Robyn. Not that Chris thought himself a great catch. No, it was just weird gazing at the man Robyn clearly wasn't over and trying to imagine what had happened.

Greg had dark hair and bright blue eyes. His smile for the camera was boyish. But was it Chris's imagination, or did his eyes seem a bit sad? As he moved onto the next photo, his gut did an unpleasant turn to see this one was a candid shot of Robyn on the same man's lap in a lounge chair. They were laughing into the camera, tangled together, looking very happy. The lounger was on some sort of flagstone patio, quite large and expensive-looking; behind them was a huge pool with a built-in waterfall and a gorgeous panoramic view of the desert.

We moved here from Phoenix, Arizona, after my husband, Greg, passed away.

Whatever had happened, Robyn's lifestyle had apparently been altered. If there was a house attached to that fancy patio, and it had belonged to her and her husband, it was a far cry from where she lived now. Chris didn't care whether Robyn had loads of money, but he hated that she had to suffer in any way. The loss of her husband and the home she knew must've been devastating.

Chris heard keys rattle in the door leading into the kitchen from the garage. Mug in hand, he went to greet Robyn, putting aside his questions about her deceased husband for now. That conversation had to happen someday if they were going to move forward. They couldn't pretend the man hadn't existed or hadn't had a big impact on her life. But he sensed she wasn't ready for that talk.

She looked so pretty in a pair of dark blue pants and a print blouse, hair pulled back from her face and secured with a clip at the top of her head. He couldn't help but stare. She set a white paper bag and her purse on the table, then crossed to him and pulled him in for a kiss.

"I'm glad to see you up and around. You were sound asleep when I checked on you this morning."

"I was wiped out, I guess. It's not every day a guy gets poisoned like Snow White. Wonder where the apple came from?"

"That's not even remotely funny."

"I thought it was, a little."

"Not one bit."

"Sorry. Us cops have to find humor where we can, even if it's grim. What's in the bag?"

She played along with his blatant redirect. "Two types of Danish, cream cheese and apricot."

"Damn, that sounds good! How am I supposed to pick?"

"I got two of each, so you can have both." She gave him a small smile.

"Sweet. Thanks, baby."

She paused, looking at him oddly before moving to the refrigerator. "You're welcome. Milk or juice?"

"I'm just going to have another cup of coffee. I don't drink a lot of milk or juice."

Glancing over her shoulder, she said, "One cup of coffee this morning is more than enough after what you've been through, sweetie."

He raised his brows. "You don't have to give me the 'mom' voice. I'm not Maddy."

"Did I do that? I'm sorry, but I just want you to go easy on your system for a few days. Your body had quite a traumatic shock."

He held up a hand. "I surrender. If it's that important to you, I'll have milk."

"It is."

"I still don't think it's that big a deal, though."

Turning with a glass of milk in hand, she froze. There was something dark in her eyes, almost like pain. Then she walked over and carefully set his glass in front of him.

"I care, that's all. Your health is a *big deal* to me."

Turning, she started to walk off, but he gently caught her arm and encouraged her to face him again. "Wait—please. I meant to say I appreciate you caring about my well-being, honest. I just don't want the person I'm with trying to dictate to me or change me."

"I'd never do that." She blinked away tears and shook her head.

His heart fell. "Shit. I didn't mean to hurt your feelings."

"You didn't."

"Then what is this really about, Robyn? Please, trust me a little." She was silent, and his heart dropped. "Does this have anything to do with Greg and his death?"

Her head shot up and anger blazed on her face. His spirits fell even lower as he realized he was right. It was clear she didn't want to confide in him, either.

"I'm sorry," he said softly. "Forget I asked."

"I can't talk about him."

"Right now?"

"Maybe ever."

He let go of her arm and she stepped back. Immediately he felt colder, desolate. "I want to be a part of your world, but I can't if you won't let me. It tells me you either don't trust me or don't have deep enough feelings for me."

"That's not true," she whispered. "You don't know how it was to be in my shoes back then. How hard it is to relive that time."

"Then tell me." So much for his resolve not to push. But he had a feeling that if he didn't, she'd never open up.

"I need more time. Please, Chris. It hurts too much."

Big blue eyes pleaded with him, and he relented. "Okay. But we have to talk about this eventually, or it will always be the elephant in the room."

"I know."

Tentatively she sat and they finished their breakfast, but the damage to their morning had been done. Conversation was stilted, and by the time she gathered her purse and keys for work, he was feeling ten kinds of remorse for trying to get her to open up before she was ready. Admittedly, the detective in him wanted to solve the mystery of Greg and Robyn and then put it out of his mind for good. At least the part about Greg.

After giving him a kiss, she started for the back door. "I'll see you this afternoon, all right?"

"Okay. Again, I'm sorry."

"Don't worry about it."

Which of course he did. After she was gone he felt restless and edgy. When he became almost overwhelmed with the cop's urge to snoop through her things—or better yet, use her computer or his police contacts to search for Greg Lassiter's name and cause of death—he did the only thing he could: he left the house.

A walk would do him good. Help him build up his strength again. He wasn't one to mope or sleep all day, no matter how tired he might be. Automatically, his feet carried him in the direction of his own house, and he wondered if the tech guys had finished searching his stuff. Probably so, and he cringed when he thought of his stack of porn videos in the master bedroom closet. Fantastic.

By the time he got to his house, he was winded and cursing himself for an idiot. He should have stayed on the sofa and watched TV. Then again, he'd be able to get more clothes, then fetch his car and drive it back to Robyn's.

He winced to see the wood frame around the front door smashed, as well as a big cracked hole the size of a heel—Tonio's—next to the knob. Someone had fixed it as best as they could, but the whole thing would need replacing.

Fortunately, Tonio had brought him his keys along with fresh clothes. Chris unlocked the door with a little difficulty and let himself in. The house was still. A glance around showed nothing much was out of place. Some items had been moved, and he wondered what the techs had removed.

He figured starting in the kitchen was best. His hunch was right—every single item of food and drink had been cleaned out. Every last one. Even his canned goods were gone, probably to be examined for tampering. Damn. It was sort of depressing not to even be able to have a snack in his own home.

Making a tour through the house, he noted things here and there that were missing. Anything that contained liquid or was applied to his body was absent from his bathroom, including cologne, aftershave, shaving cream—the list went on. His sense of violation grew, and anger began to break through the fog of shock he'd been feeling for the past two days.

A knock on the front door snapped him to attention, and he went to answer it.

He opened up to find Tonio and Captain Rainey standing there, and let them in. "Hey. I'm assuming this isn't a social visit?"

"I wish," Tonio said, looking solemn.

"You get the results of the testing?"

Rainey spoke up. "We did, and they showed exactly where the poison was placed."

"In my kitchen somewhere? In the milk or some food?"

"Nope. The cyanide had been added to both your shampoo and the body wash."

Chris's mouth fell open. He took a moment to let that sink in. "Shit. He knew that was the best place to ensure I'd come into contact with it every day. I might not eat the same foods, but I'd probably shower."

"Exactly," Rainey affirmed. "The team went over every square inch of the house, and that was the only contamination. You can come home if you're extra vigilant—and install a damned alarm system. I can't believe you don't have one."

"Never put much stock in those, Cap," he admitted. "I always thought, if I'm home I'll take care of any intruder myself. And if I'm not home, the police won't be here for several minutes, giving them plenty of time to get out, so what difference does it make?"

Rainey huffed. "Haven't you learned anything, Detective? Motive *and* opportunity. Criminals have the motive, and stupidity often gives them the opportunity. If the asshole had been faced with an alarm system, he wouldn't have been able to tote a dangerous poison into your house and spend God knows how long searching for the exact right spot to hide it. Because he wouldn't have had *time*."

His face flushed at his captain basically calling him stupid in front of his partner. But the man was right. "Sorry. You're right. I'll call them as soon as you leave."

"Good. I've already had a team in to clean your tub and shower, and it's clear of any poisonous residue. And the tech guys are bringing back the rest of your shit, in boxes, except for the perishable food and drinks, like the lettuce and milk. You'll get to have fun putting it all back."

"Awesome." Not.

"When do you think you'll be back at work?" Tonio asked.

"Miss me, honey?"

"Shut up." But his partner laughed. "I'm tired of doing all the fucking work."

"So you *do* admit I pull my weight. I'll mark this day on the calendar."

"Yeah, yeah. So, when?"

"Tomorrow, I think."

"Day after," Rainey put in. "Don't think I haven't noticed you can barely stand up. Your body had a shock, and you need to be in top form before I'll consider letting you come back."

"All right, day after tomorrow," he relented.

"See you then, bro." Tonio's mouth widened in one of his rare smiles.

Bro. It was said with such warmth, such genuine friendliness, that Chris was surprised. Almost dying changed things sometimes, for all parties. "See ya."

He saw them out and then cleaned up the house some. Nothing heavy, just made sure the drops of blood were off the kitchen floor and the bathroom was spotless. He didn't give a crap if experts had already scrubbed his shower—fuck that, he was doing it again. With gloves. Which he promptly tossed in the garbage afterward.

Next he considered whether he should stay at Robyn's house another night or come on home. He didn't want to impose and, after their conversation at breakfast, wasn't sure staying with her was the right thing to do. She wasn't ready to commit. And frankly, his staying there reeked a bit of desperation. He didn't want to force her into a relationship.

Decided, he remained at home. He still had a few things in her guest bedroom, but he could get those later. There was nothing he couldn't live without. Flopping on the sofa, he intended to watch TV but ended up falling asleep. He awoke sometime later to an afternoon talk show blaring, and he switched it off, sitting up.

First, he made an appointment with a reputable alarm company for the following day. That done, he glanced at the clock on the DVD player and saw it was almost three in the afternoon. He needed to get to the store and replace some food and, yeah, the shampoo and body wash. He'd never look at them the same way again.

Slipping on his shoes, he grabbed his wallet and keys,

then headed out. The tech team hadn't been by with his stuff, but he wouldn't be gone long. He drove to the store and roamed the aisles, stocking up on food, coffee, milk, and toiletries. His phone buzzed in his pocket as he was heading up the aisle to check out, and he stopped and checked the display.

"Hi there," he said to Robyn. "Are you on break?"

"No, I picked up Maddy from school and came home early. Where are you?" she asked, voice tinged with concern.

Suddenly feeling awkward about explaining, he was glad she couldn't see him. "Oh, I went home and took care of some things. Tonio and the captain stopped by, too. They had news about the tests on my household items."

"What did they find?"

"The poison was in my shampoo and body wash." He grimaced. "Guess what I'm at the store buying?"

"That's diabolical," she said breathlessly. "How did he get into your house?"

"I'm not sure. I never detected a break-in and my buddies didn't find an entry point when they were searching. The captain just raked me over the coals for not having an alarm system, so that's going in tomorrow."

"Good for him. So, are you coming back after you put your groceries away?"

"Well . . ." He faltered, not sure how to refuse, or how much to say about the real reason he shouldn't go back.

"If it's about earlier, I'm sorry." She sounded sincere, and a bit sad.

He blew out a breath. Hell of a conversation to have in the middle of the grocery store. "It's all right. I guess I just don't want to push so hard that I drive you off. The more I'm around you, the harder it is to take things slow."

"You're not driving me away," she insisted. "But I don't want to do the same to you."

"I don't know what you want, gorgeous. Maybe I should stay away until you figure it out." That hurt to say out loud. Much more than he'd thought it would.

"No! That's not what I want. At least come to dinner tonight? Maddy asked about you the second we came in and you weren't here resting. She was disappointed."

"Using the kid to guilt me into dinner? Why, Dr. Lassiter, that's conniving."

"Did it work?"

He laughed in spite of himself. "Yeah, I suppose. What time?"

"Six thirty?"

"Okay, sure. That sounds good. Anything I should bring? I can pick it up while I'm here at the store."

"Red wine? I have steaks."

"Mmm, red meat and wine. Two ways to a man's heart. I'll be there."

"Great! See you soon."

Hanging up, he shook his head. *Ford, you're a pussy. Face it now.*

A few minutes later, he had picked a good Cabernet. Finished at the store, he checked out and went home. He was tired when he arrived, especially after he put all his stuff away. Damned if he hadn't overdone it today, but he was too stubborn to cancel his plans. Besides, the girls would be disappointed.

You can't win her by running, either. Man up.

When it was almost time to go, he went to the bedroom and retrieved his gun and holster from the night table drawer. He rarely went anywhere without his weapon, and he'd felt naked the last couple of days. With it securely on his belt, he was nearly human again.

The drive over to Robyn's was short, but he wasn't up to his normal walk. He pulled into her driveway and shut off the Camaro, then went to the front door and knocked. Maddy threw it open and nearly tackled him in her enthusiasm.

"You left!" she accused. "Why didn't you stay?"

He gave her a hug. "I had some things to do, munchkin. But I'm here now to eat with you guys, if that's okay?"

"Uh-huh. Mommy's in the back, with the steaks."

"Lead the way."

She took him by the hand and pulled him along, which he thought was cute. He let her drag him through the living room and kitchen and out the patio doors. Robyn was grilling, flipping the steaks. Maddy let go of him and he went to her mother, pulling her in for a hug and brief kiss.

"Those smell wonderful," he said, gesturing to the meat. "Rib eyes are my favorite."

"Good. I should have asked how you like them cooked."

"Medium-rare to medium. But honestly, I'm not picky. If it has four legs, I'll probably eat it."

Maddy wrinkled her nose. "Eeewww." With that, she ran back inside.

Robyn chuckled, watching her go. "Kids. They're so funny about food. She doesn't care for steak much, but I talked her into it tonight."

"What, no lecture about the evils of red meat?" At her pointed stare, he held up his hands. "Just kidding."

"I can hardly lecture if it was my idea." She gave one a good poke. "I think they're ready."

"Here, let me." Taking the pronged grill fork from her, he stabbed the steaks and put them on the platter she had waiting. Then he followed her inside.

"Let's eat in the dining room," she said, pointing. "We'll have more room than on the small kitchen table."

He went into the dining room and set the platter on the oak table. Then he returned to the kitchen to see what else she needed help with. Robyn was handing Maddy a large bowl of salad.

"Can she get that?" His first instinct was to take over, but he was shot down.

"It's not heavy," Maddy said, frowning at him. "I can do it."

"Okay, sprite. Sorry."

After she disappeared, Robyn grinned at him.

"She's at the stage where kids want to do everything by themselves," she told him, opening the oven. Using a mitt, she started gathering foil-wrapped potatoes and put those in a bowl. "She wants to be independent, so I have to give her tasks she can complete. The salad bowl is a bit big, but it's plastic. If she drops it, nothing will be hurt but the salad."

"Good thinking."

"I've had some practice."

"So, I won't try to take over and do things for her. Got it."

"She *will* try to get you to do her math, though. Don't fall for it."

Once the table was set, they dove into dinner. Robyn served, dishing up a steak and potato for them, then putting salad in their bowls.

"Can you moosh my potato? It's hot."

He looked at Maddy's earnest face and melted. Never in his life had he *mooshed* a child's potato—or had taken care of a kid in that way at all, come to think of it. As he squeezed the potato open for her, adding butter, he was pleased that Maddy didn't want to do quite *everything* for herself. It was nice to take care of something for her.

"This is delicious," he said. He closed his eyes in bliss as he chewed his steak.

"I'm so glad you like it."

"Are you kidding? This is so tender and juicy, I'm in heaven."

They ate and he listened to them talk about their day, Maddy interjecting a million questions. A normal thing for a child her age, and he didn't mind. The chatter was happy, and he was, too. He tried to tell himself not to get used to it. Not to fall for them both, but it was hard.

He was afraid it was already too late.

"Is that a real gun?"

Maddy's question surprised him, though it shouldn't have. He knew she'd get around to asking eventually.

Nodding, he answered, "Yes. It's real. Do you know what to do if you ever see this gun, or any other one, lying on the table or anywhere?"

She thought about that. "Don't touch it."

"Exactly. That's very smart," he praised, and she sat up straighter. "I'm used to keeping it beside my bed at home, because I live alone. But since we're spending time together, I'm probably going to get a lockbox for it, to put the gun inside when I take it off."

"Okay. Even if it's not in the box, I won't pick it up."

"Good girl." The image of the gun in her small hands accidentally going off filled him with horror. He shook it off and silently vowed to buy a box tomorrow. First thing.

Whether he and Robyn stayed together, it suddenly sounded like a good practice. Being a bachelor, he'd never given it much thought. At home he had the big safe in the closet, but the box could be moved around.

They finished their meal and he helped Robyn clean up. Then Maddy skipped off to her room, claiming she had no homework. He wondered if that was true and chuckled. If he got his wish, he'd learn all sorts of things about kids.

If not Maddy, then his child someday. Maybe he could have both?

"What are you thinking so hard about?"

He smiled. "Nothing."

After they were done, he went with her into the living room to curl up on the sofa, listen to music, and talk. Domestic, sure. Some of his bachelor friends would give him a hard time, but he didn't care. They were just jealous if they made fun.

At eight, Robyn went to run Maddy's bath and he sat listening to the sounds of them talking, the little girl giggling. He also found his gaze straying toward the pictures of Greg, and resenting them. A ghost stood in the way of his moving forward with Robyn. As much as the man's death had hurt her—and had no doubt been terrible to live through—Chris wanted her to himself. If that made him a selfish bastard, so be it.

"Hey," a soft voice said. Robyn joined him again, touching his face. "I keep meaning to take those down and move them to Maddy's room for her to have. I just haven't done it yet. I don't really *see* those pictures most of the time."

Until then, he hadn't realized he'd been scowling at the photos. He shrugged, not trusting himself to say something that would upset her. "It's none of my business."

"I don't want you to feel that way. That's not how *I* feel."

"I don't know how to respond," he said truthfully. "I want to be a part of your life, and that means trust all around. I'm not sure you trust me."

"I want to," she said softly. "The past is sometimes hard to shake."

"Let me help you, baby."

"Give me time. Please."

Aching inside, he nodded and stood. "I can do that. Not forever, but for a while."

"Where are you going? You're not leaving?"

"I need to go. I've got the alarm company coming in the morning and things to do. Walk me out?" It was an excuse and he knew it. But he needed to lick his wounds in private. "And you'll be safe here. If you need me, call and I'll be here right away."

"Okay." She sounded disappointed.

Taking her hand, he walked outside. On the porch, he framed her face in both hands and covered her mouth with his. Slipped his tongue inside and licked, tasting. He inhaled her sweet scent and tried not to think about losing her. His erection pushed insistently against its confines but he didn't give in to his body's demand. This didn't feel like the right time for sex.

Stepping back, he kissed her forehead. "I'll talk to you tomorrow."

"All right. Good night, Chris."

"Sleep tight."

It was so hard to leave. Got harder all the damned time, every second. He pulled out of the driveway and was back at his own house in minutes, but the short distance between them seemed like the Gulf of Mexico.

As he stepped from his car, he was lost in thoughts of their evening. Which was why he almost missed the shadowy figure that ducked behind a bush on the side of the house.

Every cell in his body fired in alarm, and his hand went to his side, unclipping the strap on his gun. He set out in a jog, determined to catch the bastard and find out if it was the same fucker who'd poisoned him.

The prowler either heard or saw him coming, and bolted from his hiding place. He took off running, not caring about Chris's shout.

"Freeze! Police!"

Yeah, that never worked except in movies. The asshole put on more speed, crossing the alley and ducking between two houses. Chris palmed his gun and ran as fast as he could. But being knocked on his ass with the poisoning, and being fresh from the hospital, had taken its toll. He pursued for three blocks before the suspect finally ditched him, and he came to a stop. Leaning over, he braced his hands on his knees and wheezed as though he was about to have that heart attack he'd narrowly avoided before.

As he straightened, a wave of dizziness almost overcame him. He took two steps in the direction of home and knew his body was done. He'd finally pushed too far for one day.

With a shaking hand, he pulled his cell phone from his pocket and considered who to call for a ride. Robyn was out—he didn't want her to wake Maddy. He tried Tonio, but the call went to voice mail. He didn't leave a message. Shane and Daisy's place wasn't really close by, and he hated to drag them out of the house to carry him three blocks. He could call the station and have dispatch send the nearest squad car. But the thought of the guys knowing he was in such bad shape he couldn't walk home?

No. Not going to happen.

There was nobody to call. So he somehow put one

foot in front of the other and, a half hour or so later, made it home. After letting himself in, he trudged to the bedroom, undressed, and sprawled facedown on the bed.

He was so exhausted tonight, an entire marching band could troop though his house, let alone a serial killer, and he'd never know it.

With that disturbing thought, he promptly passed out.

10

"How's it going, Chris?"

"Man, that was a raw deal, what happened."

"Back already? Shit, I'd take the whole week off."

The greetings and back slaps hadn't stopped all day, and Chris was ready for the news to become a thing of the past. He was attempting to hide behind some files on his desk when his cell phone buzzed. Checking the display, he picked up quickly. This was one call he absolutely wanted to take.

"Detective Ford."

"Detective, this is Laura Eden," she said in her pleasant, smoky voice. "I'm so sorry it's taken me a few days to get back to you regarding that list of suspicious deaths that have come in to the hospital."

"I understand. I heard you were sick."

"I was stricken with the flu bug, and it wiped the floor with me. I'm back now and much better, and I've finally compiled the list. It's as comprehensive as I can make it, since not all bodies come through the medical examiner's office."

"Whatever you've got, I'll be glad to take it."

"I had some help putting it together, and it includes all the deaths we could find that were not held for autopsy—which is most of them. There's some interesting stuff on there, and I'd like to come by. Will you and the captain be around?"

"We'll be here."

Once they'd hung up, he called Rainey. The captain growled, "Yeah?"

"Someone woke up grumpy."

"What do you fuckin' want, Chris? I'm up to my ass in alligators."

"Eden is on her way with the list of suspicious deaths from the hospital. Says she has some things we'll want to see."

"Good. Call me when she gets here."

"Will do."

Immersing himself in a different case, he heard her arrival before he saw it. Eden was a stunning woman whose beauty didn't hint at the brains underneath. She was brilliant and, in a professional world dominated by men, frequently underestimated. She made no apologies and took shit off nobody.

Her arrival caused the usual whistles and immature remarks as she passed through the main room, but she ignored them all. When she spotted Chris, he smiled and waved her in, then shut the door behind them.

"Dr. Eden, how are you?"

"Good, thanks. And you? I heard about your poisoning," she said, expression serious.

"Well, I came too freaking close to having my name added to your list. But I'm good."

"I'm glad to hear it, and to see you back at work."

"I appreciate that."

There was a knock on the door, and it opened. Rainey and Tonio stepped inside and shut it again. Chris wasn't sure but he thought he saw the captain give Eden a longing look before schooling his face into a polite mask. Rumor had it that Rainey's wife was a bitch on heels, and he had a thing for the ME. Poor bastard.

"Here are your copies of the list, gentlemen. Detective Ford, you'll note that your name is at the bottom, listed as a survivor. Your poisoning was cyanide, correct?"

"Yes." He knew her lab hadn't done the tox screen, but she must have a reason to ask. He was right.

"The three most recent victims I've been able to test have had conclusive results. They died of heart failure as a result of cyanide poisoning as well."

"Goddamn," Rainey moaned. "We have a serial killer."

"That's your call, but it would appear so, Captain."

Shit. Shit. "This is bad," Chris said. "I think he came back night before last to creep around or finish me off maybe. He was hanging around my house wearing a hoodie. I chased him, but he got away."

"That would've been nice to know before now," Tonio snapped.

Chris frowned at him. "There's nothing you could've done about it. He got away and I can't identify him. But my alarm system got installed yesterday, so I'm ready if he comes back."

"My part is done, guys." Eden stood. "I'm still trying to get permission to test the other victims, but it takes time to coordinate exhumations. Of course some families simply won't agree, no matter what we tell them."

"Thanks for coming by, Dr. Eden," Chris said.

As she was leaving, Jenk stuck his head in the door and held up a manila envelope. "Got the test results back on that vial found behind Edward Burke's house. Haven't opened it yet."

"I'll do the honors," Chris said, standing to take the envelope from him. Ripping open the top, he extracted the report and whistled. "Well, this just gets more interesting. I'll give you three guesses."

Tonio stared at him for a few seconds. "Poison?"

"Yep." Chris slapped the envelope and paper on the table. "Cyanide."

Rainey blew out a breath. "The same deadly poison at the scene of one of the burglaries. What the hell is going on?"

"Let's take a look at what Laura brought and see if anything starts to make sense," Chris suggested.

The three of them studied their lists. One name near the top caught his eye. "Sarah Fell. Why does that name sound familiar?"

"I don't know," Tonio said, frowning. "It does, though."

"Fell. The only person I can think of is George Fell, who we talked to— Wait. Didn't he say his wife, who passed away, was named Sarah?" Chris struggled to recall.

"Here's her address." Tonio pointed. "Let's check it against the burglary files."

Chris pulled the file from his desk and retrieved their list of burglary victims—and hit pay dirt. "Here's the address, listed under George Fell. His wife died after the burglary," he said, excitement growing. "Do we have more of these?"

"Pauline Nicholson. We talked to her after we spoke with Fell. There's a Leo Nicholson on Eden's list of deceased. Heart attack, like all the others."

They all fell silent for a moment as the implication sank in.

"Jesus," Chris said at last. "The bastard is breaking in and slipping the poison into their homes, just like he did to mine. *That's* why nothing was ever stolen from their residences. He wasn't some voyeur—he was targeting them for death all along."

"God. But why?" Tonio sighed. "What's he getting out of it?"

Rainey interjected. "What do any of them get out of it? Smug satisfaction. A sexual thrill. Some are convinced they're doing good by eradicating people who need killing."

Chris sat back. "We have to finish cross-referencing these lists and determine which deaths are connected to the burglaries."

"That could take a while," Tonio said.

"So we'd better get started."

In the small bedroom, he paced. Filled with rage at the asshole who'd fucked up his beautiful plans.

"Who survives that?" he screamed. "Why didn't he *die*? It was supposed to be perfect!"

His mother, of course, didn't answer. Just sat looking at him, her silence damning, her eyes accusing.

"Shut up. You don't care anyway." A sob escaped his chest. "You never did, you bitch."

Neither did the others, but they'd pay. It was only fair and just, after what he'd been through. It was only right.

He'd see the last one of them burn in hell . . . And then he'd gladly follow.

A trying day at the hospital might have been made a whole lot better with a visit from Chris. She hadn't heard from him in the three days he'd been back at work, and she was afraid she'd royally screwed things up between them.

"Smile, Doc. Things aren't as bad as that frown on your face."

Robyn jerked out of her musings and turned her head to see Shea standing there wearing a sympathetic expression. "I think I messed up, and I don't know how to fix it."

"Why would you think that?"

"Chris hasn't called me or come by the house in three days," she lamented. "I told him I needed time to tell him the story of Greg, and he said it was okay. But I could tell I hurt him. What if he's given up?"

Shea set a chart on the nurse's desk and regarded her thoughtfully. "Sweetie, the man is one hundred percent over the moon about you. And Maddy. I've witnessed him around you, remember? Chris is not going to give up the best thing that's happened to him in a long time, especially not over one simple disagreement. If you can even call it that."

"You think so?"

"Everybody has baggage. Even me. For a long time, I didn't want to tell Tommy about my past, but it wasn't because I didn't trust him. It was just so *painful* I didn't want to relive it. Tommy understood, and Chris does, too. I'm sure of it."

"But . . . I haven't heard from him at all. Not a word."

"Shane said some case Chris and Tonio are working on is heating up. As in, major break. I'm going to venture a guess that's why he's been quiet."

"You're probably right again."

"In fact, I'm pretty sure I *know* he wants to see you."

"How?"

"Because the man himself just came through the doors and is headed straight for you." Shea smirked and glanced behind her.

She turned and, sure enough, Chris was bearing down on them, his eyes only for Robyn. His walk was graceful, shoulders back, golden brown hair slightly mussed. He was wearing sunglasses, which he removed without breaking stride, tucking them into his front shirt pocket. His gun sat on his lean hips as if he was born with it there.

Robyn had to concentrate not to lick her lips. Nurses parted before him like the Red Sea, and most took a good look at his ass when he walked by. He didn't so much as glance at any of them. She smiled. Broadly.

"Hey, beautiful," he said, loud enough for anyone in the vicinity to hear. That was fine by her.

Reaching Robyn, he wrapped her into his arms and held her for a moment. She wished they could stay like this or, better yet, were at home, where she could get him out of those clothes and have her way with him. He stepped back and returned her smile.

"I've missed you."

"Me, too," she admitted quietly, mindful of their audience.

"Can we go somewhere and talk?"

"The garden?"

"That's perfect."

She ignored the grin on Shea's face as they walked off. Outside, the day was gearing up to be a hot one. But at the moment it was merely warm and pleasant. Fall was coming, and not soon enough for Robyn.

Taking his hand, she led them over to a bench. She liked it that he didn't let go of her hand after they sat down. "What would you like to talk about?"

"I have something to give you." He retrieved a white envelope from his front shirt pocket, behind his sunglasses. "This is important information from the case we're working on."

"That's all you wanted to talk to me about?" She couldn't keep the disappointment from her voice.

"No! Of course not, baby," he said softly. "I've missed you so damned much, I'm not sleeping well. I've meant to call, but Tonio and I caught a break on our case and we've been burning the midnight oil ever since."

She studied him more closely and noted the signs she'd missed at first: dark smudges under his eyes, lines bracketing his mouth. He appeared a bit pale, too. He really hadn't been sleeping.

"You need to take better care of yourself," she admonished.

"I need my personal doc to make sure I do."

"I think I can handle that."

"Did you honestly think I didn't want to see you again? Whatever I said or did to make you believe that, I'm sorry.

"It's not your fault. I should have just called to see what was up instead of assuming you didn't want to see me. That was stupid and I won't make the same mistake again."

"Hey, it's okay. The phone works both ways. How about we agree not to go so long without communicating in the future?"

"That works for me." She gestured to the envelope. "So, what's the break?"

"In short? We have a serial killer."

"Holy shit," she blurted, eyes widening. "How did you find this out? Catch me up."

"To make it simple, the rash of burglaries the city has had, most of them were step one in the killer's plan to set up his victims. He wasn't stealing anything, which was what had us confounded, because we didn't know we had a killer on our hands. What he was actually doing was planting cyanide in their homes . . . just like he did mine. A vial of the poison was found outside one of the houses. The killer probably dropped it in his haste to get away."

Her mouth fell open and she stared at him, letting that sink in. "You were supposed to be the latest victim."

"Exactly. But I survived. Which is why I suppose he was creeping around my house the night you cooked steaks. I chased him, but he got away."

"My God. I can't believe this. So— Wait." She paused, brain scrambling to catch up. "Poison. These cases the medical examiner has been looking into, they're poisonings that look like heart attacks? And they're related to the burglaries?"

"Exactly—they're one and the same case. Break and enter becomes murder."

She shook her head. "Wow. I can't imagine what a sick mind it takes to come up with something so evil. He made those people suffer horribly before they died."

"I know." He made a face. "I was on the receiving end, and I've never been in so much physical pain, ever."

She didn't want to think about the day she almost lost him. Instead, she asked, "So what have you brought me?"

He handed over the envelope. "That's a list of each burglarized household in which at least one family member subsequently died. We've been working on it nonstop, and it's as complete as we can make it right now. Here's the thing. All the poisoning deaths we've confirmed so far, except one, occurred *here* and not at any other hospital in the county."

"So, they're connected because . . . ?"

"The victims so far have all lived within a few miles of each other and this hospital. We haven't come up with anything connecting them except for that. We're still digging, but I thought, what if the hospital itself is the common denominator? What I'd like to do is run the victims' names through the hospital's computer. See if anything turns up that might shed light on why the victims are all from around here. This is just a copy for you, as a consultant who's helping us with the case."

"I'm not sure I can personally authorize you to do that without a warrant or something," she said hesitantly. "You'll need permission to officially look at patient records."

His excitement waned as frustration visibly ate at him. "And in the meantime, someone's getting away with murder."

She regarded him thoughtfully. "Tell you what. I'll do some poking around when I get a chance, off the record. You can still look when you get the green light from the hospital administration, but if I *happen* to run across anything interesting—totally by *accident*, of course—I'll let you know."

At her mischievous grin, his expression relaxed. "Any help you can provide is welcome. Just *please* don't get in trouble on my account."

"I won't. Now, what am I looking for exactly?" She turned the envelope over in her hands and decided to open it later.

"That's just it. I don't know. A common thread between them, or anything that doesn't seem right. Any reason why Sterling is one of the connections between the victims. Our saying is: we'll know what we're looking for when we find it. At the moment, I'm going with the burglary angle being the starting point. But I feel like I'm missing a tie."

"Okay. I'll help however I can, you know that."

"Thanks, baby." He paused, running a finger down her face. "Tonight, I need a break from this case. I need to see you so bad I ache. And I don't mean just to get into your panties."

Laughing softly, she looked around to be sure none of her colleagues were around. It was safe. "I wouldn't necessarily complain, though."

"Goody." He grinned. "Seriously, I miss you. Can we have some alone time? I thought I'd take you down to the river again. I can take you to dinner first, or we can have an adult picnic this time. Take a stroll and watch the stars come out."

"That sounds lovely. I'll call Rachel and see if she can stay with Maddy."

"If she can't, Shane and Daisy might be able to." Worry creased his brow. "You know I adore Maddy—"

"Say no more," she assured him. "You're great with her, but we need grown-up time, too. I'm looking forward to it."

Relief smoothed out his face. "Me, too."

Reluctantly, she stood and tucked the envelope into her coat. "I have to get back to work. Pick me up at six thirty?"

"It's a date."

She found herself wrapped in his strong embrace again, and for a few seconds she allowed herself the luxury of being held against his hard body. She loved resting her head on his chest, feeling close to a sexy, confident, self-assured man. As much as she'd loved Greg, he hadn't been strong, or confident, or dependable. She now knew what she'd been missing all along.

Greg was her past, this man her future.

It was time to tell Chris what he wanted to know. Tonight.

Robyn knew why she was nervous as she waited for Chris to pick her up.

Tonight meant something different. Something more than simply a date with the man she was falling for. This evening would be a turning point for them as a couple, if her hunch was correct.

His car rumbled up the driveway and her heart lurched with excitement. Opening the curtains a bit, she spied shamelessly as he got out of the car and started up the walk. He looked cute in a pair of camouflage cargo shorts and black tank top, and sandals on his feet. His hair was artfully messy, and she wanted to run the strands through her fingers.

The man looked good enough to lick. All over.

The doorbell rang and she let him in, stepping back as he wrapped her in that wonderful embrace. "Where's Maddy?" he whispered in her ear.

"Out with Rachel, being treated to a movie." She shivered in delight at being pressed against him. "Wanna fool around, Detective?"

"Oh, I do. But later." He chuckled at her pout. "I have plans for you first."

That didn't stop him from moving in to take her mouth, though. He was the best freaking kisser she'd ever known. His mouth was heaven, his tongue was sin itself, and they balanced each other perfectly.

"Ready to go?"

"Do we have to?" She gave a little pout.

"You'll like what I have in mind. Trust me."

"I do trust you." Smiling, she started for her purse on the coffee table.

"Nah, you don't need a purse. Just yourself, and maybe sunglasses."

"Oh. Okay."

Regarding him curiously, she retrieved her sunglasses and keys from her purse and followed him out, locking the door behind them. At his car, he opened the door for her and helped her in, then shut it, walking around to his side.

As he did, she turned and caught a glimpse of the backseat, filled with bags. Getting in, he saw her looking and grinned.

"Yes, all of that stuff is for us."

"What's in those?"

"Our food for the picnic," he said proudly. "I made it myself."

"Oh, wow! That's so sweet," she said, melting. "How did you manage all of this when you had to work?"

"I took off at noon. Been working around the clock pretty much, so I got Rainey's permission to leave and went to the store. Then I took a nap, got up and cooked, packed it all up, and here we are."

"You still worked more than you rested, doing all of that. But I can't wait to see what you made."

"Well, I'm not much of a cook, but I got a recipe from Daisy that's super easy. I think you'll like it."

"I know I will."

A few minutes later he was driving down Cheatham Dam Road, which led to the river, dam, and the public state park. The view was scenic as always, and she loved coming down here. With Chris for company, it was even more special. She had to admit, as much as she adored her daughter, doing this with him alone was a whole different experience.

At the river, he turned left in the park and drove away from the dam, to the picnic area at the far end. The land was flat and smooth in that direction, the river closer to park-goers. He chose a spot by the last table and parked, then started hauling bags from the car, insisting on getting the heavy ones with the dishes, plus the small cooler.

He was always going to be a bit macho like that, she supposed, and it suited her just fine. Secretly, she liked having him fuss over her, a little. Okay, a lot.

Suddenly he froze and looked toward the trees and stared. For several seconds he didn't move, and she got worried.

"Something wrong?"

"I just remembered that man Maddy saw in the woods. You don't think . . . maybe that was *him*, stalking me. In fact, it seems pretty likely."

"My God. I'd forgotten all about that," she murmured, fear winding a tendril through her veins. "You don't think he's out there now, watching?"

Slowly, he shook his head. "I doubt it. I chased him

off, came close to catching him. I can't see him risking it again."

"I hope you're right."

Smiling, he said, "Why don't we enjoy ourselves and forget about that for tonight? We're safe here, in the open, and my gun is stashed in the new lockbox in my trunk if we need it. Not ideal, I know, but safer than lugging it around in my cargo shorts." He winked. "Can't have it go off accidentally and damage the tackle, can we?"

She laughed, unable to resist his boyish side. "No, we definitely can't."

Once the table was covered with a cloth, he pulled three Pyrex dishes out of their heated transport carriers. He'd clearly thought this out carefully, and she realized that he must've bought this stuff new, or borrowed it from Daisy. He had said himself he wasn't much of a cook. That he'd gone to this much trouble caused a bubble of happiness to swell and fill every single square inch of her soul.

No man had ever done anything like this for her before.

His final touch was a real picnic basket containing actual dishes and flatware, two long-stemmed wineglasses, and a bottle of Chardonnay with an opener.

"Wow, this is incredible! You went to so much trouble."

"Are you ready for the unveiling of the meal?" he said in a faux British accent.

She giggled. "Please." Prying the lid off the main dish,

he revealed bacon-wrapped chicken breasts. "That smells wonderful!"

"It's cooked in a sour cream sauce, and the bacon gives it a smoky flavor."

The other two dishes were wild rice and green beans. He opened and poured the wine first, and she took a sip. It was an excellent white. By the time he dished the food, she was salivating.

The first bite of the chicken was an explosion of flavor on her tongue. "Ooh, this is wonderful. I'm going to make this at home, too."

His chest swelled. "I'm glad you like it."

They ate and made small talk, enjoying the evening and each other. She pigged out on chicken and rice until she was stuffed, and was getting a tiny bit buzzed as she finished her second glass of wine.

"We're probably not supposed to have this out here," she said, wiggling her wineglass.

"No, but I like to live dangerously sometimes." He winked.

"That's what I love about you."

Electricity sparked between them as her words hit them both. The moment stretched taut and he said quietly, "Do you mean you love me literally, or figuratively?"

She swallowed hard, pulse pounding against her sternum. "Why don't we take a walk, and I'll tell you everything you want to know."

"Everything?"

"Yes."

His brown eyes softened, and he nodded. "Sounds like a good plan."

They cleaned up together, stashed all the picnic stuff and leftovers in his car, and then the time was at hand.

A whole new life awaited—if she had the guts to seize it and the man she loved.

11

This was it. The moment he'd been waiting for since they'd met.

That's what I love about you.

Had she meant it the way he hoped? Or was she about to let him down easy?

Please, don't let it be the let-down. Anything but that. I'll give her more time, all she needs.

I love her.

"Let's go for that walk," he said, with more confidence than he felt. Inside he was still a quivering little boy wanting someone to love him, pathetic as that sounded. Even to himself.

But he hadn't fallen for the first woman who came along, no matter how badly he'd wanted forever. Robyn was special, the one for him. He hoped she felt the same.

With her smaller hand clasped in his, they strolled along the riverbank. The sun was setting, sending pretty sparkles along the rippling water. A few white waterbirds strutted on their spindly legs along the opposite shoreline. He never knew whether they were cranes or something else, but they were cool to watch.

Not as interesting as his girlfriend, though. His lips curved upward as he thought about how much he liked thinking of her in that way.

They walked until coming to a nice grassy spot, not too far from the car. The sun was about gone and he didn't want to fumble in the dark. But they'd be able to see the lights over the parking lot from here.

"Want to sit?" he asked.

"Sure."

They parked their rumps next to each other and he wrapped an arm around her shoulders. Having her there at his side was right. She was soft and smelled so good, he wanted to make love to her. Right here in front of whoever wanted to see. He forced his libido to calm down and he focused on Robyn.

"You have some important things to tell me," he prompted. His nerves jangled as he waited, trying to brace himself in case this didn't turn out the way he wanted.

"You asked about Greg, and I'd like to share it with you now."

"Only if you're ready, baby." He hugged her tight.

"I am." Though her voice was strong, she paused for a while, as though gathering her thoughts. When she finally spoke, her voice was distant with memory. "I first began to realize Greg was clinically depressed about six months after we'd married. It turned out that he'd been battling depression all his life, but when we met, he and his family believed he had it under control at last. So nobody told me. I loved him with all my heart, though, so that didn't matter to me."

He didn't speak or move except to lay his free hand on her knee and stroke it. He sensed she needed his touch, but also needed him to be quiet right now, so she could get it all out.

"He didn't have a traumatic childhood, wasn't abused or bullied. None of those triggers people think of as causes of depression. He was just so . . . lost within himself. From childhood on, the demon inside him was himself, despite everything. I tried, though, to get him the best help possible. I really did. In the end, there was no help for him as far as he was concerned."

Oh, no. Chris held his breath, figuring he knew what came next.

"All the love I gave him, that Maddy gave him when she came along, wasn't enough. One day I got a call at work that Greg hadn't picked up Maddy at the day care. And somehow, I just knew."

He hurt for what she'd gone through, his eyes burning. He held her tighter and studied her profile. Tears were streaming down her face, her expression shattered with the recollection.

"He was in our four-car garage, sitting in his Mercedes with it running. Had been for hours, most likely. There was a handwritten note on the front seat next to him that just said, *I'm sorry I can't fight this anymore* and *I'll always love you both.* That was all."

This time, he found his voice. "I'm so, so sorry," he whispered.

"I was so angry," she went on. "I knew, in my head,

that depression is a disease and not something he was able to control, but it felt like he had *chosen* to abandon us. That he didn't love us enough to stay. He left me alone with a five-year-old, a delinquent mortgage on a four-million-dollar house, and a mountain of debt I had no idea he'd accumulated. I lost everything—except Maddy. She was my guiding light, and has been ever since. She was the reason I rebuilt my life when all I wanted to do was join him."

"God, don't say that," he said hoarsely, wiping the tears from her face. "Don't ever talk about harming yourself, baby."

"No, I never would've left Maddy, not for any reason." She sighed, breath hitching. "But as I healed and moved us here to start a new life, I lost my passion for *living*, if that makes sense. I never considered letting another man in my life. I was so afraid to love again, because that means possibly losing them."

"That's not always true," he pointed out gently. "Remember, you haven't lost Maddy."

"I know. But that didn't make overcoming the fear any easier. That is, until you came along."

Her words gave him hope, and he scooted to face her fully. "What do you want from me? For us?"

She smiled at him, no trace of sorrow left in her blue eyes. "I want everything. I'm so in love with you."

"I love you, too. So much."

Their lips met in a searing kiss, and he tasted her until he was hard and leaking in his shorts. His hands cupped her breasts through her T-shirt and rubbed until her nipples poked against the fabric even through her bra.

"I want you," she said, cupping his length. "Now. Where can we go?"

"Not out in the open. Come on, we'll find a place." Standing, he helped her to her feet and they took off for the car, laughing like teenagers.

Back inside the Camaro and buckled up, he peeled out of the parking lot, grinning at Robyn's delighted squeal. Suddenly he knew just the place to go, and he made a series of turns down several winding roads, slowing down quite a bit since it was fully dark under the cover of the hills and trees.

"Where are we going?"

"You'll see."

The final turn was a road that led down to the river in a different area altogether than the park where they'd enjoyed their picnic. Here, a rocky slope rose high over the river and the darkened dirt road they were now sitting on. He turned off the engine, undid his seat belt, then hers, and pulled her into his arms.

"You ever fucked in a muscle car, honey?" he purred in her ear.

She shivered against him. "No. Have you?"

"Not *this* one."

"Mmm. Are we going to fix that?"

"Oh, *yeah*."

Robyn was so hot, she thought her blood was boiling in her veins.

She couldn't remember the last time she'd lusted this badly, and she wanted her sexy cop something fierce. Right this moment, she could spread for him in front of the entire Sugarland PD and not give a damn about anything but his big cock pounding into her and making her scream.

You ever fucked in a muscle car, honey?

No, but she planned to remedy the oversight, curing herself of her staid, boring existence once and for all. Right now.

Grasping the hem of her shirt, she pulled it over her head and tossed it to the floorboard. Her bra was next. She felt wild and dirty, like she was in high school all over again, back when she hadn't always been such a good girl.

She liked the way the air kissed her nipples as her breasts bounced free. She liked it even better when her lover kissed them and licked each one as though eating the tastiest treat. Arching into his mouth, she let him have his way, enjoying his mouth and the burn of his five o'clock shadow on her skin.

When she could stand it no more, she pushed him back a bit and went for the button on his cargo shorts. "I'm glad you wore loose clothing."

"Would you be mad if I said I planned ahead?"

"Let me show you and you be the judge of how upset I am."

Lowering the zipper, she worked his shorts and briefs down as he scooted toward her some. His cock popped free, pointing at the roof, appearing dark and flushed in the moonlight. Bending, she swallowed him to the root, desire driving her to give him the best blow job he'd ever had. She wanted to make his eyes cross.

His skin was clean and he smelled spicy, like whatever he'd used in the shower. Inspired, she worked lower and laved his balls, loving his groan of pleasure. She tongued them all around, getting him nice and wet, driving him out of his mind.

"My God! Robyn, honey . . . Fuck, so good."

Jesus, she was going to burn up. "I need cock inside me. Need you to fuck me hard and dirty."

"Shit, yes. Condom. In the glove box."

Quickly she flipped open the front compartment and found the strip, tearing one off. As he yanked off his tank top, she made quick work of opening the package and sheathing him. Then she worked off her own shorts and panties, leaving her completely naked. In a sexy car with her hot boyfriend. In the dark.

Crawling over the middle hump with the gearshift, she straddled his lap. It was quite a feat of acrobatics, with the edge of the steering wheel pressed into her back. But they fit and that was all she cared about.

Reaching between them, she wrapped her fingers around him and guided the head of his cock into place. Then she slowly seated herself on him until she was totally impaled. She reveled in the feeling for a moment, watching him through half-closed eyes. The way his head was thrown back, the strong cords of muscle in his neck and chest, ecstasy etched on his handsome face. His dark eyes, staring back at her, heavy with lust.

"Fuck me," she said huskily.

"Hang on to me."

Bracing her hands on his shoulders, she prepared for

a thrilling ride—and wasn't disappointed. Fingers digging into her hips, he began to thrust, fucking her hard and deep, as he'd promised. His cock stroked her inner walls, pistoning in and out, the slap of their flesh titillating. Their coupling was raw, unbridled.

Never had she experienced anything like it before. With Chris, it was pure naughty, unfettered passion.

The quickening began to build between her legs as his length stroked her sheath, her clit. She began to unravel, bouncing on his lap with abandon and screaming in completion as her orgasm exploded. On and on she rode him, driving him to his own release. He came with a shout, thrusting through his orgasm, cock jerking inside her.

Gradually their movements slowed. Their release ebbed, leaving her sated and more blissed out than she could ever recall.

"That was freaking amazing," she breathed, lowering her head for a kiss.

He gave her some tongue, growling playfully, which she thought was cute. Finally they broke apart and she said with much regret, "Now comes the cleanup."

"Ugh. But *so* worth it." His eyes practically rolled back in his head. "I think you killed me."

"Nope. Can't do that when I plan on riding you again and again for as long as you'll have me."

His smile was white in the darkness. "That's the best thing I've heard all day. Except the part where you love me."

"And it's true. I do love you, with all my heart."

"I love you, baby." He made a face. "Guess we'd better get moving. Rachel's probably wondering if we're ever coming home."

"Home. I like how you say it that way."

He pushed a strand of hair off her cheek. "I'm coming to think of your place as home, with you and Maddy. But we can talk more about particulars later. We have all the time in the world."

"Yes, we do."

Robyn found some tissues and they got cleaned up as best as they could. Chris wrapped the condom in one of the tissues and placed it in one of the sacks without food in it to throw away later. With much wiggling around, they managed to find their clothes and get dressed again.

Before he started the car, he turned to her and said, "I'll always remember tonight. Especially making love in this place with you. I already know this is going to be one of my most treasured memories."

Happy tears welled in her eyes. "You say the most romantic things."

"I just say what I feel."

"It's the same with me. I'll always remember tonight, with you."

Reluctantly, they left their spot. But Robyn had a suspicion they'd be back.

The drive home was nice, the two of them wrapped in a fog of happiness. She did feel bad for Rachel when they pulled into the driveway and she saw it was going on eleven.

"Oh, wow," she said. "I can't believe we were gone that long."

"Worth it?"

"Every second. I'm going to give Rachel extra."

"Naw, let me cover it this time, okay?" She started to protest, but he intervened. "It's important to me."

She relented, loving him. "Thank you."

He walked her inside. She wanted to take the leftovers, but he'd said it wasn't safe since the chicken had been out so long, and he'd make her and Maddy a fresh dish for dinner one night. She couldn't wait.

"Maddy's asleep," Rachel said. "The movie was good, and then we ate pizza downtown. She was worn out, and crashed right after her bath."

"Thanks so much, and I apologize for keeping you up so late."

The younger woman waved her off. "I'm in college, Dr. Lassiter. I never sleep."

Chris paid her, giving the girl a generous tip. She thanked him profusely, blushing as she tried not to appear she was ogling him, even though she really was. When Rachel was gone, Robyn took his hand.

"Do you want to stay a while, maybe?"

"I can't think of anywhere I'd rather be. Sofa?"

"Bedroom," she said meaningfully.

"Woman, you're going to wear me out."

But he was smiling as he said it, and beat a path to her room faster than she could blink.

She switched on some music, playing low, and they got naked. For a while they simply held each other, basking in their newfound love. They talked, too, Chris sharing more about his unhappy childhood than she suspected most people knew.

"My cousin Shane knows how bad my parents got

along," he told her, "but even he doesn't know about some of the stuff that happened. The verbal abuse and screaming were kept off the radar when others visited. My parents knew how to put on a facade. Nobody would've believed me."

"I'm so sorry you had to go through that," she said, hugging him tightly.

"I'm mostly over it now, but sometimes I wonder why some guys, like me, grow up to be productive citizens in spite of their sad upbringing, while some victims go on to hurt others. My crappy childhood made me want to do better, be better. Help other people."

"You're a rare, special man. I know it, and so does Maddy."

"Thanks, but I'm just me."

"And you're perfect."

Under the sheet, her hand crept downward to explore and play. As he gradually hardened, he spread his legs for her, letting her play and stroke all she wanted. They didn't speak, but he knew to follow her lead and was quite content to do it. She ducked under the covers and pressed kisses down his flat abdomen to her ultimate prize.

This time was more about connecting on an emotional level than about lust and passion. It was about loving her man, marking him as hers. He made his enjoyment plain.

Groaning, he began to work his hips as she sucked him. This time it lasted longer, and she drove him slowly out of his mind. At last he went over the edge, moaning.

"Baby, I'm gonna—"

He shot, and she swallowed every drop of him. Sucked him through his orgasm and licked him clean, then let his softened cock slip from her lips.

"I don't have any brains left," he muttered. "You sucked them all out from the end of my dick."

Laughing, she crawled up his luscious body and gave him a kiss, sharing his essence with him. It was hot, and he apparently liked it, eating her mouth as though he couldn't get enough.

Afterward, she settled in again and drifted off, listening to his heartbeat. For now, all worries about work and serial killers faded into the background. This had been the perfect night with the man she loved.

She had another chance, and she was going to live life with Chris to the fullest.

Robyn groaned when the alarm went off.

Chris wanted to be up and dressed before Maddy woke up for the day and wondered what he was doing there. At least if they were dressed and in the kitchen, they could act like he'd come by for breakfast. They hated the ruse, but she wasn't sure what else to do. Chris was the man she loved and wanted a future with, but it felt too new to share with Maddy.

How did other people juggling kids and new lovers handle it? She could only do what felt right.

They took a quick shower, fooling around a bit. Then they dressed for work, Chris in some spare clothes he'd left in her closet, plus the gun and holster he'd brought in from his car. They were in the kitchen eating cereal and fruit by the time Maddy padded in wearing purple jeans and a pink shirt. The little girl had her own alarm clock and was pretty good about getting herself ready for school.

"Hi, Chris."

"Hey, munchkin."

She gave him a sleepy hug and then sat at the table, yawning. "I don't want fruit on my cereal. Gross."

Robyn sighed. That must be one of the standard words for kids around the globe, and described just about everything they didn't like. "Not even a banana?"

"No." She caught her mom's hard stare and amended, "No, thank you."

"That's better."

Once breakfast was finished, they parted reluctantly. It struck Robyn hard that she had been right—the turning point in her relationship with Chris had indeed been last night. They were actually becoming a family, right before her eyes.

It was fantastic.

"Chris? When can I ride in your car?" Maddy pointed to where the Camaro sat in the driveway.

"I don't know. Soon, if it's okay with your mom."

They both looked at Robyn. "Anytime is fine."

"Can you take me to school in it? Pleeeease?" She turned those big eyes on Chris, and it was apparent he was toast.

"Sure, sweet thing. Is that all right?" he asked Robyn.

"That's fine. Be sure you buckle up."

"Yay!"

Chuckling, he helped her on with her backpack, even though she'd just have to take it off again when they got to the car. When they were ready to go, he kissed Robyn, promising he'd see her tonight.

"Can't wait," she said, overjoyed. Not *When can I see you again?* but *I'll see you tonight*. As a couple, they'd turned a corner for the better.

It was beyond weird watching a man load her precious baby girl into his car and drive her to school. But he was a wonderful, special man and she knew Maddy was safe in his care. The knowledge gave her peace she hadn't known in years.

She had a man she loved, and she didn't have to bear the burden alone anymore.

Cranking up the radio, she sang along to Aerosmith as she drove to work, in high spirits. There was no masking her joyous mood, which earned her a few comments and smiles, all in good fun. She didn't care.

When Shea came on shift after noon, the other woman made a beeline straight for her and pulled her into the staff lounge, shutting the door.

"All right, girlfriend, spill it! The minute I came through the door, every single person I saw asked me if I'd seen Dr. Feelgood today," she said, eyes wide. "And that's no lie."

"Hmm, wish I'd thought of that song," Robyn joked. "I would've sung along to that one for sure."

"Keep me in suspense any longer and I'll hurt you."

"I'm about to explode," she admitted. "We're not just dating anymore. We're together."

"Get out! *Together* together?"

"As in madly in love, yes!"

Shea hugged her and they jumped around some before collecting themselves. Her friend was beaming at her, and Robyn knew she looked the same. Insanely happy and ready to bust.

Robyn took a calming breath. "I told him about Greg. It was so cathartic, and he was an absolute doll. He's almost too freaking good to be true."

"Nah. He and my brother are cut from the same cloth, both good men down to the bone. What you see is what you get with Chris. I am *so* happy for you, my friend." Shea hugged her again.

"I've never felt this way," she admitted. "Not even with Greg. He was a good man, too, but so tortured that we spent all of our years together steeped in misery. I'm not saying I would've changed meeting him or anything, because he was good at heart and I got Maddy from that relationship. But this . . ."

"I know it's different. And there's no need for you to feel guilty about being happy, you understand me?"

"I know. That part might take more time, but I know how I feel about Chris. No question."

"Good. Then be happy and don't worry about the rest. You *deserve* this."

"Thanks." She blew out a breath. "Now I've got to figure out how to get out there and be professional for the rest of the day without exploding into a shower of glitter."

"Now there's an image. Don't worry about what anyone else thinks—just roll around in that feeling."

"I will."

One more hug, and then they left the lounge to attend to their duties. The ER got busy, and her relief doctor called in sick. She left Chris a message to let him know she had to work overtime, and that Rachel would still pick up Maddy if he wanted.

She saw the typical number of scrapes and bruises from falls, strep throat, the flu, and one broken arm from a teenager's skateboard trick on a metal stair railing. She shook her head over that one and said a prayer for Maddy not to try stupid shit like that.

When the inflow of patients waned, she excused herself, letting the staff know she would be in her office for a while. Really she just wanted to get off her feet and maybe eat part of the granola bar hiding in her desk. But then she remembered the list Chris had given her, and her promise to do a little digging.

She rarely got to try her hand at amateur sleuthing, only when chasing a medical cause for an illness. As a doctor she liked to think she was pretty good at that, so maybe she *could* find something helpful to Chris and Tonio.

On the fourth floor, she let herself into her office, shutting the door behind her.

Let the hunt begin.

12

Sitting behind her desk, Robyn chewed on a pencil and thought through what they knew.

Chris's list of burglary victims overlapped with the cyanide deaths at the hospital.

After poison was discovered in Chris's shampoo and body wash, tests had shown the poison to be hidden in bathroom products of other victims as well.

The hospital could be the common thread. Chris said all of the victims except one had died here. They all lived in the area, near each other and close to the hospital.

Chris was looking at it from a different angle, starting with the burglaries and ending at the hospital. Now, the more she thought about it, she wondered whether it was the other way around—whether something about the hospital tied the victims together to begin with.

Unlocking the bottom desk drawer, she extracted the copy of the cross-referenced list of known burglary and poisoning victims. She decided to search starting with the earliest burglary victim, bring up the hospital records, and study his case history.

A startling pattern began to emerge. The victims didn't only *die* at Sterling; they had all been treated at Sterling before they were burglarized!

Charles Adams had first been to the ER two months prior to his death from what the ME and police now knew was poisoning. He was burglarized two weeks after that hospital visit. Attending physician, Dr. Alan Chin.

Jean Caplan was treated in the ER six weeks before she died in the same manner. The burglary occurred a mere week after her hospital visit. Again, the attending physician had been Dr. Alan Chin.

On the list went, eight people total. *Eight that they knew of!* Robyn could barely believe it. Had someone at the hospital first encountered his future victims at the hospital? Did he study all the patients, select his targets, break in to their homes to plant the poison, and kill them? Suddenly cold, even with her white coat on, she sat back and rubbed her arms. Alan could not have done this. Would not have. The sweet, gentle man who was such a good friend and mentor to everyone around him just wasn't capable of this sort of evil. Of course, that's what everyone said when their coworker or their neighbor turned out to be a killer, wasn't it? He was such a nice guy, he never could have done such a thing . . . But Robyn felt it, deep down.

This killer was systematic. A planner. He had a specific reason for choosing his targets, and the method of killing them. So he was no doubt smart enough to make sure suspicion fell on someone else, such as Alan Chin.

There was some other connecting thread they were missing. She was sure of it. Something that tied all the victims together, that explained why they were chosen out of the thousands of patients seen in the ER over the past few months.

Idly, she wondered what each victim did for a living. Did that matter? It might. Here she was playing amateur detective when she should be talking to the real one and giving him what she had. Picking up her cell phone, she punched the button for Chris's contact.

His phone rang several times, finally going to voice mail. Damn. She left a message, a sense of urgency nagging at her.

"Hey, it's me. Still working, but I'm leaving soon. I'm in my office and I've been doing some digging on your current case. I'm guessing you didn't get permission yet to come by and look at the records since I haven't heard from you. An interesting pattern has shown up regarding the burglaries and the visits. I don't want to say too much on the phone, so call me back. Or I'll be home in about an hour. We can talk then." She hesitated. "I love you."

That was still so new, saying those words. But she meant them and was no longer afraid to express how she felt. That made her smile.

Evening rounds went much too slowly, since all she wanted to do was get home to Maddy and Chris. At last, another doctor arrived to take over. Making sure the list was in her purse, she gathered it and left her office. She said good-bye to Shea and Cori on the way out and took the elevator down to the staff parking garage.

Her shoes squeaked on the concrete, echoing in the cavernous space. The sound always gave her the creeps even though there was nothing to be afraid of. There were plenty of cars here, doctors, nurses, and other staff members coming and going at all hours.

Just not tonight. There was nobody else around as she crossed to her car, which was weird. Keys in hand, she punched the automatic unlock button and was reaching for the handle when she heard a scuff of shoes from behind.

Fear shot through her and she whirled, only to be caught by a strong pair of hands and hauled back against a hard chest. Opening her mouth to scream, she stomped on the assailant's foot and shot her elbow backward, into his stomach. But one of his hands immediately clamped over her mouth, muffling the sound, and her counterattack had little effect.

Twisting, she fought him for all she was worth. And as she turned her head, she got a good look at her attacker. The shock was profound.

"Noo!"

She scratched, bit, and clawed. And she almost got free—

Then there was a sting in her arm, followed by a rush of cold numbness that spread through her body. He held her tight as the drug swiftly took effect. *No, no! Chris!*

Against her will, the world dimmed and vanished.

"Maddy, eat your peas," Chris said patiently. Or with what he *hoped* was patience and not a frightening growl.

"No! I hate peas. They're *gross*." Scowling, she flicked one of the green orbs away from her chicken strips. "When is Mommy coming home?"

He sighed. "I don't know, munchkin. She had to work late. Please, eat just two bites?"

"I'll throw up," she warned him seriously. "It'll come up *green*."

Jesus. How had Robyn done this by herself for the past two years? Maddy was a great kid, but parenting was exhausting. He didn't know what the hell he was doing. With his luck, he'd scar the little girl for life and Robyn would never forgive him.

"Fine," he said, giving in to defeat. Because he was *not* cleaning up green pea puke. He didn't care how annoyed Robyn got with him for letting the kid have her way.

Happy, she attacked her chicken with renewed gusto as the danger of consuming mushy vegetables was past. Chris finished his meal and took his plate into the kitchen, rinsed it, and put it in the dishwasher. Dinner accomplished, even if it was with the help of frozen, ready-to-cook chicken strips.

Patting his front jeans pocket, he wondered where he'd left his cell phone. Then he recalled taking it out of his pocket and laying it on the nightstand in Robyn's room. He'd forgotten it in the midst of making their dinner.

Padding to the bedroom, he picked up the phone and checked the display. One missed call from Robyn. Figured. Checking the voice mail she'd left, he frowned as he listened. The first part give him a slight chill, and he wondered what she'd found.

The *I love you* part of the message made him feel warm and content inside.

He called her back, but her phone went to voice mail. Seemed they were going to play phone tag this evening. But she'd be home soon, so he guessed whatever she had to tell him could wait.

However, when two more hours had passed, long after she should have been home, he tried again. Again the call went straight to voice mail, and he started to grow worried. He knew she must be with a patient, but trying his luck anyway, he called the direct line to her office. She didn't answer, so his last gasp was the ER.

"Sterling Emergency Room, this is Barb. How can I help you?"

"Hello, I'm Detective Chris Ford with the Sugarland PD, and I'm trying to track down Dr. Lassiter. Is she available?" He had no guilt whatever at pulling rank to get through to his lady.

"Oh, I'm sorry, Detective Ford. Dr. Lassiter left for the night some time ago."

His gut clenched. "Are you certain?"

"Yes. I know because she told us good-bye on her way out, and she had her purse with her. Can I leave a message or anything?"

"No, thank you. I'll catch up with her later."

"Okay. Good-bye."

Dread crept over him as he hung up. *Where the hell are you, baby?*

How long had she actually been gone? Checking the call he'd received from her, he noted it had been placed while he was cooking dinner, a little over three hours before.

She could have gone by the store, he reasoned. That

was pretty much the only place she would have gone so late at night, but even that explanation didn't satisfy him. He was almost positive she would've let him know, because she wouldn't want Maddy to worry.

That was the clincher for him. There was no way Robyn would leave her daughter to wonder where her mother was. No fucking way.

He had to go look for Robyn. But he had to see Maddy safe first. Looking on the fridge for Rachel's number, he called to ask if she could come sit with the little girl. But Rachel's mother answered the phone and told him that she was studying at the library for a big test and there was no way she could come. She apologized, but Chris told her it was fine, even though he was starting to panic.

Next, he called Shane and explained the situation.

"Hang tight. We're both on our way," his cousin said in a tone that brooked no argument. "Daisy will take care of her while you and I check out the hospital."

Glad to have backup from his cousin, he exhaled in relief. "Thanks, man. See you soon."

The wait was only about twenty-five minutes, but seemed interminable. Chris paced the floor, checking his phone constantly and leaving more messages for Robyn, each one more tense than the last.

"Baby, please call me. I'm getting worried. I love you." Thank God Maddy was in her room getting ready for bed, and hadn't a clue what was going on.

When the doorbell rang, Chris practically ripped the door from its hinges to let them inside. "Thank God you're here. I'm going crazy."

"Still no word?" Daisy asked. She and his cousin wore identical expressions of concern.

"None. This isn't like her," he said, pacing, running a hand through his hair. "I know Robyn. There's *no way* she'd go this long without letting Maddy know where she is. Me, maybe, but not her daughter."

Shane nodded. "I believe you. Let's start at the hospital and go from there. We'll find a reasonable explanation, I'm sure."

"I am, too, but I'm scared of what that's going to be."

Moving forward, Daisy gave him a tight hug. "She'll be all right, Chris. You guys go. I'll make sure Maddy gets tucked into bed."

Chris kissed her cheek. "Thanks a million."

"No problem. I know you'd do the same for us."

It was true. There wasn't much of anything he wouldn't do for Shane and Daisy, and Drew as well. They were his family. He hoped Robyn and Maddy would be his one day, too.

Shane drove, and Chris stared out the window. Darkness had fallen a while before, leaving the city under a blanket of lights. Everywhere people were going about their business, completely unaware of the drama unfolding around them. They had no clue that one of their own was racing to find his lover, fear growing with every mile.

When they arrived at the hospital, Shane parked and they hurried into the ER. Chris stopped at the sign-in desk and schooled himself to be polite and not snap at the woman working there.

"Hello, I'm Detective Chris Ford and this is Detective Shane Ford," he began.

"Oh!" the perky young nurse exclaimed. "Brothers?"

"Cousins." He resisted the urge to roll his eyes. "I called earlier looking for Dr. Lassiter, but Barb said she'd left a while ago."

"Yes, she's gone. I mean, I didn't see her go, but that's what I heard."

"Did she maybe come back?"

"I don't think so, but I can get Barb for you if you'd like."

"Could you, please?" he asked in his most polite tone.

The girl beamed. "Sure."

She disappeared through the double doors into the exam area, and he glanced at the clock on the wall. Each tick seemed sinister, marking the passing of more time with no answers.

At last the young nurse came back with an older woman he assumed was Barb.

"Hello," she said in a friendly tone. "Are you the detective I spoke to on the phone?"

"I am. I'm still looking for Dr. Lassiter. Has she been back here since she left?"

"Not to my knowledge," the woman said. "But if you'd like, you can check her office on the fourth floor. She keeps it locked, though. If she's not there, I wouldn't be able to let you in."

"Who can?" he pressed.

"Maintenance has a set of master keys. Rafael is around somewhere, so he could open it up for you guys."

"Would you mind having someone find him and meet us there?" He had a strong feeling Robyn wasn't in her office. If not, he wanted to see if she'd left any papers, notes, or other information behind for him to look at regarding the cases.

"Sure." The nurse pointed toward the bank of elevators. "Take those up to the fourth floor, and turn right. A few doors down on the left is Dr. Lassiter's office. The door has her name on it."

"Thank you so much, Barb."

She nodded, expression concerned. "I hope you find her and nothing bad has happened."

"Me, too."

Chris was practically vibrating by the time they reached Robyn's office. He tried the door and it was locked, so he knocked just in case. No answer. Some sixth sense told him she wasn't inside, but he had to be sure. If she *had* come back and something had happened to her, she could by lying in there, unconscious. Or worse.

"What's going on, Shane? Where is she?"

"I don't know, bud. We're going to find her, though. Try not to worry."

The maintenance man arrived, and Chris was impressed that he asked to see their badges. Chris had to dig out the one he kept in his wallet, since he normally just wore his clip-on badge while on the clock. He was wearing his holstered gun, though, which he'd put on his belt before Shane and Daisy arrived. Rafael eyed both of them before nodding and unlocking the door.

Robyn's office was dark except for the glow from the streetlights outside coming through the window blinds. Reaching in, he flipped on the lights. Empty. He wasn't sure whether to be relieved or not.

Shane followed him inside. They poked around the

modest space, but there wasn't much to see. Robyn was apparently tidy, leaving her desk clear and free of the haphazard papers or files that might be found in a different office. Given that she was a doctor, however, and most of her information was confidential, that wasn't surprising.

Upon trying her desk drawers, he found them unlocked. But other than the usual office supplies and some innocuous papers that didn't mean anything to anyone but her, there wasn't anything to give him a clue what she'd been looking at when she'd called him earlier.

"I wonder if she took the list with her," he mused.

"What list?"

Belatedly, he realized he hadn't told his cousin about her call. He got Shane up to speed, telling him about her sleuthing, comparing the burglary lists to happenings at the hospital. "She didn't say what she'd found, though. She wanted to talk to me when she got home."

Shane's eyes narrowed. "I hate to say this, but it's quite a coincidence that she'd disappear right after she supposedly found something. I'm not trying to scare you; it's just—"

"I know. In our experience, that's not a good sign." The idea was taking that kernel of fear inside him and spreading it to fill every inch of his soul.

"Why don't we trace her steps to the staff parking garage, check on her car," his cousin suggested.

"Good idea." As they left, he pulled the door shut behind him and nodded to Rafael, who was hovering at the end of the hall. "We might be back."

"No problem," the man said.

Downstairs, they headed for the nurses' desk again and the same perky young nurse smiled at them. "Did you find anything helpful?"

Chris shook his head. "Not yet. Could you tell us exactly what route the doctors use to go from here to the staff parking garage?"

"Sure." She pointed. "Go down the hallway past the elevators you just used, then keep going all the way to the end. After that you'll see a set of double doors leading outside. Go straight ahead and the lower level of the garage in front of you belongs to the staff."

"Do you know if there are security cameras?" Chris asked.

"There's some up in the corners all around the garage, but I couldn't tell you if they actually work." She shrugged. "Hopefully their presence is enough to keep anyone from getting mugged or whatever."

He doubted that very much. Crimes were committed on camera all the time, and he rarely found the devices to be much of a deterrent.

"All right, thanks."

They took the route she suggested and walked into a garage that could have been lit more brightly, in his opinion. There were too many dark shadows in the corners, places for an assailant to hide. Looking around, he searched for Robyn's car.

"What does she drive?"

"A silver Lexus, four-door sedan."

There weren't many silver cars, so it didn't take long to spot one that looked like it could be hers. As they approached the back of the car and started around it,

Chris spotted what was on the ground—and his knees nearly buckled.

"That's Robyn's purse," he said, voice rising in panic. Even when he'd almost died, his heart hadn't beat this fast or hard. "Someone's got her, Shane."

"Shit," his cousin said in shock. "I'll call it in."

He couldn't answer. Could only stare at the purse with small items scattered around it—lipstick, a nail file, her keys. And the corner of a paper sticking from the top.

On shaking legs, he walked over and knelt by the purse. Then, very carefully, he extracted the paper. Unfolding it, he saw it was the cross-referenced list he'd given her, with her own handwritten notes all over it.

He stood and scanned them quickly, deciding he needed more time and a quiet place to study them thoroughly. And another set of eyes, like Shane's, to look as well, so he didn't miss anything.

Tonio and Taylor arrived, along with the captain and a couple of techs to dust for prints. That included the list Chris was holding, so he surrendered it for the time being. Rainey said the circumstances were enough to call it an abduction, though it was a horrible shock to hear the word out loud. He couldn't catch his breath, and didn't realize he was about to hyperventilate until a hand fell on his back and steered him away from the scene.

"Try to calm down and keep a clear head," Shane said. "That's it—deep, slow breaths. You won't be able to help her if you pass out."

"How are we going to find her? She could be anywhere by now!"

"I think whatever Robyn found in those papers is going to help us identify our culprit, or at least give us a clue what's going on."

"God, I hope you're right."

The techs let him have the papers back, stating there were two sets of prints, probably belonging to him and Robyn, though they lifted them to be sure. They pointed out that the perp probably hadn't touched them, because if he had, he would have taken the list with him. Chris was even more sure Robyn had gotten too close to the truth and their man had kidnapped her because of it.

Either that, or to get back at Chris—the one victim who'd foiled his would-be killer's plans.

"I want the video feed from these cameras," he told Rainey, gesturing to the corners next to the roof.

"I'll make it happen."

They wrapped up quickly, then Chris and the other three detectives, plus Rainey, remained behind to obtain the video footage from the security office. Chris still had Robyn's notes in hand and was itching to read them. But looking at the video had to come first since it might show her kidnapper. Something was about to shake loose—he was certain of it.

In the office, security was already waiting for them, thanks to Rainey's intervention. A beefy guard pulled up the feed and started the conversation.

"We scanned the footage from the past four hours, and we've got something you should look at."

Pushing play, he ran the segment. In the film, Robyn could be clearly seen walking to her car. When she was almost there, a tall, dark-haired man dressed in jeans and a T-shirt emerged from his hiding place on the other side of the car next to hers and grabbed her from behind.

"Son of a bitch," Chris swore. His hands clenched into fists. He'd never felt so goddamned helpless.

A brief struggle ensued, and Robyn did her best to break the man's hold, stomping on his instep and elbowing him in the stomach, dropping her purse and keys in the process. She almost managed to twist free, then the asshole fumbled for something and jabbed her arm. Chris realized it was a syringe and saw red. The bastard had drugged her.

"I'm going to kill that motherfucker." His voice was cold, deadly.

"Any idea who he is?" Tonio asked the guard.

The man peered at the screen. "Can't really see his face very well with the grainy footage, but he looks familiar."

Chris nodded. "We think he may be an employee here. We'd like to bring people in—especially those who work with Dr. Lassiter—and see if anyone recognizes him."

"No problem. I want to help catch this fucker."

They started with people already on shift, nurses who knew Robyn, bringing them in one at a time so they wouldn't leave the ER shorthanded. But Chris was as patient as he could be under the circumstances.

Kasey, the girl from the front desk, thought the man looked familiar, but couldn't place him. The same with Barb and Cori, which was disappointing. With each new person, he hoped *someone* would identify this guy. He'd just about given up hope when Shea, working a late shift tonight, showed up.

One look at the screen and she gasped. "That looks like one of our nurses. Lee Miller."

Chris bolted upright from his seat next to the guard. "Are you sure?"

"Run the tape again," she asked. They did, and she frowned. "The guy's face is too grainy, so no, I can't say with one hundred percent certainty that's Lee, but given his build and hair, the way he moves? I'd be shocked if it wasn't."

Chris almost pumped his fist. But they weren't in the clear yet. "Can you get us his full name and address from the personnel records?"

"You bet. I'll be back as soon as I can." She rushed out the door, and Chris looked to the captain.

"It's not enough for a warrant," he said in frustration.

"If she was sure and the video was sharper, we could swing it," Rainey admitted. "But we're not giving up. Once we have his name and address, we're going back to the station to dig up every single fact about Lee Miller we can possibly learn, as well as how he might tie in to our cases."

Chris blew out a breath. "I say we just walk up and knock on his door, ask him some questions. Maybe he'll get nervous and screw up, make a break for it."

Rainey snorted. "Yeah, and tip off a possible serial killer that we're onto him and waiting on his doorstep? Are you hearing yourself?"

"Fine. Then can we put surveillance on his residence?"

"Yeah. That we can quietly do. If he makes a move with her in tow, we'll get him. I'll put Shane and Taylor on that now." Before Chris could protest, Rainey continued. "In the meantime, I need you and Salvatore doing the digging and making the puzzle pieces fit. We need that warrant."

"Yes, sir." He wanted to hit something. Hard.

They waited for tense minutes until Shea came back with Miller's full name and address, even his social security number. "I also managed to pull some personal info from his file and sort of make a copy of it," she confessed. "He's received a number of complaints and reprimands since he's been here. There's even a note in here about trouble at the last place he worked, a hospital near Clarksville."

"Interesting," Tonio said.

"Thank you, Shea," Chris said. "I hope you're not going too far out on a limb."

"No, it'll be all right. Believe me, if he's guilty of murder, the hospital won't raise a fuss about how the information was found. They'll spend all their time hoping the victims' families don't sue them."

Sad but true. That seemed to be all anyone cared about these days. Lawsuits and money.

They thanked her again, and then Chris caught a ride with Tonio back to the station. They had a long night of work ahead of them if they were going to break this case open—and then get Robyn free of that diabolical bastard's clutches.

Hang on, baby. I'm going to nail this fucker. Then I'm coming for you.

Robyn's brain began to come awake. Gradually she became aware that she was lying across the seat of a car.

The vehicle was moving, which made her slightly sick. Might be the sedative Lee had given her.

Lee Miller. She never saw that coming. Not from someone she worked with, who was supposed to *save* lives, not take them. Why had he gone to such trouble to poison all those people? What madness was behind his reasoning? Or was he simply insane, capable of no reasoning at all?

Instinct told her there was an underlying cause. But before she could think more about his motives, the car pulled into a driveway, from what she could tell. Then it slowed to a stop and the engine was shut off.

Next he got out and came around to the back, opened the door, and pulled her out by her feet. She kept her eyes closed and pretended to still be out, leaving him no choice but to carry her. He slung her over his shoulder, and she wondered whether he lived where his neighbors might see and call the police.

A quick glance from under her lashes sent disappointment and fear spiraling through her. His car was parked in a driveway next to a garage, and there were tall bushes and an equally tall fence blocking any view from outside. Basically, she was screwed.

How Chris or anyone would figure out Lee was responsible, she didn't know. Couldn't think too hard right now. She couldn't wrap her brain around much beyond the terror of what he was planning to do to her.

She knew this man, could identify him. He wouldn't let her live.

Lee carried her through a house she assumed to be his. Since he couldn't tell her eyes were open, she made note of the route and where he was taking her. The interior was drab and depressing. The worn furniture looked like it hadn't been reupholstered since the fifties, and the drapes were dark olive green and dingy. There was even an old rotary-style dial phone on an end table next to the sofa. *Who still has one of those? How weird.*

She kept up the ruse of being asleep, all the way into a bedroom where he gently laid her on the bed. Then he said something chilling.

"There," he said happily. "Now you can keep Mom company until I get back."

Mom? What the fuck? With that, he left the room. So she turned her head to speak to "Mom" and find out if she was her son's prisoner as well.

And found herself staring into the vacant eyeholes of the skull attached to the well-dressed skeleton on the bed beside her.

Robyn screamed herself hoarse, and thought she might never stop.

13

Chris bounded into the station with Tonio, and they retrieved every single bit of information on their case before hurrying to the conference room.

"Okay," Rainey said, shutting the door behind them, "let's have a look at Dr. Lassiter's notes on that list."

Chris unfolded the paper and flattened it out. "This is a copy of the cross-referenced list of burglary victims who later died from what we now know was poisoning. Robyn offered to do some poking around for us and see if she could find anything interesting."

"Seems she did," Tonio said, pointing to the first of the notes. "Check this out."

Leaning over, they read together:

Charles Adams—fracture treated in ER May 5, Dr. Alan Chin. Burglarized May 19. Died July 14, poisoning.

Jean Caplan—laceration treated in ER July 16, Dr. Alan Chin. Burglarized July 24. Died Sept. 30, poisoning.

On the list went, as the three of them stared at Robyn's notations. She hadn't done the entire list, but she had a good start. Enough to show a pattern they had all missed through their own investigation.

"Fuck me," Tonio exclaimed. "All of the victims were treated in Sterling's ER *before* their homes were broken into. Then they later died of poisoning."

Chris buried a hand in his hair. "Shit! Why didn't I think of this angle from the start? The hospital was the perfect place for our suspect to come into contact with each victim and them be none the wiser. He could just sit back, pick and choose them, like he was ordering from a damned menu. And he had access to all of their information, including names and addresses."

Tonio sighed. "We would have thought of it sooner or later. At least we know now. The question is, does Dr. Chin have anything to do with all of this?"

"Robyn doesn't seem to think so," Chris said, pointing to one of her notes on the back of the page.

Alan Chin?? NO.

The word *NO* was underscored three times.

"He may or may not be guilty," Rainey mused, "but we need to get the good doctor in here to speak with us, fast."

Tonio pulled out his phone. "I'll call the hospital, get in touch with him. Hopefully he's got nothing to hide and he'll be cooperative."

Tonio left the room to make his call and Chris stared at the list and Robyn's notes. "So now we know he chose these specific people out of the hundreds who come into the ER on a weekly basis. What do they have in common that we haven't ruled out yet?" Chris racked his brain. "Hmm. All of these victims were authority figures. A school principal, a doctor, a teacher, a lawyer, etc."

"And a cop—*you*." Rainey eyed him in speculation. "So he hates authority. Some kind of rebel?"

"Yeah, maybe." They thought some more. "All of those types of people are in their jobs to help others. Maybe he needed help somehow, and they failed him, so now he's taking revenge."

"Where the hell did he get the cyanide, though? Not from the hospital."

"No. But if he's in the medical field, he could possibly have purchased it legally, claiming it was for research purposes. Or he could have falsified medical credentials, or stolen it outright."

"There haven't been any thefts of cyanide reported anywhere in the state, or elsewhere that we know of, within this time period," Rainey reminded him. "That leaves purchase, either legally or illegally."

"Or stole it from someone who didn't want to report it."

Their speculation was interrupted as Tonio strode into the room again. They quickly filled him in on their discussion, then Chris asked about his phone call.

"Dr. Chin is on duty tonight. He'll be in to speak with us after he gets off at seven in the morning."

Chris let out a vicious curse. "That's too fucking long! Robyn is out there waiting for us to make some damned progress and we're sitting on our hands!"

"Not quite." Tonio took a seat at the table. "Dr. Chin

was shocked at what I told him, which didn't include a lot of details. I just said we're investigating the cyanide deaths and he was the attending physician in some of the cases, if not all. He volunteered to pull up records of who was on staff and working in the ER with him on the days the victims were first seen and treated."

"That rocks," Chris said in relief. "You didn't mention Lee Miller's name?"

"Of course not." He paused. "Also, I spoke with Taylor. He and Shane are outside Miller's apartment staking it out, and it's dark. There's been no movement at all, and it's possible he's not home."

Anger surged in his veins. "He *has* to be there. Where the hell else could the fucker be?"

"We'll find him. And we'll find Robyn, too. I think he'll make it easy for us. Care to guess why?"

Chris stared at his partner. Shook his head.

"Come on, my friend. This is Psychopath 101. He had a horrible life, and the people around him were an epic fail at protecting and nurturing him. So he kills people in a way that makes a statement—poison. And now, why is he breaking his routine to take a woman who's not on his agenda?"

Slowly, the truth dawned. It was like a window opening to reveal the sun. "It's a cry for help. He *wants* to be caught."

"*Ding ding!* You've got it."

"That's why he won't kill her," he said, hope flaring. "At least not yet. He wants the confrontation, some sort of final justice. That's what this has all been about."

"It could be he wants to grandstand, but we don't

know for sure," Rainey emphasized. "Robyn is a doctor and an authority figure, so he could have taken her because of that, or simply because she was onto him. Or he could be enraged that Chris survived and is seeking revenge by taking her, or wants to lure him into a confrontation so he can finally kill you."

Chris deflated some. "All true. But I know what my gut is telling me."

Whatever Miller's sick reasoning, he prayed they had some time. He held on to that thought, because they had long hours ahead of them before they could gather enough for a warrant to search Miller's property.

He, Tonio, and the captain spent hours poring over the case files, making sure they had all the details down that they knew so far. Sometime shortly after four in the morning, Dr. Alan Chin arrived early, much to their surprise.

There was a knock on the door, and another officer showed the doctor in before closing it behind him. The doctor was a small Asian man with a kind, open, and honest-looking face. He was also very anxious to share what he knew.

"I was able to get another doctor to come in and cover the last part of my shift for me," he said, glancing around anxiously. In his hand was a sheaf of papers. "I was most distressed by the detective's call, and I want to help however I can."

Chris had learned long ago not to put too much stock in appearances, but his instincts shouted this man was sincere. "We appreciate that very much. Do you have something to share with us, Dr. Chin?"

"Yes. I compiled the names of the staff members who were on duty with me on the dates that Detective Salvatore mentioned." He slid the papers across the table without commenting further. From the intense way he watched them, it was obvious he was waiting for them to reach their own conclusions.

The cop in Chris did a victory dance as he scanned the documents. "Some of these staff members were there when you treated more than one of the victims. But only one nurse was on shift when every single one of them was treated."

"Yes." Chin nodded.

"Do you recall Lee Miller assisting during these cases?"

"Some of them, though it's hard to remember all. We see so many people."

"What is your opinion of Mr. Miller's performance as a nurse?"

Dr. Chin shook his head. "That young man has been on the verge of termination for some time. He's sloppy, as though his head is always somewhere else."

"Why hasn't he been fired?" Chris studied the doctor's expression, which turned disgusted.

"His father was an important man, Detective. Dr. Jonathan Miller was chief of staff many years ago, when Lee was a young boy. Not at Sterling, at the old hospital before Sterling was built. But many of Miller's old cronies opened Sterling and memories are long, if you know what I mean."

"So he was hired and keeps his job because of who his daddy is," Chris summarized.

"Who his daddy *was.*" Chin's tone clearly communicated that the man's demise was no great loss. "I worked under him back then, and the man was an asshole. The kind to find fault with everything and satisfaction in nothing. When he died, I opened a bottle of sake and drank it all in celebration."

Tonio coughed to cover a laugh. "You gave us your professional observation of Lee, but what of your personal opinion?"

Chin thought about that for a long moment. He spoke with a slight shrug. "The boy is a complete enigma. The nurses I work with are close. They talk and gossip constantly. They chatter like magpies, gossip until my ears bleed. They socialize. They smile. Lee Miller does none of those things. Ask anyone and they'll tell you the same."

Chris exchanged a look with Tonio and the captain. Miller was antisocial, which meant working in an atmosphere such as an emergency room had to be sheer torture. He had to have a deeper motive for doing a job he hated.

A futile attempt to please a dead father who could never be satisfied? To show the old man he could succeed?

And to make those who had failed him—such as his authoritative father—pay.

"Dr. Chin," Chris said, "is there anything else you feel is pertinent that you'd like to tell us?"

The doctor hesitated, then gestured to the list. "I realize this may be irrelevant, but something stands out in my mind from when I saw that first man, Charles Adams, in my ER. Mr. Adams came in because he had fractured his wrist in a fall. Lee told me he was glad Mr. Adams would be okay, because the man was his elementary school principal here in Sugarland."

Chris's eyes widened. "You're positive about that?"

"Yes. Because of my exchange with Lee, that particular patient stands out." The doctor shrugged.

"One more question, Doctor," Chris said. "Would someone like Lee typically have access to cyanide?"

Dr. Chin's brows shot up. "No, not typically. It would be very difficult for him to obtain, outside of stealing it. I just don't believe the young man has the kind of clout to get such a substance legitimately."

"What about his father?"

"Jonathan Miller could have obtained anything he wanted," Dr. Chin stated with absolute confidence. "No matter what it might have been. He had connections."

"Anything else?"

"Nothing that comes to mind."

Chris stood and held out his hand. "Thank you for coming and being so open with us, Dr. Chin."

The doctor shook his hand and gave a small smile. "My pleasure to be of assistance. Someone is doing terrible things, and I want him caught, whoever it is. If I can help again, please don't hesitate to call me."

"We'll keep that in mind."

Chris waited until the door had closed firmly behind Dr. Chin before he pounced, practically begging his captain. "We've got Lee tied to every one of the victims. So far, he's the sole common denominator. We've even got his elementary school principal as the first victim, and there could be more who were part of his past we don't know about yet."

"The last part is unverified."

"Not for long," Chris said desperately. "We'll make the connections."

"Yes, but for now it's all circumstantial."

Chris wasn't ready to give up the fight. He was so tired, ready to drop from being awake almost twenty-four hours. And he had much longer to go—they all did. "We've got bodies! We've got Lee in the room with every victim before they died!"

"We need something solid and you know it," Rainey growled. "Dammit, Chris, I'm doing what I can."

Just then, there was a knock on the door. "Come in," Rainey called out, and Jay Stover, one of the techs who worked the scene around Robyn's car, came in holding a cell phone sealed in a clear plastic bag.

"Got something for you guys," Jay began, holding up the bag. "Dr. Lassiter's phone was just under the edge of her car, with the screen smashed. From the casing, we were able to lift a print. Three guesses who the print belongs to."

Chris bolted upright. "Lee Miller?"

"Yep." The man looked pleased with himself. "Seems Miller was an army medic for four years before he came back to town to be a nurse. Fingerprints were on file."

"Yes! Got that bastard," Chris yelled, slamming his hand on the table. "Now can we get the fucking warrant?"

Rainey stood. "Yeah. Now we can get the fucking warrant. I'll call the judge."

The exhaustion vanished and a rush of adrenaline fired through him. There was no way he'd sleep.

Not until the woman he loved was home safe and sound.

Robyn sat huddled on a chair in the far corner of the bedroom. As far away as she could get from the woman's skeleton—which wasn't nearly far enough.

Lee's mother. How totally, unbelievably sick.

How long had she been there? Years, if the condition of the skeleton could be believed. What little skin there was clinging to the bones was mummified, and the clothes were moth-eaten. Her death hadn't happened weeks or even months earlier.

Had Lee lived here with her since her death? Had he killed her?

Questions chased themselves around in her brain, each more terrifying than the last. She couldn't understand what would drive a person to do those things. To live this way. She had heard it said that the inside of your home was a reflection of your soul. If that was true, Lee Miller's soul was a very dark, desolate, twisted place.

It was a place she was desperate to escape. She'd tried the windows, only to find them sealed tight. She'd screamed, pounded on the door, done everything she could think of. Even tried to pick the lock, but it was no use.

She wasn't sure how long she sat there, nerves jumping with fright every time the house creaked or she thought she heard footsteps, her captor moving around. Her eyes were bloodshot and her head hurt from lack of sleep. But there was no way she could've closed her eyes even if she wanted to.

Her agonized thoughts turned to Chris and Maddy. Her lover could take care of himself, and she had no doubt that, as scared as he might be, he was also pissed as hell and would move heaven and earth to find her.

Maddy, however, was probably still asleep and hopefully hadn't yet realized that anything was wrong. But she would, and what would happen then? How would Chris or anyone explain that someone sick had taken her mother? Her little girl would be scared, and she'd need comfort. Robyn knew her friends and Chris's would step up to help, but that wouldn't necessarily reassure Maddy that everything would be all right.

She ached to hold her baby and reassure Maddy. And herself.

Footsteps coming down the hallway made goose bumps break out on her arms. In the back of her mind, she'd been holding out hope that Lee would make himself scarce, staying away until Chris and the other cops found her. A futile hope, she realized, as the keys rattled in the lock and the door opened slowly, with a squeak.

Lee stepped inside, smiling as though they'd just run into each other casually, in a restaurant or somewhere. "Hey, you're awake! Did you have a nice nap?"

"I didn't take a nap," she muttered. *No, I screamed until I'm sure I ripped my vocal cords. Thanks for that.*

"Oh? Well, maybe later. Have you and Mom been having a nice visit?"

She stared at her captor. If he was acting, it was an

Oscar-worthy performance. "No. She's being a bit antisocial today."

That clearly threw him, and he frowned. "Oh. That's not like her at all." He looked to the remains of his mother. "I expect you to treat our guests better than that, Mother. What will the ladies think if it gets around that your hospitality is less than perfect? What will Daddy think?"

"It's quite all right. I'm sure she's . . . tired." He wasn't acting, she was sure. This man's elevator didn't go all the way to the top floor.

"Yeah, probably so." Lee gave a sigh. "We're always tired, Mom and I, putting up with my dad's bullshit night and day."

The doctor in her rose to the fore, her interest piqued. Suddenly she saw Lee as a troubled, psychotic man who'd obviously suffered some sort of breakdown. She was willing to bet he wasn't evil—but had suffered through something evil.

"Tell me about your dad," she encouraged. "What kind of bullshit?"

His expression became grim, dark eyes haunted. "You wouldn't understand."

"Try me."

"He yells at us. Like, all the time. He likes to make Mom cry." The man's lip quivered.

"How?"

"He hits her, calls her names. Like 'worthless bitch,' 'fat cow.' He'll even treat her mean at dinner parties and nobody ever says a word. None of those sons of bitches on the board ever do anything."

And there's his first problem with authority figures. Not just his father, but those who wouldn't stop what was happening to a boy and his mother.

"What else does he do?"

"He hits me with his fists," Lee said in a small voice. "He told me not to tell, but one day she found out."

God, how horrible. "I'm sorry he hurt you, Lee. Can you tell me what happened next, after your mom found out?"

"I wasn't supposed to hear, but I did anyway. Dad screamed at Mom and said if she wasn't so fucking useless he wouldn't have done what he did. She said she was going to tell someone and get him in trouble."

"But she never did?"

Tears filled his eyes and he looked away. "She would've. But he made her sick and she died, real fast."

Horrendous. No child should suffer such atrocities.

"How did he make her sick?" she asked gently. But she had a good idea.

"There was some stuff in his garage. He got some into an eyedropper and put it into her food. He laughed and said, as a doctor, he found it fascinating to watch her meet her end writhing like a hooked fish. How could something so small make her stop breathing?"

He sounded so sad and confused.

"I don't know. But that's why I became a doctor, so I can help people like your mom."

She knew instantly that was the wrong thing to say.

"You can't help me or my mom!" he shouted, jabbing his finger at her. The scared boy was gone, and an angry, delusional adult was in his place.

"I'm sure somebody—"

Crossing the short distance between them quickly, he backhanded her across the face, snapping her head to the side. Tasting blood, she brought her shaking hand to her face and licked her lip. She remained very still, not wanting to set him off further.

"You don't know anything about it," he told her coldly. "Don't pretend you do."

"I'm sorry." Taking another risk, she gestured to the bed. "How is it that she's here, in the house?"

"This is where my dad put her, after he killed her. Then he told all his friends she ran off and left him. He was such a bastard nobody had any reason to doubt that."

"Where's your dad now? Is he retired, or did he move away?"

Lee snorted. "Of course not. He's right where he deserves to be—dead and buried in the local cemetery. I put him there right after I gave him a taste of his own medicine." He shrugged. "Now Mom is at peace, and I have my own apartment. But I visit Mom sometimes."

Robyn thought she was going to be sick.

This whole messed-up family should've been carted away to an asylum years ago. Starting with the father.

If she got out of this alive, it would be a miracle.

Please, Chris. Find me before it's too late.

Chris checked his weapon, secured his bulletproof vest. All around him, the others were doing the same.

In his line of work, there was no such thing as too much precaution. One seemingly average nurse was very possibly a serial killer, and really, there was no such thing as *average* when it came to people.

Armed and ready, he faced Rainey, Tonio, and two uniformed cops Rainey had chosen to go along as backup. Rainey wouldn't accompany them, but they would give him an update when they had Robyn secure and Miller under arrest.

He refused to consider any other outcome.

Outside, they took Tonio's car, and the two uniforms followed. At a time like this, Chris couldn't help but be grateful for his partner's innocuous vehicle. It would sure attract less attention from their suspect than his own flashy Camaro, and for the first time Chris wondered whether there was a method to Tonio's madness.

"Say, is this the only car you own?" he asked, curious.

His partner snorted. "No, man. This is my work vehicle. You think I take this piece of shit out cruisin' when I want to get laid?"

Chris chuckled in spite of the situation. "Why didn't you tell me? All those times I ragged on the grampsmobile, and you never said a word."

"You never asked. You *assumed* I had no cool anywhere in my body."

Huh. Simple as that. He'd never asked. "Sorry. What's your *real* car?"

"1978 Corvette Stingray," Tonio said, unable to hide the pride in his voice.

Chris whistled. "Whoa, that's some serious mojo. How'd you afford that?"

"Bought her cheap, been fixing her up for years as my project car. And she's cheaper than a girlfriend."

Chris laughed at that. "No doubt. Attract the babes with the hot car, then love 'em and leave 'em, eh?"

"You got it."

His humor drained the closer they got to Miller's apartment. The complex was situated in a nice area of town, but not affluent. It featured the pleasant if cookie-cutter buildings and landscaping found everywhere from malls to office complexes.

Chris much preferred his older house with its sucky plumbing. At least it had character.

Dawn was just breaking when they parked one building over from Miller's. The tiredness was still being held at bay by the sheer anxiety pulsing through him. She had to be all right. He couldn't wait to pull her into his arms and watch Miller be led away in cuffs. Or a straitjacket.

"These buildings have only one entry and exit," he pointed out to Tonio as they got out of the car. "The front door."

"Makes it a little easier that he can't flee out a back way."

Shane and Taylor, who'd been staking out the apartment, got out of their vehicle and fell into step with them. The two uniformed cops brought up the rear. One carried the battering ram; kicking in doors with one's foot, even with shoes on, was a great way to break an ankle.

"Yeah." They walked toward the building in question, and Chris frowned. "Something's bothering me about this whole setup. Like how did he get an unwilling victim into his apartment without half the neighbors seeing them?"

"Good point. But it was nighttime. They could've thought she was drunk."

"Maybe. I don't like it, though."

"Let's see what we can find. She could be here."

The whole thing felt off. The hair was prickling on the back of his neck, like this was too easy. Way too simple, even if the crazy bastard wanted to be caught.

At the door, Chris banged on the surface with his fist. "Lee Miller," he shouted. "Sugarland Police. We have a warrant to search your property. Open up."

No response.

"Let's bust it in," Tonio said, then turned to the two uniforms and reached for the battering ram.

Tonio took the tool from the other cop, and Chris grabbed the front end of it. Tonio counted to three; then they swung the heavy ram into the door near the handle with crushing force. The wood began to splinter, and it only took one more solid blow for the door to cave, rocketing inward to bang against the inside wall.

Quickly they passed the battering ram back to one of the other cops, and then Chris took the lead, rushing inside with his weapon drawn.

Nothing but silence met their arrival. The apartment was pristine, almost too much so. There were no throw pillows on the sofa, no framed photographs. No magazines or books lying around, no mail or other papers. Cautiously, he crept toward the kitchen and found the same lack of personality.

Moving down the hallway, Tonio on his heels, Chris checked the rest of the place. The bedroom was similarly bare; the bed had not been slept in last night, if ever. A quick glance revealed just a few items of clothing in the closet. In the bathroom, there was one small container of body wash.

Yeah, he wasn't touching *that* shit with a ten-foot pole.

Frustrated, Chris walked back to the kitchen and yanked open the fridge—not only was it empty, but it wasn't even cold.

"He doesn't fucking live here," Chris groaned, anger mounting. "This is his dummy address. He's screwing with us."

Tonio didn't necessarily agree. "I don't know if he's messing with us so much as he's got this whole separate life that doesn't belong here. Maybe this apartment was his attempt to be normal, you know?"

"Could be. Does it matter? Miller and Robyn aren't here, and neither is any of the evidence we need," he ground out. "Shit!"

"We'll regroup." His partner looked tired, but determined. "He's got another bolt-hole. We won't stop until we find out where it is."

"Yeah." He blew out a breath, his body sagging now that the adrenaline rush had passed. "Damn, I've got to call Daisy. She's been watching Maddy, and I don't even know if the sitter is coming, or if she's staying. Is this a school day? Who'll take her? I can't screw up the very first time Robyn really needs me to take care of her daughter—"

"Chris, calm down, man." Tonio eyed him with concern. "Take a deep breath. You said Daisy's with the little girl?"

"Yes." He inhaled, then let the air out slowly, trying to calm himself.

"Then the kid is fine. Daisy works with juveniles all the time, and she loves them. What's more, Daisy is a cop, too, and she knows the score when it comes to being tied up at work. Maddy's in good hands."

"That's true," Shane put in, glancing around the living room. "They're fine."

"You're right. I'm just worried about the munchkin." He swiped a hand down his face. "She's such a good kid, Tonio. A ray of light, just like her mom. She doesn't deserve to have anything bad happen, not after all she's been through."

Chris's heart hurt thinking about the ragged hole Greg's suicide had left in Robyn and Maddy's lives. They had come through the grief, but how would Maddy survive losing her mother?

"Go home, get some rest," Tonio urged. "We'll find Robyn, and you won't be any good to her if you're dead on your feet."

He shook his head and started out the door, his friends trailing behind. "I can't sleep. Not yet, and not until she's home safe and sound. There's no reason why you can't get some shut-eye, though. I'll keep working on getting a second address, and I'll call you when we get a hit."

Tonio gave a humorless laugh. "You're shitting me, right? You're my partner, man. Where you go, I go. We're in this together, until the end."

Relief swamped him, and gratitude. How could he have ever doubted Tonio would be a good partner? He wouldn't make that mistake again. "Thanks. That means a lot."

The two uniforms took care of letting the building's manager know about the broken door, while Tonio drove them back to the station. Shane and Taylor followed. When they arrived, he learned that Rainey had gone home for a while and Chris phoned to let him know things hadn't gone as planned.

When the call was finished, he slumped over the conference table, brain scrambling to think where to start next.

Suddenly, he straightened. "Shea got Miller's social security number from his records. If he owns any other property, his social will be tied to it, right?"

"Probably, because of the taxes." Tonio grinned. "And I think I know somebody at the county clerk's office who can get her hands on that tidbit of information. She owes me."

"I'm not even going to ask."

"You don't want to know." Scrolling through his contacts, Tonio finally found the one he wanted and punched the contact button. After a few seconds, the call was answered and he poured on the charm. "Hey, gorgeous. How's it shakin'?" Pause. "Yeah, I enjoyed that, too. I'm up for a repeat if you are."

Chris sighed and did his best to tune out his friend's attempt to wheedle information out of his current bed buddy. It appeared the guy's lifestyle wasn't as stale and boring as Chris had previously believed. Ignorance really was bliss sometimes.

After a couple of minutes of playing verbal footsie, his partner hung up the phone, his expression victorious. "Score. She's going to poke around the county records and see what she can turn up on Lee Miller."

"I hope she finds something. Anything. I can't take much more of this."

"She will. Just a little longer, and we'll have something to go on. I'm sure of it."

The four of them talked quietly, waiting for the important call. Chris tried to distract himself listening to their bull as they razzed each other about this and that, but he couldn't focus on anything but getting Robyn back.

He loved her so much, he ached. He needed her back in his arms, in his bed.

Conversation came to an abrupt halt as Tonio's cell phone rang. The man answered, then asked for the address and started writing it on his notepad. When he was done with the call, he nodded to them and gestured to the address he'd written.

"Miller owns some property outside of town, an old house that sits on a two-acre lot. The records show the place used to belong to his parents, then apparently passed to him after his father died. We ready to do this?"

"I've been ready," Chris said, pushing to his feet. "I want to bury that fucker."

Shane threw in some caution. "Remember, that's what he wants as well. We can't play into his hands if we can help it."

"I know, but part of me wants to, and save the taxpayers a lot of money." At the looks his friends exchanged, Chris held up a hand. "Don't worry. I'm solid. I promise not to go Rambo on his ass unless I don't have a choice."

"Good enough," Shane said.

A bit more waiting was involved as Rainey called the

judge again, revising the warrant to include the second property. With that taken care of, they were set.

Chris headed for the door. "Let's go."

Tonio put the address into his GPS and they were on their way. This time the four detectives rode together, the same two uniforms following again in their patrol car. When they reached the turn that led into a rural area with the houses spread apart every few acres, Chris began to tense. This was it. Miller wanted them here, for this. One way or another, the ordeal would be over soon.

At last the address came into view, and Tonio slowed, but didn't stop. This allowed them to get a good look at the property as they went past.

"Jesus, look at that big house. It used to be quite a showplace," Chris remarked. "He's let it go totally to ruin."

His partner snorted. "If what we suspect about his home life growing up is as bad as Dr. Chin indicated, or even worse, then it makes perfect sense that he'd allow his father's symbol of wealth to rot. The place is as broken and hopeless as Miller himself."

From the backseat, Taylor chimed in. "Damn, you should be an FBI profiler or some shit."

"Nah. The stress would suck."

"True that," Taylor agreed.

Tonio drove down the road to the next driveway, then turned around and went back to the house. Miller knew they were coming, but his partner still parked out on the road behind cover of a stand of trees instead of pulling down the driveway. Every bit of surprise they could hold on to until the last minute, they'd take.

Quietly, they exited the vehicle and made their way to the house. Chris and Tonio took the front, Shane and Taylor the back in case he tried to escape. The two uniforms passed over the battering ram and positioned themselves on either side of the house, which was now virtually surrounded.

Holding the ram, Chris repeated the action he'd taken at the apartment earlier. He had to follow procedure, though it made him burn with anger. Banging on the door, he yelled:

"Lee Miller, this is the Sugarland Police! Open up—we have a warrant!" He waited the space of about three heartbeats before he hefted the tool. "Fuck this."

And he splintered the bastard's front door into a million pieces.

14

Robyn's head was nodding.

Despite her best efforts not to fall asleep, the constant vigil, remaining alert for the sounds of Lee moving about, was taking its toll. But she didn't want to be surprised by his return.

In fact, she'd spent hours fashioning a little surprise of her own.

After the weird conversation with Lee the previous night, he'd disappeared and mostly left her alone. She could hear him pacing, sometimes ranting to a person she suspected wasn't really there. But he kept to himself, thank God for small favors.

Well, except to offer her breakfast, which she refused. A human could live for weeks without food. Water was a different matter, and she had accepted a sealed bottle with some trepidation. She had taken a sip and thanked him warily, but she was still trying to be alert to any possible side effects. As she drank, he'd beamed at her as though she'd given him a gold star. She couldn't fathom how his messed-up brain worked.

When he left, she spent long moments examining the bottle itself. She considered dumping the water and trying to shape the bottle into a sharp weapon, but the plastic was too flimsy. She needed something sturdier. Besides, if he asked for the bottle back to throw away, she'd be in trouble.

Next she forced herself from the corner and prowled around the bedroom as silently as possible. The house was old, and she didn't need her footsteps giving her away. The room was a sad little time capsule filled with bric-a-brac she suspected had belonged to his mother. Whom Robyn studiously avoided looking at.

It was almost a shrine. On the antique dresser were lace doilies, an old figurine of a ballerina, a small doll, and a gorgeous jewelry box. Robyn wondered whether this stuff had belonged to one of Lee's grandmothers, since his mother wasn't nearly old enough to have used these things when they were brand-new.

She was drawn to the jewelry box, so she walked over and opened the lid. Idly, she began to sift through a string of pearls, brooches, clip-on earrings, and other trinkets ladies wore long ago. Briefly, she considered a brooch as a possible weapon. Picking one up, she turned it over, examining it from all angles. It wouldn't do. The edges weren't sharp enough and the pin was too small to do any damage.

Finished examining the box, she went on to the small writing desk against an opposite wall near where she'd been huddled. The desk was small and plain, and other than some stationery, pens, paper clips, and such, it didn't reveal much. Until she dug toward the back of the middle drawer . . .

And found an ornate letter opener.

Her pulse sped up as she stared at the slim silver object with its pretty, swirly handle. This might be her savior. Footsteps sounded from down the hallway, closing in fast, and she quickly pocketed the opener. Since it was slippery, she pointed it down and stuck the sharp end through the seam of her pants pocket to keep it in place.

And none too soon. The door was flung open and Lee hurried inside, stopping when he saw her away from the corner.

"What are you doing?" His eyes narrowed.

"Your mom has some lovely things," she said calmly, gesturing to the dresser. "Did they belong to *her* mother?"

"Yeah," he snapped, moving toward her. "We don't have time to talk about that. We've got company."

"Who—?"

But her question was aborted as he grabbed her arm and dragged her from the room and down the hallway. Stumbling to keep up, she managed the stairs without falling. At the bottom he kept going, pulling her into the middle of the living room. Spinning her to face the front door, he stood behind her and hooked his left arm around her neck in a tight hold. With his right, he pressed something sharp into her side. A knife? Oh God.

"What are we doing?" She couldn't keep the fear from her voice.

"They're here," he said, sounding excited. "Are you ready?"

"Ready for what?" The police? She fervently hoped so. Terror threatened to steal all rational thought, and she held on by a thread. Carefully, she started to inch her fingers into her front pocket.

Just then, a loud banging sounded on the front door. And it was followed by a very welcome voice.

"Lee Miller, this is the Sugarland Police! Open up—we have a warrant!"

She didn't have time to celebrate. There was a murmur from the other side of the door, and then something huge slammed against the wood. The old door exploded inward, no match for whatever tool they'd use to break it down. It banged against the opposite wall and Chris rushed in, gun drawn on her captor, followed by three other detectives who were also armed and ready to shoot.

Briefly, Chris's eyes met hers, but revealed nothing. No indication of how to handle this situation. So she did the only thing she could—watched and waited. And trusted her lover.

"Drop the knife, Lee," Chris said in a firm, even voice.

"I can't do that."

"Yes, you can. Put it down and we'll walk out of here, get you some help."

His laugh was maniacal. "Help? That's rich! Where were you when I needed help before, huh? When Daddy was terrorizing me, beating up Mom for more entertainment, and then having cocktails with his buddies like nothing happened? Where were you then?"

"I wasn't around then, Lee."

"Lying cop!" he yelled. "I saw you take my dad's

money and just walk away! I saw that smirk on your face. He bought you, and you were my last hope!"

Chris's eyes widened. "No, Lee. That was another cop, not me. I'm not much older than you are. I was in grade school, just like you. I couldn't have done anything back then, but I can help now. I'll get—"

"It's too little, too late! Don't you see?"

"Not true." Chris's body was tense, but it was obvious he was trying to convey sincerity. "People believe you now. You've showed them how it was. With a good lawyer explaining those extenuating circumstances, you can get a lighter sentence. Maybe even go to a hospital instead of prison. You could have a new life."

"Bullshit!" The point of the knife dug deeper into her side. "I knew a long time ago there would never be any help for me. Everybody failed me. Nobody cared. That's why I had to do what I did, to get people out there to understand how fake they are! The people who are supposed to save kids from monsters are fake and they don't give a shit!"

He was losing it. The sting in her side became a burning sensation, and warmth trickled down her skin. This was what Lee wanted. She was his sacrificial lamb, his way to commit suicide by cop.

Lee wanted to die. But, by God, she wasn't going to go with him.

Chris's gaze strayed to hers again, then dipped for a second to the hand she was still inching into her pocket.

With a slight smile, she mouthed, *I love you.* And braced herself to end this thing.

* * *

Sweat rolled down Chris's spine.

Miller was done, had given up. The truth was in his dead eyes, the rage in his tone. The bitter defeat.

Lee no longer wanted help; he wanted peace. In the abused man's mind, there was only one way to achieve that. But Chris wasn't going to allow it to go down on Lee's terms.

Chris tried changing tactics. "You were smart, hiding the poison in the shampoo bottles. We never figured out how you got the cyanide, though."

The man's stance eased some. "The army. Made all kinds of contacts in the military. Helps to know people who can get you stuff under the table."

"I'll bet. Yeah, you were the smart one all around. Nobody had a clue for a long time. Once you're treated, you can turn your life around. Put that intelligence to use reaching out to people like you, who've been through so much."

For a few seconds, Lee seemed to consider the idea. Then he sneered. "I know what you're trying to do and it's not going to work. It's lip service, just like I've gotten my whole life. And you know what? I'm tired of fighting, tired of everything."

"It's not lip service," Chris said, easing closer. "If you'd just—"

"Sorry, Detective. This ends now."

Before Chris could blink, Lee drove his right arm forward. Robyn cried out and Chris had a split second to realize Lee had stabbed her before she jerked a long, silver blade from her pants pocket, drew her arm back, and thrust it into his thigh as deep as possible.

With a roar, Lee let go of Robyn and she fell.

"Drop the knife!" Chris shouted.

The man had to be in agony, but that didn't stop him from straightening and rushing at Chris, knife raised to attack. He had no choice but to fire. Rapidly, he pulled the trigger, feeling no satisfaction as the man jerked and red bloomed on his shoulder. Lee staggered backward and sprawled on the floor, moaning.

Tonio bounded past Chris to kick the knife away from their suspect and make sure he was subdued. Chris's sole attention was on Robyn as he rushed to her side and fell to his knees, studying her side.

Red was staining her blouse and white doctor's coat and was starting to pool on the floor. She was staring up at him with scared blue eyes, panting, in obvious pain.

"Chris," she whispered.

"Shh. You're going to be okay, sweetheart."

Shane appeared beside him. "Taylor's calling the paramedics."

He struggled to keep the tremor out of his voice and his hands as he stroked her face. "You hear that? Help is coming. You're going to be fine."

"This shit hurts." She attempted a smile, but it didn't quite form.

"I know, baby." He took one of her hands in both of his. "Just focus on me, okay? Listen to my voice. I know Maddy is going to be so happy to have her mom back."

"Maddy! Where . . . ?" Her lids began to droop.

Fear surged into his throat. "Daisy's been taking care of her when Rachel's not there. I'm not sure what they've told her but we'll deal with that when— Robyn? Baby, stay with me," he begged.

But her eyes drifted closed despite his pleas. Tears stung his eyes and he kept talking, probably not even making sense, hoping she could hear. Finally the paramedics arrived, and he was forced to move aside.

"I love you," he told her. "Stay with me."

Shane stood next to him with a hand on his shoulder, squeezing in support. "She'll be fine. These guys are the best and they'll take good care of her."

The lump in his throat made speech impossible, so he simply watched, knowing now how helpless she must have felt when he had come into her ER poisoned. And then she had endured the added stress of treating him. He had a whole new respect for her.

Activity on the other side of the room caught his attention. He hadn't realized another team had arrived to work on Lee's shoulder wound. Searching his soul, he knew he didn't want the man to die, in spite of what he had done. Inside he was still a little boy who'd been tortured behind his mind's capacity to cope.

He never had the loving family unit Maddy did, and never would.

Taylor strode up to him and Shane. "We've got all the evidence we need. The office off the living room is full of the victims' profiles—all the stuff we had gathered on them and more. One of the uniforms just told me the garage is full of poison. Like enough to gas a city block if the house ever caught fire and burned."

That was it. They had him.

The medics loaded Robyn, and almost refused to let

Chris ride. The city was cracking down on riders, but the badge and gun probably helped change their minds. He kept a watchful eye on her during the trip, terror gripping him when her blood pressure started to take a dive. Like a champ, she held on until they got to Sterling and she was rushed into surgery.

At loose ends, Chris prowled the ER, pacing every square inch. Then he expanded his walk to include the entire lower level. Like a tiger in a cage he walked, feeling trapped by circumstances out of his control. He wanted to fix her and he couldn't. That job belonged to someone else, and the wait was maddening.

When he noted he'd been gone almost two hours, he wasted no time getting back to the ER in case anyone came out to talk to him. But there was only Shane, who'd come to sit with his cousin while the others were wrapping up the crime scene.

"You're not going to believe this." Shane took a seat beside him, expression grim.

"At this point? Try me."

"There was a skeleton upstairs in one of the bedrooms. From the clothing and condition of the body, the forensics guys are saying it could be Lee's mother."

Chris blinked at him. "Say what?"

"Yep. She'd been dead for years, nothing left but bone and a bit of hair and skin. Isn't that goddamn creepy as hell?"

"Jesus. Is Lee talking? Did he kill the woman, whoever she is?"

Shane sighed. "I'm sure he will, once his public defender gets his head out of his ass. Lee's got nothing to lose and everything to gain by telling the truth at this point. He really *is* insane, unlike most killers. I did manage to get one tidbit before he lawyered up."

"What's that?"

"Lee claims he killed his father, that it wasn't a natural death as everyone thought. He says doing in dear old Dad was his first taste of revenge."

"If his father really did all the stuff Lee claims, then I'm not sorry to hear that. Just sorry he didn't stop there."

"Yeah."

Chris was silent a moment. Worry for Robyn bombarded him anew, and he clasped his hands tightly. "I love her, cuz."

"I know you do," he said. "You guys are lucky you found each other. And Maddy is a doll, too."

He gave a watery laugh. "Isn't she? I never thought I'd have an instant family, a woman and a first grader. But you know, I wouldn't trade them for anything." He paused. "She has to be okay."

"She will be."

His cousin seemed so sure, and he clung to that. Another half hour passed before the double doors opened and a familiar man spotted them and walked purposefully over. Dr. Alan Chin stopped in front of them, wearing a serene expression.

"Detectives," he said in greeting. "I assume you're waiting on news of Dr. Lassiter's condition?"

Chris stood and nodded. "Please."

"I'm happy to say she's come through surgery just fine."

"Thank God," he rasped. "What was the damage? Anything permanent?"

"No. The wound was a bit deep, but clean. No major organs were punctured or torn, so we had the best possible scenario to work with. She lost a lot of blood, so we gave her more, sewed her up, and she rallied nicely."

Grabbing the doctor's hand, he shook it. "Thank you so much. When can I see her?"

"After she leaves recovery and is settled into a room. About forty-five minutes to an hour." The man smiled. "Dr. Lassiter will be our guest for a couple of days at least, and I know she won't be happy. You'll keep her company, I trust."

"You bet your ass I will." He laughed, the darkness gradually lifting from his soul. It would take some time to forget the sight of Lee shoving a blade into the woman he loved, but he'd get there.

"She'll probably sleep until tomorrow," the doctor said. "I'll be by later to check on her."

"Thank you again."

He waved a hand. "It's what I do."

Then he was gone. Chris turned to Shane. "Tell Daisy and Maddy I'll be home in a little while. I want to talk to Maddy and explain what's going on as best I can without scaring her too much."

"Good idea. What will you say?"

"I don't know yet. I don't want to lie, but I'm thinking that keeping the truth simple is best."

"I agree."

They parted ways and Chris waited impatiently until a nurse he didn't recognize came to get him. She told him Robyn's room number on the sixth floor and pointed him toward the elevators.

His knees were shaking as he entered her room, and he had some idea why. If the knife had been higher or lower, in a different spot, the wound could have been lethal. He could've lost her.

Pulling up a chair, he sat at her side and held her hand. Her skin was too cold and he rubbed gently, careful not to disturb her IV. Her beautiful face was waxen, and he saw a bruise on her cheek he hadn't noticed before. The idea that Lee had hit her made his blood boil. Nobody was ever going to get the chance to lay a hand on her again. He'd keep her under lock and key if he had to.

He drank in her long lashes, arched brows. The way her auburn hair tumbled around her face. She looked vulnerable now, but she was the strongest woman he knew. Too many times in her life, she was forced to be brave. To take it on the chin and keep going.

He would be brave for her, and let her lean on him for the rest of her life. If she would have him.

Not so brave right this second, however, he bent his head and let the tears come. There was nobody to see the release of the terror that had held him in its grip, kept him awake for two days straight, and left him dead on his feet. If anyone did happen to see, he didn't care.

So he bawled like a baby, until the darkness and fear were cleansed.

And all that was left was love.

Maddy met Chris at the door when he walked into the house that evening, Daisy and Shane hovering close behind.

"Chris! Where's Mommy? She didn't come home with you?" Launching herself into his arms, she wrapped him in a hug.

"No, she didn't, sweet pea." Lifting her up, he hugged her fiercely before setting her on her feet again. Then he took her hand and led her into the living room, to the sofa. "Sit with me for a few minutes?"

They sat and she scooted close, so he turned slightly so he could look into her face. His friends sat, too, ready to interject if needed. Taking a deep breath, he began. "You know how your mom takes care of sick people and makes them well?"

"Uh-huh. She takes their temp-ra-ture and gives them medicine."

"Right." He ruffled her hair. "Well, it's your mom who doesn't feel well this time, so she's in the hospital, where some of the doctors are taking care of *her* now."

"She's in the hospital?" Her little brows furrowed.

"Yes, just for a few days."

"Is she—is she gonna die?"

"Absolutely not. I *promise* you."

"She's going to come home?"

Chris made sure to smile broadly. "You bet! In two or three days, I'm going to pick her up and bring her home. Then we'll have to give her lots of TLC until she can walk around better."

"Why?"

"Because she's going to have some stitches right here." Lifting his shirt a bit, he pointed to the spot on his side.

"I had stitches on my arm one time!" she exclaimed. "And I didn't cry."

"Good for you! Well, she didn't cry, either, so we'll have to make her something special, like chocolate chip cookies."

"Yeah. She likes those." Maddy seemed pleased at the idea of rewarding her mom for being brave.

"Do you have any questions?" *Please don't ask how and why the stitches happened. I don't want to lie.*

"Can I go see her?"

"I don't know if they'll let you in, munchkin."

Her anxiety returned. "But I want to see Mommy! I want to help her get better."

"You will," he assured her. "I promise she's going to be fine. Tell you what, though. I'll ask tomorrow and maybe they'll let you in for just a bit, okay?"

"Okay. But I miss Mommy." She pouted adorably.

"Me, too. She'll be home before we know it. In the meantime, I'll try to be a good dad, okay? I think I'm getting the hang of it." He held his breath, wondering how she'd react.

Maddy smiled at him. "Yep. Hey, you ready to eat dinner? Daisy cooked again—she cooks good."

"Is that why the house smells so great? I'm starved."

"Me, too!" With that, she bounded off the sofa and bolted for the dining room.

He looked to his cousin and Daisy, vowing not to get too emotional. "You guys are awesome. Thanks for everything."

"We know we're fabulous," Daisy said with a grin.

Standing, he strode across the room and pulled her into a hug, then Shane, too. It was a mostly happy group who sat at the table and ate chicken pot pie. One of their number was missing, but the situation would be put to rights soon. Just not soon enough for his liking.

Once the kitchen was clean, Shane and Daisy left, promising to come by in a couple of days, after Robyn was home. Chris allowed Maddy to watch some TV, and then ran her bath and made her turn off the program. She complained some, but did as she was told, splashing until she pruned and he had to make her get out again. Kids. Who could figure them out?

He tucked her into bed that night and read her a story, loving how she scooted close and paid rapt attention to the tale of a brave knight saving his lady from a dragon.

When the story was done, he laid the book on the nightstand and turned out the light. "Bedtime, munchkin."

"My daddy always said that to me," she told him sleepily.

A pang shot through his heart. "He did?"

"Uh-huh. But he called me 'pumpkin.' He read me a story and said, 'Bedtime, pumpkin.'" She yawned. "He read the stories good. But he never smiled and laughed like you do."

God help him, he had no idea what to say. What came out was, "From now on, we're going to smile and laugh all the time. You, me, *and* your mom."

She grinned up at him. Then she said shyly, "Can I call you Daddy?"

If ever there was a time in a man's life when he suddenly knew the purpose of his entire existence, for Chris, it was *that* moment. Somehow speaking past the huge lump in his throat, he managed to answer. "I'd love that very much, if it's okay with your mom. And if it's fine with her, can I tell people you're my daughter?"

"Yep! That's what daddies do."

Indeed they did. Heart overflowing, he gave her a hug, kissed her head. "Good night, baby girl."

"'Night."

He lasted until he made it to his and Robyn's bedroom before he gave in and cried for the second time that day.

From sheer joy.

This was the life.

Robyn knew the pampering had to come to an end, but after the pain had become manageable, she'd enjoyed the attention from Chris and Maddy. Yeah, she'd shamelessly milked it for all it was worth. They didn't seem to mind, though.

From her lounge chair on the deck, she watched the two people she loved most running around the yard like a couple of wild banshees as they played tag, their new yellow Lab puppy, Rocky, yapping and throwing himself into the game. Maddy had gotten her way on the new family member with a sweet pout at Chris and a bat of her eyelashes.

Shouts and squeals drifted across to where she sat, and she smiled. Chris was funny, trying to pretend he wasn't fast enough to outrun Maddy and the pup, and they were both loving it.

After she "tagged" Chris, he rolled on the grass and

she leaped on him, tickling. She managed a good dig in his ribs and he let out a loud "Ahh!"

For several more minutes they played, and then Chris stood and brushed the grass off them both. Taking her hand, he led her to the deck and up the steps.

"Hey, beautiful," he said cheerfully, coming over and leaning down to give her a solid kiss. "How are you feeling?"

"Good, just like I was when you asked thirty minutes ago." She ran her fingers through his brown-gold hair.

"Can't blame me for worrying."

"You will whether I want you to or not," she teased.

"True. Say, Maddy and I think it's time to start the grill. Ready for some hot dogs?"

"Yes, I'm starving," she said, stomach rumbling.

"It's a plan. Can't have my girls go hungry." He turned to Maddy. "Would you do me a big favor and go get the weenies and the buns while I start the grill?"

"Yes, sir!" She ran off to do as asked, the puppy hot on her heels.

Smiling, he shook his head. "I wish I could bottle and sell that energy."

"Same here. Some days I'm not sure whether watching her makes me feel young or old," she joked.

"Young, because you *are*." Ignoring her snort, Chris went about lighting the gas grill. In a few seconds the flame was dancing, and he closed the lid to let the inside get hot.

Maddy came back with the weenies and buns, and had even thought to bring a plate for the cooked hot dogs.

Chris praised her good thinking, and she puffed out her little chest, proud to have pleased him.

Robyn was fascinated seeing them interact. Anyone who didn't already know she wasn't his biologically would never guess, except for their slightly different coloring. They were easy around each other, and got along well. He took a real interest in what she had to say, and he listened. They had fun and laughed a lot.

But he wasn't afraid to discipline her when needed, though it wasn't necessary very often, and he never exacted a punishment without discussing it with Robyn first. He was well aware he was new, still establishing his authority, and he was deeply respectful of Robyn's wishes where Maddy was concerned.

In short, the man was a dream come true on every single front.

Soon the weenies were cooking and the delicious aroma filled the air. They might not be the most nutritious things ever, but hot dogs were normal and fun, and God knows they needed plenty of both in their lives right now.

Her two angels fixed the patio table with paper plates, napkins, chips, chili, cheese, relish, and onions. Maddy fetched the three of them bottled water, and Chris put the dogs on the plate, and they were ready to eat.

The meal was nice, the company even better. Robyn couldn't remember when she'd been happier in her life. They just fit together, birds in a nest.

They talked about all sorts of things, like Maddy's school work, happenings at the police department, Shane and his family. The one subject they didn't broach in front of Maddy was Lee Miller. She shuddered when she recalled Chris telling her that Lee had confessed to following Chris around. That Lee had been the man who'd spoken to Maddy in the woods that day. He was truly insane. There was a possibility that his psychiatric evaluation would result in his being rendered unfit to stand trial. In this case, Robyn knew being sent to a facility where the man could undergo treatment was the appropriate measure.

Whether the judge would agree, time would tell.

"Any change with Clay Montana?" Chris asked.

"No," she said sadly. "We're holding out hope he'll wake up, but it's far from certain."

"That's just awful."

"Yes, it is." She paused. "On a lighter note, Daisy told me Drew is seeing someone."

His brows raised. "Really? Who?"

"That's the mysterious part—he won't say." She paused for dramatic effect. "But he and Blake are spending an awful lot of time together. Daisy said she and Shane haven't seen a girl around at all."

"Oh, wow. Blake's nineteen, and Drew's seventeen. So that makes Drew jailbait, at least for a few more months."

"That could be why they're keeping it hush-hush. Well, that and the question of Drew coming out . . ."

"Coming out of where?" Maddy chirped, not understanding the gist of the conversation.

"Um, that's a talk for another day, sweet pea," Robyn said, then looked at Chris again. "Anyway, Daisy also said it's just speculation on her and Shane's part at this point, and asked us to keep it in the family for now, so to speak."

"Did she sound like they would be upset about it, if it turns out to be true? 'Cause I've got to tell you, it doesn't sound like my cousin to judge." He seemed really concerned on Drew's behalf.

"No," she assured him. "Just worried about Drew being able to handle it with his peers. Especially with Drew's deceased father being a super-macho NFL legend."

"That could be tough. But if it's true, I know he'll be fine. He's got a great support system."

"Yeah."

Chris stretched and sat back in his chair. With a smile at Maddy, he said, "Is it time?"

"Yes!" the little girl shouted, jumping up from her seat. "Finally!"

"Time for what?" Robyn studied the two of them, confused.

"I'll help Maddy. Be right back."

Her daughter had already raced inside, and Chris followed. In a couple of minutes, they were back, Maddy carefully holding a big glass vase of beautiful spring flowers mixed with red roses.

"Oh my! Are those for me?"

"They most certainly are," Chris said, hovering in case Maddy slipped or started to drop them.

"They're so gorgeous!" She inhaled, reveling in the fragrant aroma as Maddy set them on the table. "What did I do to deserve these?"

"Are you kidding? Maddy and I thought you deserved something extra special after all the stress you've been under. Flowers seemed just the thing."

"Thank you, guys. They're so perfect."

She fussed over them a bit more and noticed that they were standing in front of her, not moving, studying her as though they knew something she didn't. They were wearing broad smiles, the kind that made them look like they were up to something. Or knew something she didn't.

"There's a *card*," Maddy stressed, pointing to the plastic stand with the small square on it. "Open it!"

"Oh, sorry."

Robyn was reaching for the card when she spotted the red ribbon tied to the top of the plastic stand. Her gaze followed the ribbon downward, but it disappeared into the greenery. Curious, she pulled the ribbon up. And she was stunned by what was dangling from the end of it.

There, tied to the other end of the ribbon, was a beautiful diamond ring. It had a marquise diamond in the center and a few smaller ones scattered around it.

"Oh my God," she whispered. All she could do was stare, dividing her attention between the ring, Chris, and Maddy. "Is this what it looks like?"

Instead of answering, Chris carefully untied the ring, palming it. Then he dropped to one knee right there on the patio, with Maddy for a witness.

"Robyn, I knew from the moment I saw you that you were the woman for me. I knew that *here* was the smart, beautiful lady that I wanted in my life forever. You've completed my heart and soul. You *and* Maddy."

As he paused, she put her hand over her mouth, happiness filling every part of her.

"I love you both. I want to call you my wife, and Maddy my daughter—which is fine by Maddy, by the way." The little girl chimed an agreement. "What I'm trying to say is, would you marry me?"

"Say yes, say yes," Maddy chanted, bouncing up and down.

There was no other answer to give. Reaching out, she drew him in for a fierce hug and kiss. "Yes, yes, I'll marry you. I love you so much."

Their kiss wasn't quite as steamy as she'd have liked it to be, considering their rapt audience, but every ounce of emotion was conveyed between them.

Drawing back, Chris took her hand and reverently slid the ring onto her finger. Then Maddy cheered and a group hug ensued, and promises of ice cream all around.

"So I thought I would sell my house and move in with you guys," Chris said between bites of ice cream. "Makes more sense than uprooting Maddy. She's had enough of that in her short life. Right, munchkin?"

"Uh-huh." She was more focused on her treat now that the main event was over.

"That sounds great. You're here now more than you are at your own house anyway. Especially since you've been taking care of me."

He'd put on a show of staying in the guest room—even if he didn't stay there for long after Maddy was out for the count. Robyn thought it was funny, two adults sneaking around like teenagers.

The evening was wonderful, full of laughter. Joy. Later, after Maddy was long in bed, Robyn and Chris snuggled on the sofa surrounded by lit candles. Soft music was playing and they were drinking each other in, savoring the warm closeness. It was hard for her to believe she would have this sexy, kind man as hers for the rest of her life. But she'd have forever to get used to it.

"If it was any other couple, I'd say the boyfriend would be taking a chance to let the child in on the proposal."

His chest rumbled in a smoky laugh under her ear. "I don't want to sound arrogant, but I wouldn't have done it if I thought there was a chance you'd say no. I wouldn't hurt Maddy that way."

His first thought was for her—their—daughter. This was a big part of the reason to love him for eternity.

"I know you wouldn't. I thought that was very classy of you to let her be a part of it."

"Hey, she'll always be a part of anything concerning our family."

"Well, not a part of *everything*."

Turning in his arms, she began to nuzzle his neck. Nip and lick at the skin at his throat, hopefully driving him crazy.

"Point taken," he moaned, tilting his head to give her better access.

One of her hands slid between his legs, palming the crotch of his soft sleep pants. Well, soft except for the steely rod underneath begging for attention. Apparently he couldn't take much teasing tonight, because he stood and gently scooped her into his arms, carrying her to their bedroom.

Theirs. She loved that.

Chris took his time undressing her. Pushing her onto

the bed and making sweet love to her. He was careful, not wanting to hurt the tender area around the scar, even though the wound had healed.

Parting her thighs, he pushed inside of her, keeping his weight from pressing down too hard. He moved with exquisite slowness, stroking the flames higher with every thrust.

All too soon, they were shattering together. Coming down to earth.

Then he wrapped her into his arms, making sure she was lying on her left side, and pulled her head onto his chest.

"I love you, my sexy detective."

"I love you, my smart and gorgeous doc."

She raised her head and kissed him deeply, then relaxed into him again and started to drift off to sleep.

Please be happy for me, Greg. Wherever you are.

Just before she went under, she could have sworn she heard him reply, *I am, honey. So happy for you. Time to let me go.*

And so she did, her soul finally free to love a man who would cherish her, keep her safe.

For the rest of their lives.

Turn the page for a special preview of
the next book in the Sugarland Blue Series,

On the Run

Coming from Signet Eclipse in April 2015.

The stench reached his consciousness first.

Then the pain. All over, racking agony, which proved he wasn't dead yet, though he didn't have a clue how that could be.

Awareness of being trapped came next. Buried. But not in the dirt. As he tried to move, various items surrounding him shifted and rolled away. With his fingertips he felt . . . cans. Paper. Slime. Old food? Cold knowledge gripped him, turned his blood to ice.

After the bastards were finished with me, they threw me out with the garbage. Literally.

Move, Salvatore. Move or you're dead.

Using his hand, he sought the air. Pushed and clawed, twisting his body in the stinking refuse. The weight on top of him was heavy but not crushing. They'd meant to hide his body, completely confident he wouldn't awaken, or make it out even if he had. He tried not to think they might have been right.

At last, fresh air. But as he broke through the pile, the heap sloped downward sharply and he was tumbling sideways. For several feet he fell, being jabbed and poked by sharp edges until he landed in the dirt at the bottom, the wind knocked out of him. Breathing was almost impossible, his lungs burning. He was hurt inside and out.

His eyes opened to slits, and he tried to peer into the darkness. All he could make out was a sea of garbage. No moon or stars. Worse, little hope.

They'd thrown him into the dump miles outside the city, where nobody in their right mind would venture. *Don't give up.*

Drawing his legs under him, he pushed upward. His legs were like rubber, his strength almost nonexistent. He made it halfway to a standing position before crashing back to the ground with a hoarse cry. God, the pain. His entire body felt hot and cold by turns, and swollen like a balloon. Any second, he would split and spill onto the ground like the plastic bags all around him vomiting their guts. His skin and clothing were wet, too, from head to toe.

He knew it wasn't all from the slime of the trash.

Shaking, Tonio crawled forward on his belly, inch by inch. Time lost meaning. An hour or three might have passed, though he didn't think it had been so long—he would have already been dead.

Wetness ran down his forehead, down the bridge of his nose. Gradually, he grew cold. So cold he knew he'd never get warm again. What was he doing? Why had he been abandoned in this godforsaken place? Too much blood loss. Confusion. He tried to remember, couldn't. Knew it was the beginning of the end.

Anthony. I'm Anthony Salvatore, and I'm a cop. Have to get out of here, get help. Let them know—what?

Her name whispered through his mind like a promise.

Or a nightmare. He didn't know which, and now he might never.

Angel.

Have to let Chris, somebody, know about Angel. Because if I fail . . .

Sister or not, Rab would kill her. He would show her no mercy, and she would end up here, in a grave next to Tonio. No matter what she'd done, her betrayal, he couldn't let that happen.

"Angel."

Her name was on his lips, her beautiful face in his mind, and the memory of her warm, supple body close to his heart when his strength finally deserted him.

Angel's or devil's mistress. Dark or light. He'd wanted years to learn her secrets, and been granted only weeks. It would have to be enough.

"Be smart, baby," he rasped. "Stay safe."

Against his will, his eyes drifted shut.

And Tonio surrendered to the darkness.

Five weeks earlier

Detective Tonio Salvatore leaned against the bar in his favorite dive, where the regulars only knew him by his first name, and sipped his whiskey, neat.

They didn't know what he did for a living, either, and nobody ever asked. He figured, if anything, they had him pegged for a dangerous thug of some sort, maybe into drugs or fencing stolen goods like three-quarters of the guys there. Because he was dressed as he always was when he came here, in leathers, a tight black Metallica

T-shirt, heavy boots, a five-o'clock shadow on his jaw, and a bandanna around his short raven hair, it was a reasonable assumption.

It didn't hurt that he was six-four and muscular and looked mean, even though he wasn't unless he had to be.

Stroker's was a rough place with an even rougher clientele, but it suited him despite his job—or maybe because of it. It was the perfect place to keep his finger on the pulse of Cheatham County's criminal activity without risking being seen and recognized in his nearby city of Sugarland, Tennessee. He wasn't here in any official capacity, though. He just wanted to relax, incognito.

And maybe see some action that involved the weapon in the front of his leathers and not the one strapped to his ankle.

Taking another sip of his Dewar's, he savored the smooth flavor and recalled the sweet little piece of work from last weekend. The blonde—what was her name? Trish? Tess? Didn't matter. She'd been all over him from the minute she spied him at the bar, and it hadn't taken her long to maneuver her way between his legs as he sat on the stool, then proceed to check his tonsils with her tongue.

His cock stirred as he remembered giving her a ride on his Harley to the motel down the road, his go-to for one-night stands, which provided him and his chosen partners with relief. No way was he taking any of them home. He wasn't stupid.

The blonde had hugged him tightly from behind, pressed her breasts against his back, her hot crotch against his ass, and he'd nearly wrecked trying to get them to the motel.

Inside, they'd been naked in seconds, and he'd eaten her out, enjoying the moaning and breathy little whimpers coming from her throat. She'd dug her fingers into his short hair and held on for the ride as he'd thrown her onto the bed, slid his cock deep, and fucked her so hard, the headboard had cracked the plaster on the wall.

Looking around, he hoped she'd be back tonight.

"Another round?" the bartender asked. The guy's name was Rick, and he was as tough as anyone here. Had to be to work in a place like this. Tonio knew for a fact the man kept a baseball bat behind the counter and wouldn't hesitate to use it.

"Sure," he answered. Fuck it, he was off duty tonight.

"Comin' up."

His night improved when the little blonde with the perky bust and tight jeans strolled through the front door. He turned back to his drink, making sure not to clue her in that he'd noticed her arrival. As he thought she might, pretty soon a warm body sidled close to him, and a woman's voice whispered in his ear.

"Fancy meeting you here, Tonio." Small teeth nibbled at his ear lobe. "Buy a girl a drink?"

"You bet." Damn, what *was* her name?

"Hey, Tess," Rick said in greeting. "What's your poison tonight, baby girl?"

Settling on the stool beside Tonio, she brought a long manicured nail to her lips in thought. Then she grinned. "How about a Screaming Orgasm?"

Rick snorted and winked at her, then smirked at Tonio. "Don't think you need me for that one, but whatever the lady wants."

While Rick mixed her drink, she swiveled to face Tonio. Leaning over enticingly, she showed every bit of the rosy nipples under her plunging blouse and eyed him like a cat ready to pounce on a mouse. They both knew she wouldn't have to work real hard to catch him.

"Watcha been up to, sexy?" she asked.

He shrugged. "Not much. Messing with my bike, doing a little business to keep a roof over my head. The usual." All true, even if he'd just effectively skewed her perception of him possibly being a criminal even further. Why he was playing this game, he wasn't sure.

But they were both enjoying it, so what was the harm? He might learn something interesting.

"What do you do to keep that roof over your head, hmm?" She took the drink Rick slid over and took a healthy swallow.

He'd stepped into this willingly. But there was no question he had to develop a cover now. Besides Tess, Rick and a couple of other men were very interested in his answer and were trying to pretend they weren't. Who knew? He might luck onto a case that would lead somewhere, eventually to arrests for drugs, or who knew what else. Sure, his captain would have his balls for going out on his own, but if it lead to something big, he'd forgive Tonio just as fast.

"I acquire things," he heard himself say. "For those who want them."

She arched a brow. "What kinds of things?"

"Whatever you want, for a fee."

"Anything?"

"Pretty much."

Tess wasn't fazed. "Good to know. I might be persuaded to pass that along."

"Up to you." Pulse kicking up a notch, he tossed back the rest of his drink, letting his demeanor say he didn't give a shit whether she did or not. But he'd gotten a nibble that might lead to something bigger, and the game was on. The high was better than any drug.

Almost better than sex. But not quite.

After taking another drink, she slid a hand up the thigh of his leathers and brushed her fingers across his tightened crotch. "I can provide something *you* want, too."

His dick was throbbing in his pants. Hot.

"Yeah?"

"Oh, yeah." Leaning into his chest, she took his mouth and tangled her tongue with his. Her nipples grazed his chest and peaked to tiny eraser points, rubbing. Driving him crazy.

"Want to get out of here?" he asked between heated kisses.

"Sounds like a great idea," a woman's voice said. And it wasn't Tess's.

Tonio and his hookup turned toward the woman who'd stalked up to them without either of them noticing—and Tonio's breath caught. The woman was several inches below Tonio's height—perhaps five-nine—long-limbed with a killer body that looked like she'd just stepped from the pages of a skin magazine. Long dark hair fell past her shoulders, almost all the way to her waist. Her eyes were large and green, and her nose was a sharp blade above a full, lush mouth made for sucking cock. Full, ripe breasts pushed at the snug cotton shirt, which had been cut with scissors or a knife to make it a low V-neck and sleeveless as well. She wore tight jeans and black ankle boots with silver conchos studded around them. Encircling her right upper arm was a surprisingly feminine Celtic tattoo. His mouth watered. The look, which would have come across as tacky on anyone else, was stunning on her.

Definitely centerfold material.

"What the fuck do you want, Angel?" Tess was clearly less than pleased with the other woman's presence.

"Are you really that stupid?" Angel stared at her, then shook her head. "You know this is Rab's territory. He's not going to be happy to find you here again, and he's not taking you back."

What? Stuck in the middle of Tess's trying to make another man jealous? Fuck.

"You think I give a shit what that asshole thinks, or what makes him happy?"

Angel sighed. "Look, I'm telling you this for your own good. My brother— Crap, too late. Here he comes now."

Angel really did look worried, Tonio had to admit. When Tess glanced toward the door, she did, too. Who was this Rab guy who had the women so nervous? Tonio followed their gazes and cursed inwardly.

The man who held their attention was a frigging tank, maybe even an inch or so taller than Tonio himself. He was about thirty or so and bald, and wore his tats proudly as sleeves down both thick arms. Several pendants bounced against his broad chest, and he wore jeans that emphasized his muscular thighs.

Rab headed straight for their group, a steely expression on his face. Tonio slid from his stool and planted himself slightly in front of the women on pure instinct. This wasn't even his fight, for God's sake.

"Bitch," the man growled, throwing his sister the barest glance. "What the hell are you doing here?"

Tonio's back went up. He absolutely *hated* any man who addressed a woman as *bitch*. Only bottom-feeders resorted to that kind of talk to make themselves seem like bigger men.

"What do you think?" she purred slyly. Curling into Tonio's side, she wrapped an arm around his waist. "I'm here for a drink, same as you. A little company, too. No harm in that."

"There is when you know goddamned well I don't want to see your face." His eyes were dark and cold, like black marbles. He hadn't acknowledged Tonio at all.

"Fine," she said airily. "I guess I won't introduce you to my friend Tonio here, who has a special talent."

That icy gaze settled on Tonio for the first time, and inwardly he actually shuddered. That didn't happen often. There weren't many people who scared him. But there was something about this man he perceived as dangerous. Even deadly. Maybe it was because he was too still, too calm. As though watching and calculating.

"What talent might that be?" Rab drawled, checking him out from head to toe, his disdain clear.

"Acquisitions," Tess said pointedly.

And here we go.

That caught the other man's interest. "What's your specialty?"

"Don't have one. Someone wants something, I get it."

That was taking a risk, not specializing. It might have sounded too close to fishing on Tonio's part. Too suspect.

Rab studied him for a long moment. Tonio held his gaze, not backing down. *Never, ever volunteer more than you're asked. That's the first rule of being undercover.* Eventually, the other man spoke again.

"You got a last name?"

"Reyes," he lied.

"You got a number?"

Shit. He couldn't give out his real cell phone number—he'd have to get a burner, fast. And have an unpleasant conversation with Rainey first thing tomorrow. He was onto something here. He could feel it. The room had hushed, every single person there tense. Belatedly, Tonio noted all the men dressed in a similar fashion who'd risen to their feet and moved subtly behind Rab. None of them appeared to be the stereotypical bumbling backwoods yokel. They looked tough and serious. He'd bet most of them had done hard time.

This man was no small-time player.

"I'm around," was his only reply.

Several men flexed their fists. Looked to Rab, who held them off with a slight flick of a hand. *Jesus*. He'd escaped getting the motherfuck beat out of him by the skin of his teeth, and all he'd wanted was a cold drink and a hot woman. In that order.

"I expect you will be," Rab said, his warning unmistakable. "Same time tomorrow night. Here. We'll talk."

Dismissing Tonio, the man strode away, taking up residence at a table in a corner of the bar. The only vacant table in the place, which must have been reserved for him. Angel stepped closer to Tonio and tilted her head toward the corner.

"You've got his attention," she said, sounding less than pleased. And still concerned. "I hope you know what the hell you let in when you opened that door."

"Interesting way to talk about your own brother."

A second of unease flickered in her jade eyes. She glanced around and apparently decided Rab's men were no longer listening. "My advice? Don't come back."

"Noted." Angel, warning him off. He was even more intrigued than before—and he knew he'd be back.

About the Author

National bestselling author **Jo Davis** is best known for the popular Firefighters of Station Five, Sugarland Blue, and Torn Between Two Lovers series. As J. D. Tyler, she's the National bestselling author of the dark, sexy paranormal series Alpha Pack. *Primal Law*, the first book in her Alpha Pack series, is the winner of the 2011 National Reader's Choice Award in Paranormal. She has also been a multiple finalist in the Colorado Romance Writers Award of Excellence, a finalist for the Bookseller's Best Award, has captured the HOLT Medallion Award of Merit, and has been a two-time nominee for the Australian Romance Readers Award in romantic suspense. She's had one book optioned for a major motion picture.

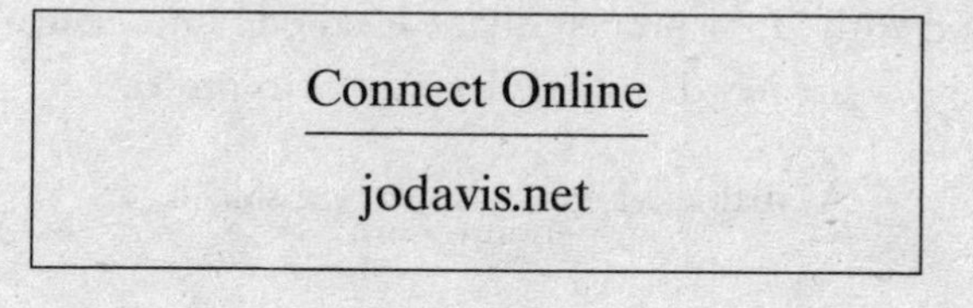

Also Available From

JO DAVIS

Sworn to Protect

A Sugarland Blue Novel

After recovering from a near-fatal gunshot wound, Detective Shane Ford receives yet another shock: the sudden death of his best friend, which makes him the legal guardian of his godson, Drew—a bitter sixteen-year-old harboring a terrible secret. Shane is determined to pry the truth out from Drew, but his actions only alienate the boy further and pit him against Juvenile Detective Daisy Callahan, whose job is to protect Drew's best interests. Shane has feelings for Daisy, but he vows not to allow his attraction to interfere with his duty. But the realities of Shane and Daisy's blossoming love and their growing bond with Drew propels Shane headlong into danger for the new family he has sworn to protect.

Available wherever books are sold or at penguin.com

facebook.com/LoveAlwaysBooks